Crossing a Fine Line

by

W. L. Brooks

The McKay Series

Crossing a Fine Line

Cover Art by *The Wild Rose Press, Inc.*

The Wild Rose Press, Inc.
PO Box 708
Adams Basin, NY 14410-0708
Visit us at www.thewildrosepress.com

Publishing History
First Edition, 2023
Trade Paperback ISBN 978-1-5092-4704-2
Digital ISBN 978-1-5092-4705-9

The McKay Series
Published in the United States of America

Dedication

For my dad, who believed in the McKays first. And for all the readers who love these characters as much as I do.

Noah walked barefoot to his office and poured himself a scotch. He closed his eyes as the liquid traced a molten path to his stomach. Shaking it off, he sat at his desk and flicked on the TV for background noise.

On top of his stack of mail was a letter with his name on it, one that hadn't been there before. Opening the drawer to his left, he pulled out a pair of latex gloves. Using every precaution, he unsealed the envelope and dumped out the contents. He picked it up with his thumb and forefinger and unfolded the paper.

Reed around the rosy
Someone's too damn nosy
Ashes to embers
Make sure he remembers
Ashes take flight
Someone dies tonight

What the hell? Someone had been in his house. He squeezed his eyes shut. She'd broken in before. Hadn't she? Damn it; this had gone too far. He got a plastic baggy from the kitchen, put the note inside, slipped on his loafers, and grabbed his keys. So much for getting any sleep tonight.

Praise for W. L. Brooks

The Secrets that Shape Us, McKay Series, Book 2
"W.L. Brooks has given readers the total package in this novel."

~ *Reviewer InD'tale Magazine*

Let the Dead Lie, McKay Series, Book 1
"…you find yourself unable to put your eReader down until you get to the end. Because, it's that good."

~*The Romance Reviews*

The Truth Behind the Mask, McKay Series, Book 4
"The love scenes are searing hot, so readers may want to keep a cool glass of something next to them while reading."

~ *InD'tale Magazine*

Acknowledgments

For twenty years, I've been working with or thinking about the McKays. I wrote the first drafts of their stories over the course of two years, then packed them away. Life happened, and when the opportunity arose where I could try to do this author thing for real, I jumped at it.

My dad was my biggest supporter when I created these characters. In fact, he's the reason Emmit got his own story. I wish he would have lived to see them published; he would have gotten a kick out of it.

I wanted to take a minute to thank all the readers who've loved my McKay girls from the beginning. To the people who asked when the next book was coming out, thank you. You have no idea how much it means to know other people love these characters too.

To my family and closest friends for reading all of my books and supporting my craziness—I appreciate it. Thank you for following me on social media and liking all of my posts to help me out—you're awesome!

I would also like to thank The Wild Rose Press for taking a chance on me. For being a supportive and instructive publisher, teacher, mentor, and partner on this journey. To Eilidh MacKenzie, who helped me get all of these books where they needed to be, and for believing in my girls…thank you so much.

Being a writer isn't easy. Being a writer with social anxiety, general anxiety, depression, and inattentive ADHD is definitely a task, but I've met some ladies who make it easier. I want to give a special shout-out to my best book bitches, author April D. Berry and author Kate Prada, for being amazing Queens, writers, and friends. I can't tell you how glad I am we found each other.

And to The Romance Riot, who are the coolest kids around, thanks for being my kind of crazy.

Chapter One

Noah Reed grimaced and set the mug down; the coffee was cold. How long had he been standing here, staring? He leaned his muscled shoulder against the wall and continued to study the woman on the other side of the two-way mirror. At twenty-five, his suspect could easily be mistaken for a teenager. She was young, brash, and bewitching. Her long, tawny hair was in twin braids on either side of her head, her overalls were frayed, and her boots were muddy.

By all appearances she was dismissible, but underestimating her would be absolute folly. Not only was this woman intelligent and resourceful, but she was also his nemesis, and he had charges that would stick. Murder in the first degree; he had her dead to rights. And he hated it.

Her gaze landed on him through the glass. She couldn't see him, but that didn't stop Noah's gut from clenching at the ice in her blue-green gaze. Fletcher McKay didn't try to disguise her feelings. No, her hatred of him radiated off her slender form like a plume of smoke.

Noah straightened from the wall and rolled his neck. There was no doubt he would be walking on dangerous ground.

He had given up being a homicide detective in the city, a job he'd loved, to take over as interim sheriff when Jasper Hart asked him to. Noah had been honored. But that was before this.

Technically, Daemon Randle's murder wasn't his jurisdiction, but Noah had called in a couple of favors so he could take the lead with this particular suspect. He had her. Fletcher returned from her "vacation" the same day as Randle's transfer. A sniper had shot the victim—and Noah loathed calling Randle a victim— through the heart. Fletcher was a damn fine marksman. She also had a reason for killing the bastard—a world-class-bordering-on-justifiable motive. But murder was murder, and he was the law in this town.

****

Fletcher held Reed's steely gaze when he entered the room. It wasn't the first time she'd sat on this side of the interview desk, and with Noah as sheriff, she doubted it would be her last. Reed outweighed her by a good hundred pounds, was over a foot taller, and was fucking massive—linebacker huge. Plus, he had it in for her. The man was a dumb jock turned cop. Okay, he wasn't a jock, and he was far from dumb. But he drove her batshit.

He'd had her sitting in this small-ass drab room stewing for almost two hours. She could wait; her lawyer was on the way, though Reed wasn't aware of that yet.

Reed had been kind enough to give her a cup of sludge passing as coffee to fight the chill in the interview room, which would have been nice of him if he had given her time to use the restroom. If he had come in and offered her a bathroom break, she would have accepted, then told him they needed to wait for her lawyer. But he hadn't come back until now—the asshat.

Was it the oldest trick in the book? Give the perp a beverage, withhold the bathroom, and watch them squirm? Yes, yes, it was. But that was beside the point.

The legs of the chair scraped against the concrete floor. "Did you kill Daemon Randle?"

An image of Daemon invaded her brain. Not how he looked after he'd received a new face and had taken her hostage, but before. When all she'd suspected him of was murdering his brother.

And she'd wanted answers bad enough to do or say whatever she had to. Not only had he believed her, but he'd also sworn his everlasting love and devotion.

She had sacrificed so much to trap him, and he had taken the easy way out. Or so she thought, but she had been irrevocably wrong. The actual ramifications of his "devotion" came later…with the torment.

Fletcher jerked when Reed rapped his knuckles against the table. Fuck. She'd gone down the rabbit hole again. She inhaled through her nose, then exhaled through her mouth in such a way that it went unnoticed. She had practiced. She straightened in her chair and shot Reed a droll look. "What was that?"

"Did you murder Daemon Randle?" Reed asked again, looking over his shoulder when the door opened.

A dark-skinned man in an impeccably tailored grey suit entered the room. "Don't answer that, Fletcher."

Pure delight shot through her. Reed was going to be *so* pissed. She slapped an eat-shit-and-die grin on her face.

"And who the hell are you?"

The man held his hand out for Reed. "I'm Malik Watson, Ms. McKay's attorney."

Noah shook Malik's hand, but his eyes never left

hers; one dark brow rose. "Attorney?"

Fletcher shrugged.

"Fine," Noah grumbled. "I'll leave you to speak to your client alone."

Fletcher waited until the door shut. "You got here fast," she said, her bladder forgotten.

Malik smiled. "Your voicemail was persuasive."

Fletcher grinned. Mal hadn't changed since college. He was several years older than her and incredibly handsome in a bookish way.

He stared at her for a moment with his dreamy hazel eyes and sighed. "Did you kill him?"

"No. Did I want to? Yep." More than anyone could fathom; more than she would ever admit. Daemon Randle had kidnapped her, kept her prisoner, and that was the least he'd done to her. Did she want him dead? You bet your ass.

Malik's lips quirked upward. "I'll advise you not to mention that to anyone else."

Fletcher snorted. "No shit! But if it makes you feel any better, I have an alibi."

"Why didn't you say so in the first place?" He undid the button on his suit jacket and sat. "Is it solid?"

Was it ever! "Rock."

Raising a brow, Malik opened his briefcase. "Then why not tell Sheriff Reed and save yourself all this?"

" 'Cause, Reed's had a vendetta against me for years. Now he's getting his chance to get his revenge. I want him to think he's got me, and then when he goes to arrest me, I'm gonna lay it on him." It was going to be sweet.

He waved a hand in the air. "And I'm here because?"

"It'll make Reed think I've got something to hide. Convince him he's won. Then wham!" She slammed a fist on the table. "It'll be great. The look on his face alone will be worth it. I'll be paying you either way, so stop pouting."

He smirked. "The higher they rise, the harder they fall. Let the games begin."

Chapter Two

Fletcher took her time filling Malik in on the goings-on of the last few years. There was a lot of territory to cover, and Mal wasn't used to the kind of life she led; hell, most people weren't. Despite unhinged people trying to kill her and her family from time to time, Fletcher loved her life. Sure, things hadn't always been a basket of roses, but roses had thorns, didn't they? Yep, big sharp suckers that could tear the flesh and leave marks. She was an expert on scars.

"Damn, Fletch." Malik squeezed her hand, then sat back in his chair. "You and Reed have a history?"

Fletcher stiffened. "He hired me to track down a lead on a family member; I found them, then things went off the rails." That was an understatement. Her insistence that Noah move on the information she'd obtained had come at an exorbitant cost. He had wanted her to take her fee and never speak of it again. Fletch had refused. But Noah said it was the least she could do; after all, if not for her, both of his parents would still be alive. It hadn't mattered that she'd—"All Reed cares about is whether or not *he* gets a good night's sleep."

"Have you thought about talking to a psychologist?"

Her mental health was her business. She tapped her temple. "My head's fine, thank you very much."

He pursed his lips, then glanced at his watch. "Want to tell me your alibi?"

Fletcher grasped the straps of her overalls. "You got somewhere you need to be?"

"If I leave here soon, I might be able to get back to the city for a late—"

"You can stay at my sister's. She runs the bed-and-breakfast in these parts."

"She has rooms available?"

"Yep. We'll tell her you worked your magic and got me out of here. It'll get you dinner too." Fletcher winked.

"Sounds good to me." He spun his pen between his fingers. "So?"

Fletch shifted in her seat. "My alibi?"

"If you please."

She sighed. "I was with an old friend."

"Whose name is?" Mal asked, but the door opened before she could respond.

"Fletcher McKay, you're under arrest for the murder of Daemon Randle. If you could please stand while I read you your rights," Noah began, the handcuffs swinging in his grasp.

Mal stood. "Your evidence is in no way sufficient to warrant an arrest."

"I've got motive and means."

Mal stepped back. "What?"

"We found a rifle in her vehicle," Noah began. "It matches the make of the one used to kill Randle."

"Fletcher?" Mal said.

"I always carry protection when I vacation in the mountains. There're all kinds of wild creatures that would like nothing better than to bite your ass off. I have the permit."

"Ms. McKay, stand up," Noah said with a bite to his voice.

"Fletcher…" Mal warned.

She stood and moved as close to Noah as she dared. Given his recent dating history, the man was sure to have something deplorable. Her head barely reached him mid-chest, and she had to look way up. "I didn't kill Daemon Randle. That's the truth." Fletch cocked her head to the side. "I'll give you this one chance to trust me."

His strange silver eyes went smoky. "The evidence is too strong to ignore. I *am* sorry," Noah whispered.

She gave him a once-over, then pointed to Malik. "Tell him."

"My client has a rock-solid alibi."

"What?" Noah roared.

Fletcher couldn't stop herself from jumping.

Mal cleared his throat. "My client was with a friend during the time of the murder."

"Who?" Noah gripped the back of a chair.

"The honorable Judge Mason, first name Rebecca," Fletcher said. "You can call her if you want. I have the number." She wrote it down on Reed's notepad, then took her seat.

"I will." The slamming door echoed in the small room.

Mal stared at her. "A judge?"

She bobbed her eyebrows. "I bet Noah shit himself too." Life was good.

"How do you know her? Judge Mason?"

"She approved my sister's adoption. Nothing sissy about that woman and that's the truth." Fletcher had never met a female judge before meeting Rebecca, and Judge Mason was beyond anything she could have hoped for in a mentor or friend.

Malik tented his fingers. "You stayed in touch?"

"Never burn bridges that lead to the law. Or so my granddaddy Judge J. T. Vaughn always said." Ten minutes later, she shot to her feet when Noah returned to the room.

"You're free to go," Noah said between gritted teeth.

"To be clear," Mal began, "there will be no charges brought against my client?"

"No. Judge Mason was with Fletcher at the time of the murder. You can't buy an alibi that good."

"Then we're free to go." Mal headed for the door.

Noah sneered. "Isn't that what I said?"

"I'll meet you out front, Mal," Fletcher said. "There should be an older man with white hair walking a hole in the floor out there. That's Jasper Hart. Tell him what's going on." She shooed him out the door.

"Something you wanted to add, McKay?" Noah began pushing in the chairs. "I should charge you with obstructing justice."

"Me? What about you? If this isn't a conflict of interest—"

"How so?" he asked, going ramrod straight.

Fletcher narrowed her eyes. "You helped me investigate Daemon in the first place." Why had she gone to Reed for help? His connections? Because she hadn't wanted her family to know she was putting her nose into the Randles again? Those were the answers she kept telling herself. But why had *he* helped her? That was a question she was afraid to ask.

He grunted. "Helping you investigate Randle is a long way from being complicit in his murder."

"I didn't kill him."

"If you had told me your—"

"All you had to do was have faith in me." Fletcher grasped the straps of her overalls. "If you hadn't jumped to conclusions—"

" 'Jumped'?" He crossed his massive arms over his chest. "There's no one on God's green earth I can think of who wanted Randle dead more than you. You had motive, means, and, until you told me your whereabouts, you had opportunity. What the hell conclusion did you expect me to come to? Not to mention calling Mr. Magnificent out there."

"Malik?" Fletcher smirked. "Yeah, that's apt."

"Why didn't you tell me your alibi to begin with?"

"Maybe I wanted you to trust me!" She turned to go, stopping when Noah grabbed her.

He narrowed his eyes. "Why would you care what *I* think?"

"I don't!" She snatched her arm back, pissed at herself. She didn't need his trust, didn't want it. Or him. She didn't. Not at all.

"Why don't I believe that?"

"That's the problem, Reed. You never believe a word I say." She saluted him with one finger and headed to the lobby. Fletcher grinned when she came upon Mal and Jasper.

"Girl, I swear you're gonna be the death of me," Jasper shouted, disheveling his white hair. "I've been here for three hours and had six cups of coffee. Bad coffee too."

"I know, Jasper. Hold that thought; I've gotta pee

10

something awful!"

Malik laughed, and Jasper grumbled.

She came back from the restroom to find Jasper by himself. "Where did Mal go?"

"I gave him directions to the B and B, and I called your folks to let them know what was going on. Something you should've done, missy!"

Fletcher shook her head. "Stop getting yourself worked up, Jasper. You could have another heart attack; then who would take my late-night calls?"

He held the door open and rolled his weary greenish-blue eyes. "Always about you, isn't it?"

"Damn straight!" Fletcher snickered. She followed Jasper to the parking lot and got into his old pickup, which she called the uproarious rust bucket.

He turned the engine over, then pointed to her. "You want to be telling me how you got yourself outta this one?"

She buckled her seatbelt. "I had an alibi."

He stopped and stared at her. "I waited around for three hours, and you had a dagnab alibi?"

"What part of 'don't worry' didn't y'all understand? It's not my fault you don't recognize plain English. Sheesh!"

"I'll remind you it was 'I called my lawyer, so don't worry.' Who the hell needs an attorney when they haven't done anything wrong?"

"When a body is subject to calumny—"

"Who ain't talking plain now, missy?"

"Let me put it this way: when a person's character is maligned, they shouldn't leave anything to chance." She rolled her eyes when he wanted to hear more. "Reed's trying to ruin my good name."

11

"Why in tarnation didn't you say that?" Jasper asked with a growl.

"What fun would that be?" Fletcher laughed and turned up the classic-rock station.

Jasper turned it off. "You still haven't told me what your alibi was."

"I was with a judge at the time of Daemon's death," she said and gave him just enough details to satisfy him.

"You know whatcha gotta do now, missy?"

"I'm sure you're going to tell me, old man."

Jasper harrumphed. "Find out who killed Randle."

The hairs on the back of her neck rose in remembrance of icy fingers. "I don't have to do a damn thing."

Chapter Three

Noah locked his truck and headed toward the diner. It was almost six a.m., so McKays should open any minute. One would think eating in a place that embodied the name of his nemesis would turn his stomach, but it didn't. He waved at Charlie, who was unlocking the door.

"Morning, Noah," Charlie McKay Sutton said with overpronounced sweetness and a forced smile.

"Good morning."

McKays was everything a small-town diner should be, and Noah could admit it was one of the reasons he'd made Blue Creek his permanent residence. The counter was stainless steel with red vinyl-topped stools. One wall boasted a string of booths, while tables for two or four took up the center section. Not long ago, Charlie had added a pastry case with various delights baked by one of her brothers-in-law.

Charlie always put fresh flowers on every table and offered homemade meals that brought a crowd. Not to mention the woman herself. Even without the baby bump, Charlie gave off a sense of home and motherhood that comforted her customers—comforted him. Her personality was sunshine and rainbows when she wasn't upset with you.

"I'm guessing you're mad at me this morning," he said, taking his usual seat at the counter.

Charlie narrowed her brown eyes, then poured coffee into the mug before him. "You couldn't have asked Fletcher what was going on? You had to take her to the station like some criminal."

Noah sipped his coffee. "She could have saved both of us the trouble if she'd told me she had an alibi. She's the one who got an attorney."

"Fletcher never does anything like normal people, or so Mama always says. Speaking of the lawyer, Malik Watson"—she fanned herself with a napkin—"now that's one secret I don't blame Fletch for keeping!"

"Does your husband know you feel this way?" He smiled. Charlie had married Noah's cousin Craig a while ago. Despite now being forever linked to the McKays, Noah was happy for the couple. Not to mention becoming an honorary uncle for Charlie's five-year-old daughter Mack.

Charlie snorted, making the blonde curls of her ponytail bounce. "My husband is the biggest flirt this side of the creek, and you know it!"

He toasted her with his mug. "I plead the Fifth."

Charlie took his order, went to the kitchen, then came back with a divided tub of napkins and cutlery. She rolled a few settings of silverware, then asked, "Any word on Marylou?"

Noah shifted on the stool. He loathed this subject but answered her anyway. "No, I ended it with Marylou several months ago, as you and everyone else in Blue Creek knows." He damn well didn't want to see her either. It was karma; he had stooped to a new level of despicable by dating Marylou Thomas. He'd only done it to get a reaction out of Fletcher, and he had succeeded.

Charlie looked up from the silverware. "You mean because of the whole fraud thing?"

His gut clenched. Another sore subject. "The DA wouldn't prosecute with what I had."

"So that's a no on having seen her?"

"Mrs. Thomas said Marylou was on an extended vacation in Europe."

A wide grin broke out on Charlie's face. "As in never coming back?"

"I don't think so. Sorry to disappoint you."

Charlie sighed. "That's okay, Noah. Just keep looking for the evidence to put her away."

"Sure thing," Noah said and thanked her when she put his plate in front of him. Eggs, bacon, toast, and grits; his stomach rumbled. He took a bite, then turned to see who she was greeting. "Morning, Jasper," Noah said. Was he in for a lecture?

"You're out and about early." Charlie poured Jasper a cup of coffee. "Craig said you closed the bar last night."

"That I did." Jasper sat.

"You're not tired?"

"Oh, I'm tired," Jasper began and swiveled on his stool to point at Noah. "I'm sick and tired of someone besmirching the sheriff's badge!"

Noah set his fork full of grits down on the plate. He glanced at Charlie, who made a mad dash for the kitchen. "You asked me to take the position."

"That I did, boy. That I did." Jasper sipped his coffee. "Didn't know you were gonna let the power go to your head. Or that you were going to use that badge for personal vendettas!"

"Are you implying I'm abusing my position?"

Jasper put his hands up. "I'm observing facts, is all."

The kitchen doors swung open, and Charlie came to stand in front of Jasper with her pen and pad. "What can I get you?"

"My usual, Charlie girl, thank you."

Charlie, bless her, tried to lure Jasper into talking about something else. Noah took a few more bites from his plate, but it was like ash on his tongue. When Charlie went to put in Jasper's order, Noah set his fork down again. Breakfast was ruined. "Let's continue this"—Noah waved a finger between them—"discussion. Where you were making accusations against me?"

The older man grumbled, "I said 'observations,' not accusations."

"It's the same damn thing, Jasper." Was he pissed, hurt, or offended? All of the above.

"No, it's not. *You* make accusations. A sheriff should observe, then form an unbiased opinion based on the facts!"

Was he serious? "You let the McKays skate away too many times to count. Sorry, Charlie, I'm not talking about you," he added when she returned to the counter.

"You kinda are, Noah."

"I never let anyone 'skate' away with anything! I listen to what they have to say, and they explain themselves. If you would just listen, boy."

"And let's stop with the 'boy' crap, shall we? Damn it, Jasper, you asked me to fill in for you. You came to *me*. Obviously, you thought I had some worth."

Jasper's fists were clenched on the countertop. "That was before."

"Before what?" Noah shouted. "Before I brought Fletcher in for questioning? Or before you realized I might uncover your secrets?"

"What you need to be 'uncovering' is who killed Daemon Randle!"

Noah sipped his coffee. "It's not my case or jurisdiction, as you well know. I called in favors to take the lead on interviewing Fletcher."

"Interrogating's more like," Jasper grumbled.

Noah set down his mug. "If she had told me her alibi—"

"That's a bunch of bologna. She—"

"That's enough!" They turned on their stools to find Fletcher glaring at them.

"Thank God!" Charlie cheered. She pointed at the men. "You're in for it now."

"What in tarnation are you doing here, missy?" Jasper huffed. "And in your jammies, no less!"

Noah couldn't help staring. Fletcher was in pajama bottoms with a tank top over a sports bra. It wasn't her clothes that held his gaze but the scars marring her flesh. They covered her arms, shoulders, and back. Her body was a testament to the hell she'd endured. His gut twisted.

Fletcher inspected herself. "I'm decent, Jasper, so don't bitch at me! Tiny called, and I had to rush up here 'cause your sorry ass is causing trouble. Thanks, Tiny!"

Jasper wagged a finger at her. "Don't be talking at me like that, dagnabbit!"

The kitchen door swung open, and Tiny Wellington came out. Tiny was about Noah's size, years older, wiser, and one of the best people the good Lord ever created. He crossed his arms over his massive chest, tattoos shifting on his ebony skin, and leaned against the doorjamb. "You're welcome, shug," Tiny said, his gold tooth flashing with his grin. "Happy to help."

Jasper ducked his head.

Noah shifted. He considered Tiny a friend and didn't want the other man to witness this humiliation. Not only had Tiny been a marine and a semi-professional boxer, but he also had an open invitation to the gym in the basement of the station house. Noah worked out with him regularly. Tiny taught a self-defense course a couple times a year, and he held boxing classes for the deputies twice a week.

"Tiny," Fletcher began, "make Jasper's order to go and double it for me."

"Already got it going," he said, eyes twinkling, and went back to the kitchen.

Jasper thumped the counter. "I'm eating here, dagnabbit! I'm not a baby you have to coddle."

Fletcher pulled cash out of her pocket and tossed it at her sister. "For the jar—to cover my bases and whatever commotion these two asshats caused."

"I already added what they owe to their checks." Charlie smirked, holding up her order pad. Then made a production of putting the bill in the blue glass jar labeled Pay for Profanity.

Jasper grumbled something Noah couldn't make out, but Fletcher did.

"You should have thought about that before you went upsetting shit, old man," Fletcher said. "You know it makes Charlie batty. And you"—she turned to Noah—"don't ever disrespect Jasper."

"Shut it, McKay," Noah hissed. He wasn't

disrespecting anyone.

"This is my sister's place, remember, and I can say whatever I feel like. Until Charlie tells me to stop," she added when Charlie cleared her throat.

Jasper fidgeted with the breast pocket of his shirt, then dropped his hand. "Don't know why they called you anyway."

"Someone has to get your ass in line, and Tiny's too busy to be dealing with your petty crap. Besides, you just had heart surgery; you're not thinking properly."

Jasper sputtered. "That was months ago! I'm fine now."

She threw her arms in the air and shouted, "Of course you are!"

The action pulled her tank top up, exposing the flesh of her lower back. Noah tensed, but he didn't look away fast enough.

Fletcher yanked the shirt down. "Keep your eyes to yourself, Reed."

Noah raised his hand in mock surrender. Her back looked like someone had whipped her with a heated instrument and for good reason…someone had. Daemon Randle, may he rot in hell.

"Told you not to wear them tops," Jasper said.

"I ran out of the house in a hurry, for fuck's sake. I didn't have time to grab a sweatshirt."

Tiny came out with to-go boxes and handed them to Charlie. Jasper grumbled but paid for the meals. Noah asked Charlie for a box as well. Maybe he'd get his appetite back later.

Fletcher and Jasper said their goodbyes to Charlie and Tiny, then Fletcher flicked Noah off. The door closed, and Noah squeezed his eyes shut. "That went well," he said, more to himself than anyone else.

Tiny leaned on the counter with a mug of coffee. "Could've been worse."

"I should be thankful?"

Tiny grinned, then asked Noah if he had any leads on Daemon Randle's murder.

Chapter Four

"You don't have to stay here all damn day," Jasper said for the fifth time.

"I know." Fletcher emptied the dustpan. She'd convinced Jasper he needed to do some cleaning; that was, let her do some cleaning. She reminded him that sloth was one of the deadlies. He'd told *her* to call his landlord, but here they were washing up.

Jasper harrumphed. "You need to be out there finding whoever killed Daemon Randle."

This again? "I thought we agreed to drop it."

"You agreed!"

"I don't give a shit who killed Daemon. I'm glad he's dead." She got out the mop. The place was looking livable. Jasper's wife, Laura, had died a few years ago from cancer, and other than putting in new carpet, he hadn't done anything else to maintain the place.

Fletcher had offered to hire a housekeeper for him, but Jasper had refused. It wasn't like she didn't have the money. Noah had guilted her into taking a ridiculous sum for finding his mother. A big part of her had wanted to burn it all, but she was practical enough not to listen to that side.

No, she had taken Noah's blood money, invested it, and come out on top. So, she could certainly afford some upgrades for Jasper, but the old man refused. The only thing he had let her do was buy a brand-new, big-ass flatscreen, so they could watch movies. She shook her head, then said, "Huh?"

Jasper crossed his arms over his chest. "I said, someone's got it out for you, missy. Whoever killed Daemon knew you were gonna be blamed. They set you up. Even used the same type of rifle you have. If that's not worth looking into, then I don't know what is."

"Someone's always got something against me, Jasper; that's a constant in my life. Hell, I don't know what I'd do if someone didn't want me dead."

"It's not funny, dagnabbit. You need to go see what you can find out!"

She gripped the mop handle. "Not today, I don't." Not tomorrow either if she had anything to say about it. Should she find who had killed Daemon? Without a doubt. Jasper was right—she was the perfect scapegoat. But the idea of getting involved…going anywhere near Daemon again—even his dead body—sent a wave of panic crashing over her.

"What did McKay say? I'm sure he agrees with me about finding whoever went after Daemon."

Fletcher wrung out the mop, her knuckles going white. Her father was not her favorite subject at the moment. "It's what he didn't say."

"What's that mean, missy?"

She stretched her neck. "Pops fought with me for months about my investigation into Daemon. He gave me hell and said I'd gone too far. I paid a price, didn't I? And Pops can't even say Daemon's fucking name without looking like he's going to puke." She blinked away the sting of tears. Her first instinct was to apologize for the outburst, but she was so tired of saying sorry.

Jasper reached up to fiddle with the breast pocket of his shirt, then dropped his hand. "Your dad's got a soft stomach when things get overwhelming. Been like that for ye—"

"Don't stick up for him." She had been making excuses for her father for a long, long time, and her ma had defended Pops plenty yesterday. Fletch sighed. She couldn't fault her mother. Savannah Walker McKay was always fighting for or defending their family.

"I'll do what I please, missy. And give me that thing." Jasper snatched the mop out of her hands. "You're pushing wet dirt everywhere."

"Fine." She hopped up on the counter. It was a small kitchen, but bigger than the one at her place. "I think I might sell my cabin."

"Don't talk crazy, or folks'll think you're getting doped again. And I know a dagnab subject change when I hear one."

She snorted. "But seriously, I've been considering it."

"You built that place with your own hands. Almost every square inch; the parts on and off the blueprints. It's yours, and you don't need to be selling it."

"That's true enough. I dreamed of building that cabin when I was a kid." She shrugged. " 'Course, I thought big sister would be doing it with me."

He wrung out the mop and shot her a glare. "See what keeping secrets does, missy?"

"If Casey hadn't run away, things would be different."

"If y'all hadn't kept that letter a secret, *maybe* things would've been different."

She fiddled with the locket she wore around her

neck. "I reckon it worked out for the best; if we hadn't hidden the letter, Casey wouldn't have left, and Alexandra wouldn't have hired Ryan to find her. Casey and Ryan wouldn't be married. And neither would Alex and Jake. See, things happen for a reason."

"That's what I've been telling ya. 'Bout time you started listening." He looked up from mopping. "What happened to the lawyer?"

"Mal?" At Jasper's nod, she said, "He went back to the city before I even got up this morning." They'd had a fun night reminiscing.

He looked her up and down. "Never did put any clothes on either."

Fletch rolled her eyes and hopped off the counter. "Fine! I'll go change. You've got more complaints than anyone I know." It was a good thing she kept extra clothes here for when she stayed over.

He harrumphed. "Here's another. You stink."

Fletcher let out a dramatic gasp. "You say the sweetest things!"

Jasper pursed his lips and nodded. "That explains the smell."

"What?"

"You're full of crapola!"

She burst out laughing and headed down the hall to freshen up. It only took about twenty minutes before she was back on top of the counter with another cup of coffee. Jasper was wiping down the table. "Just so you know, the outfit I had on counts as clothes, old man. They're 'leisure wear' or some shit like that."

He snorted. "Since when do you know anything about fashion?"

"I asked Alex before I left there this morning."

"Wait, you were staying at Alex's B and B?" He pointed the sponge at her. "You sleeping with that lawyer boy?"

Fletcher snorted coffee out of her nose.

"What's so damn funny?"

"Jasper, you're more Mal's type than I am."

He perked up. "Well, at least the boy's got taste."

"That's why you were thinking he was sleeping with me." She snickered.

"I can hope, can't I?"

She threw the arm without the mug in the air. "What in hell's that supposed to mean?"

"You need to find you a man and settle down."

Her mouth dropped open. "Jasper Hart! That's about the most sexist thing you've ever said. I don't need a man."

"What about a woman?"

She stared at him and bit her lip. "Are you asking if I'm gay?"

His cheeks got ruddy. "Wouldn't bother me if you were. Hell, you could like both for all I care. It happens nowadays. I just want you to be happy s'all."

It was her turn to blush. "I prefer men, if you must know. And I don't need anyone else to make me happy." A body had to be content with herself. Able to live with her demons, and she was working on that.

Jasper put the sponge in the sink, then topped off his coffee. "All I'm saying is you'd like married life. I did."

Fletcher jumped off the counter, slipping on a wet spot. "On that note, I'm so outta here." She kissed his cheek. "I'll talk to you later."

"Fine. Don't cause no trouble. And cut McKay

some slack. And make sure you talk to Casey about working at the garage—"

"Casey and Ryan are on their babymoon, remember?"

"What the hell's that again?"

"It's a couple's trip, like quality time before the baby's born. Though they should have gone way before now. How Casey convinced Ryan it was okay to wait until the third trimester is beyond me."

Jasper snickered. "Ryan can't resist giving your sister her way. As it should be…which reminds me. You need to—"

"Should I get a piece of paper for this long-ass list you're giving me?"

He huffed. "Don't get smart with me, missy. I may not be sheriff anymore but—"

"As if I need reminding. Sorry," she added when he glared at her. Sheesh!

"Don't sell your cabin. You worked too hard on it. And you're—"

"Talking crazy!" She rolled her eyes and grabbed her keys. Feeling guilty, she said, "The weather's supposed to get colder in the next couple of days. I'll put on a pot of chili tonight, so it'll be good and tangy for dinner tomorrow."

Jasper's eyes brightened. "And you'll make your cornbread too?"

Fletcher grinned. He loved her chili and cornbread. "What good would the chili be without it?"

"If this is a bribe of some kind…I'll take it."

She winked. "Thought you might."

****

Fletcher decided to stop by the bed-and-breakfast

26

before she went home. There had been a few guests last night, other than Mal and herself, but those couples would have already checked out, so she felt free to intrude. Did her choice have anything to do with the fact that it was lunchtime? Maybe.

Fletcher parked in the guest parking lot and got out of her truck. Her sister Alexandra had named the B and B Granny Vaughn's, after the house's previous owner and their beloved granny, Sadie Madison Vaughn. Ever since Alex had moved in, it had become the McKay sisters' gathering place. They'd had some grand adventures here, like going through all the secret passageways Granny's first husband had built in the house. Then there were some not great experiences, like when she got shot for the second time and her family was taken hostage. But such was life. Or hers anyway.

She went through the back porch door, as was family custom, and was enveloped by a heady aroma the moment she stepped into the kitchen. "What smells good?"

Jake Keller looked up from where he was pulling a dish out of the oven. "Jake's chicken and dumplings casserole."

Jake was almost a foot taller than Fletcher. His face was covered with a few days' worth of beard, his jeans had a hole at the knee, and his black T-shirt was coated with flour. Seeing him like this made her happy.

"Yum," she said, as if she hadn't known she would arrive at precisely the right time.

Jake bobbed his eyebrows over his dark green eyes and set the oven mitts aside. "You hungry?"

Alexandra breezed into the room before Fletcher could answer. "Your friend left early this morning."

27

Fletch rolled her eyes. "I was here, remember?"

Her sister nodded and kissed her husband. Fletcher shook her head. Alexandra McKay Keller was the prissiest of her sisters. They'd had their issues, but they'd been working on them.

"He's the guy you dated in college, wasn't he?" her sister asked.

"Yeah." Fletcher snorted. Alex knew about Malik's "sexless" remarks.

She looked up from pouring herself a glass of iced tea. A full red brow rose over a blue iris. "Interesting."

"What is it, Alexandra?" Fletcher plopped into a seat at the kitchen table.

"I wouldn't have pictured you employing someone who'd wronged you."

"I'm talking to you, aren't I? And you wronged me." Well, Alex had wronged Jasper, but it was basically the same thing.

"Let's not start, ladies," Jake pleaded and set the food on the table.

Alexandra grabbed the plates and silverware. "Nothing's being started, Jacob."

He grunted, his mini man bun bobbing, and served the meal.

Fletcher took a bite. "God, that's good."

Jake grinned. "Eat up!"

Fletcher made a circle in the air with her fork. "And she's right, I'm not trying to start shit." She didn't give herself the leeway to wonder if things would have turned out differently with Daemon if Alex hadn't done what she did. That was a dangerous road. And it wasn't fair to her sister.

It had been Jake who had given Fletcher a place to

crash with no questions asked, while she sorted shit out. One morning when Jake was out of town, the bell rang, and there was Daemon standing in front of her with his brother's face. She'd about pissed herself.

Daemon had faked his suicide and put another body in his place; then he had Dan Henderson, boyhood chum and renowned plastic surgeon, turn him into his dead brother. Fletcher had been stunned. Then he had taken her—

Jake kicked her under the table. She met his gaze, and he winked. She'd gone down the hole again. She took a moment to do her deep breathing, then shoved her mouth full of food and asked Alex what she was babbling about.

"You weren't listening to me at all, were you?" Alex huffed. "And you're purposely speaking with your mouth full to—"

Fletcher made a production of swallowing. "Go ahead and finish what you were saying."

Jake shook his head. "Kid, stop fucking with her."

Fletcher held up her hands in mock surrender. "Sorry, Alexandra."

"It's odd that out of all the lawyers in the world, you hired Mal." Alex sipped her iced tea.

"He didn't mean what he said. He was confused about his sexual orientation and transferred his pain into lashing out at me." Fletcher took the time to enjoy her food. Jake's cooking was the best. It was a good thing too, because Alexandra didn't cook. Couldn't if you wanted to get down to it. She burned everything and had since they were children. A fact that tickled Fletch.

"Oh." Alex strummed a small tattoo against her glass with her nails. "That makes sense then."

Jake pointed his fork at Fletcher. "What's the deal with Reed dragging you into the station?"

Fletcher took a breath and over the course of the meal filled them in on what happened.

"Your next step is to find out who killed Daemon, right?" Alex asked from where she loaded dishes into the dishwasher.

"Why is everyone asking me that?" Fletcher hovered by the coffee maker as it began to brew. What should she do? Go to the city, gather all the information she could on Daemon's murder, and find the person responsible? Yes, that's what she should do, but—

"Someone wanted to pin it on you," Jake said.

"They did the world a service as far as I'm concerned." Which was true. On one hand, she thought someone should give the shooter a fucking medal. On the other, she still had questions for Daemon, ones she needed to ask face to fucked-up face. She hadn't been ready to get that close to him again, not yet. Seeing him at the trial had been bad enough, but now she would never get her answers.

"I agree, but—"

"You and your 'buts,' Alex." Fletcher rolled her eyes.

"*But* Jacob's right," Alex continued. "Someone wanted you to take the blame. Someone's framing you."

"That's nothing new." Woohoo, the coffee was ready! Alexandra made the best brew, and Fletcher often wondered if that was why she put up with her sister. Taking a sip of the hot liquid, she turned to find Alex staring at her. "What?"

Alex raised a brow. "That doesn't bother you?"

30

"Princess, if the kid wants to drop it, let her."

"Thanks, Jake!" Fletcher said. "Alexandra, don't stress yourself out about this. Stress causes wrinkles and gray hair; look at Jasper." She grinned when her sister paled a bit. Vanity was the deadly Alex had the closest relationship with, and Fletcher couldn't resist pressing that particular button of her sister's.

Alex ran a hand down the skirt of her dress. "If you want to delude yourself, Fletcher, I can accept that."

"That's mighty big of you, Alex, thanks," Fletcher said, got a to-go cup, and headed out.

Chapter Five

Fletcher parked her truck in front of her cabin. Two years of blood and sweat had gone into building her hideaway. She had hired professionals to assist with the well, septic, and a couple of other things. The power was solar, which she had also gotten some help with, but the rest she had done herself.

She took in the wooded area and decided to do a perimeter check. When Fletcher had been drugged, someone had been here, nudging her over the edge of sanity, and she had never found that person. Now, with all that was going on, it was best to be vigilant.

There were the normal animal tracks and some ATV tire treads. People liked to ride their four-wheelers out here in the woods, so it wasn't unusual. But...had they ever been this close to her cabin? A tingle ran up her spine, and she wouldn't ignore it.

Fletcher walked the perimeter again. The ATV tracks hadn't breached the boundary, so they weren't close enough to have been caught by her cameras, but they were near enough to give her pause. This was still McKay land, and there were No Trespassing signs posted. Her blood chilled when she came across the partial footprints by the kitchen window. She squatted down. They were relatively fresh, maybe the last couple of days, but what was there of the tread wasn't distinctive. She had to check her surveillance.

What were the chances of someone getting this close to her cabin within the same time frame as Daemon getting his head blown off? Coincidence? The odds were *not* in her favor.

Fletcher kicked off her muddy shoes and left them on the porch next to the old pair of Tiny's boots he'd given her to keep out there. If someone saw her small shoes, they would think woman alone, but two pairs implied a couple, one of whom was big as fuck. It was a cheap and useful deterrent.

Once inside, the kitchenette was to the left with a breakfast bar and stools. The den was the first room you entered. The fireplace worked, but only if you knew what you were doing. Books were stacked in different places around the cabin. There was a bedroom, a small workroom, and a bathroom. It was her haven, or it had been.

She hustled to the fireplace. She'd wanted to do most of the work on the cabin herself so no one would know about her secret rooms. Her family knew about them, but that had been unavoidable.

Pushing in the third brick from the left, she stood back as the fireplace wall slid apart. After she descended a few steps, the entrance shut and the twinkling lights came on. She took the short, wide tunnel to the next door and pressed in the code.

She rolled her shoulders and entered. Other than a cot, a desk, and some framed prints on the wall, this room was empty. Fletcher had created it as a red herring. Anyone looking would stop here, thinking they'd found the actual bunker.

Fletcher grabbed the folded metal chair leaning against the wall. She stuck the predominant legs into the two holes on the floor and lifted; eight joined slats came up, revealing her second door. Moving the chair and slab out of the way, she maneuvered the key card out of her back pocket and slid it through. The light blinked green, and the trapdoor opened. She took two steps down into yet another tunnel lit by Christmas lights, then went a few feet to the next entrance. She pressed another button and entered her additional bunker.

These accommodations resembled a small RV and were directly under the main cabin. There was a tiny kitchenette, an office nook, a cot, a small shower stall, and a toilet. All the comforts of home.

This was the room she primarily used. Hitting the light switch, she sighed at the mess. Like Jasper, she needed to do some cleaning. She'd been putting off coming down here again for months; whenever she'd been home, she'd chosen to stay topside in the main cabin. When she'd been investigating Daemon, she'd spent days on end down here, researching and surveilling. Devising her plans. This room still contained that energy, and she hadn't been ready to deal with it yet. Avoidance was not the healthiest of coping mechanisms.

Fletcher eyed the desk, which sat against the wall, and the array of pictures lining the floor. She had come down here the day after her escape, but that was months ago. She hadn't picked the photos up. No, she'd left them there to rot and left the past to putrefy.

She stepped around the pile, booted up her computer, and hovered above the keyboard. Once the home screen came on, her fingers flew over the keys. She pulled up her surveillance programs and fast-forwarded through the past couple of days.

Fletcher leaned closer to the monitor. Someone had been here; she could make out a shape, lurking by the window, but that was it. Why hadn't the floodlights come on? They were motion activated. She checked the other cameras, but they hadn't picked up anything useful either.

She scratched her shin, then glanced down and flinched. Daemon Randle's face peered at her from the photographs on the floor. She swallowed, her concern over the floodlights forgotten. The pictures were from before he'd had his plastic surgery. Fletcher knelt and picked up the photo. She stared at his once-handsome face and crumpled it in her hand. He'd been a murderer and a psychopath who'd claimed to love her. Desire her.

Tears prickled her eyes. The days she had spent as Daemon's captive hadn't been the worst of her life, but they came close. He had taken her from place to place, murdering anyone who got in his way or was no longer useful. She had seen plenty of death, but she knew firsthand that witnessing a life stolen took longer to come to terms with. It hadn't fazed Daemon.

All Daemon had seemed to care about was molding Fletch into some sort of Stepford wife. He'd demanded she dress, speak, and walk properly, and always, always be a lady. It had been a private type of hell, everything she hated, everything she was not...

She shook herself—stupid rabbit hole. Fletcher inhaled through her nose, then exhaled through her mouth; she did it several times, then began stacking the photographs. She wouldn't forget anytime soon. Her brain made sure of that. The nightmares replayed her worst memories like the cassette tape Jasper had had stuck in his uproarious rust bucket's old-ass stereo for over a decade.

She dropped the stack of pictures in the small trashcan, then hurried back through the hidden passageway topside. Not for the first time, Fletcher cursed her stupidity. She should have put in a quick exit for the bunker. Maybe she should get that done now. If she didn't sell the cabin that is. Of course, if she sold the cabin, whoever purchased it would know her secrets, her paranoia. Fletcher snorted as the fireplace closed behind her. Jasper was right; better to keep this shit to herself.

She grabbed lighter fluid and a box of matches from under the sink, then took the trashcan outside. Fletcher slipped her shoes back on whilst eyeing her surroundings. There were no unusual sounds, no movement.

With a sigh, she went to the side of the cabin and dumped the photos on the firepit. There were still charred logs in the center from the last time she had sat out here enjoying a fire and gazing at the stars. This was not that. She used both hands and squeezed the bottle of lighter fluid in a zigzag pattern over the face staring at her. She tossed the container aside, then lit a match, and dropped it. *Whoosh.*

Heat rushed up and warmed her cheeks. Fletcher shivered as the flames turned Daemon's likeness to ash. Fire was the quickest way to destroy. Was she conceding to him by using this particular medium? Daemon hadn't only been psychotic; he'd also been a pyromaniac. He had taken pleasure in burning things;

now it was he who would burn. That wasn't a concession; it was fucking apt.

"Have fun in hell, motherfucker," she whispered.

Chapter Six

Noah pulled into his driveway and swept a hand through his hair. He was sweating, and it had more to do with the second summer than his run-in with Marylou's mother. Mrs. Thomas was a piece of work; he'd thought so when he dated Marylou, and the observation still held true. Now, however, Mrs. Thomas was a major thorn in his ass.

She'd called him for the fourth time in two months, threatening to sue the sheriff's department. He'd told her, repeatedly, it was only slander if the accusations were false. She was welcome to take him to court. On the other hand, she was the only person in Blue Creek who was disappointed Fletcher was released.

The minute he'd walked into the station, Noah had been asked by five of his six deputies for an update on "Deputy McKay's" situation. It didn't matter that she was no longer on duty. Even Hector Diaz, who was a damn fine deputy, if rather reserved, had cornered Noah in his office and given him a list of reasons why Fletcher wasn't capable of cold-blooded murder.

As if that wasn't enough, he'd been called out to Mildred Lawrence's home to investigate her ruined flowerbeds. The sixty-year-old retired school secretary and part-time manager of the diner was the hub of Blue Creek gossip. She had plied him with coffee and donuts, then filled him in on a few things he should be made aware of. Like the fact that everyone had expected Jasper to pick Fletcher as his replacement. And there was no doubt McKay would win if she were to run against him in the next election.

His day had been full of drama. McKay drama. He shook his head, grabbed his stuff, and headed up the walkway. The irony of his home having once belonged to the McKays was not lost on him either. J. T. Vaughn had built the estate. The judge had left it to his former son-in-law, Emmit McKay, who had sold it to Noah. The staircase was the first thing you saw when you entered the house. Done in dark oak with a taupe carpet inlay, the staircase dominated the entryway.

Noah had let Alexandra talk him into decorating once the renovations were complete, and he had never regretted it. He liked the ambience of the B and B, and he loved what she'd done with his place even more. There was no denying the woman had talent.

The downstairs boasted the great room that Noah used as his office/den. Three of the rooms on the bottom level Noah didn't even use. There was one full bath, one half bath, and a decent-sized kitchen. Not that he cooked much, but the place was similar to the home he'd grown up in, and he didn't have to duck when he walked into a room.

He put his briefcase on his desk, then went to the kitchen to grab a beer. Though, considering who his last visitor had been, maybe he should have something stronger. When Emmit had entered his office, Noah had been sure he was in for another lecture; he'd been wrong.

Before resigning from the FBI, Emmit had been a sharpshooter and worked a few cases with Noah's father, so their having a private conversation wasn't out of the ordinary. They, along with Mrs. McKay, had been out to dinner on multiple occasions. They'd met at Craig's bar several times for a beer. Despite Noah's feud with Fletcher, he and Emmit had a mutual respect, even friendship. But why had the McKay patriarch come to see him today of all days? To form an alliance or to unload his conscience? Noah wasn't sure which.

Emmit had said Noah was the only one who could or would appreciate his position. Until he'd heard his daughter's alibi, Emmit thought she could have killed Randle. She was more than capable. Hell, the man had made sure all his daughters could defend themselves. To the death. They'd had to use those skills on more than one occasion.

It had been the man's almost desperate need to be heard without reproach that had kept Noah silent. There was no doubt Emmit loved his daughters, but his presumption of Fletcher's guilt was telling... It also presented Noah with another question, but he knew just where to get the answer.

****

Headlights flashed across Jasper's makeshift workstation in his garage when someone pulled into the driveway. He grumbled when Noah got out of his truck. Hadn't he seen enough of the boy today? Yep. With a sigh, he covered his work with a drop cloth, then wiped his hands on the bandanna he kept in his pocket. "Whatcha want?"

"To talk."

Jasper harrumphed. "Didn't we do enough of that this morning? You fixing to ruin my evening as well?" Noah towered over him, in both height and bulk. Jasper was on the shorter side, but he made up for it in pure cantankerousness. Or so Fletch was always telling him. It looked like he was going to have to invite the boy in. "Come on, then."

They went through the garage door, into the hall, then entered the kitchen. Jasper had to admit it was nice to walk into a clean house. He'd forgotten the sensation. Not that he didn't keep things shipshape, he did, but he had slacked off on the dusting and mopping and things like that. His dishes were washed, and the bathrooms were—

"Do some tidying?"

His cheeks heated. Had it been so bad that other men noticed? Well, hell. "Damned girl was trying to spread dirt everywhere and pass it off as cleaning. You want a beer?"

Noah eyed him. "I didn't think you were supposed to be drinking."

"Doc said I'm fit as a fiddle and can have a beer if I want one. But these are for guests, dagnabbit, and I'm trying to get rid of 'em. So take it," he said. "You ain't on duty, right?"

"No," the younger man answered with just enough sass that Jasper almost smiled. Instead, he shoved the ice-cold can into his hands.

Jasper grabbed a bottle of water. The doctor said he needed to drink nearly a gallon a day. Jasper sighed. He'd rather have the water boiled, poured over ground beans, and percolated. Oh, well. He leaned against the counter and toasted Noah.

The younger man took a seat at the kitchen table, dwarfing it. "Are you working at the bar tonight?"

"Nope. I plan on watching a movie or two, and

then I'll wait for the phone."

The younger man's lips quirked. "Get a lot of late-night calls, do you?"

"Damn girl rings me up at three in the morning, which is fine if I'm closing the bar." Jasper shook his head. "She can't sleep." The nightmares kept her awake. Horrible nightmares, where she would scream bloody murder, then jump up and act like it never happened. She stopped staying over as much after one of her episodes had frightened him to tears. Her screams still haunted his old ass, but no one needed to know that. So he said, "Could be that insomnia."

Noah looked at his beer. "She could call her father."

"Hell and tarnation, just spit it out," Jasper hollered. Noah wasn't squirming, he was too damn big to squirm, but there was something he wanted to get off his chest.

"I think Emmit feels excluded."

Jasper reached toward his breast pocket to fiddle with the badge that was no longer there, then dropped his hand. "McKay needs to give her some dagnab space," Jasper said with more heat than he'd meant to. His sigh was weighted. "Fletch was knocked down, but she's pulling herself back up. Gonna take some time s'all. We all gotta respect that."

Noah nodded.

"And maybe I owe you an apology for this morning."

Noah held up a hand. "No need."

"Then I'll explain it."

"You don't have to."

Jasper glared at him. "The missus and I couldn't

have children, which didn't bother me none, truth be told. But when Emmit adopted those girls, Laura, my wife, took right to 'em. And after everything they went through, they kinda became ours."

Noah opened his mouth, then closed it when Jasper held up a finger.

"When I say ours, I don't mean Laura's and mine; I'm talking about the whole damn town. Most of us didn't give those girls a fair shake. We make light of it now, but we called them heathens because we didn't take the time to get to know them. People still feel like they owe the McKays for that—the harsh judgment because they were orphans—different. You need to consider that before you jump to conclusions. I'm not saying to let anyone break the law; I'm telling you to be one hundred and ten percent certain before you go accusing a McKay—any McKay—of a crime."

"I can do that."

Jasper sighed. "Then you'll go far."

Noah set his beer on the table. "Why do you protect Fletcher when she's more than capable of protecting herself?"

"It's that damn locket." He could still remember it in his hand. The weight of it—weight of the dagnab world.

Noah pursed his lips. "Explain?"

Jasper motioned to his throat. "That locket she always wears ended up being evidence, and I had to take it from her—"

"I read the file on that case."

Jasper found that both interesting and encouraging. "I'll never forget it. We were in the kitchen of Savannah's apartment, and I had to collect the locket as evidence. The look on that girl's face when—" Jasper cleared his throat. "Fletcher could take down a man your size in two seconds flat if she caught him off guard. She's too damn smart for her own good, and she can defend herself from a physical blow. It's the emotional stuff; she's got no real guard against matters of the heart. She takes things personally. Real personal."

Noah rubbed his jaw. "Can I ask you another question and get an honest answer?"

Jasper harrumphed. "Honest is how I answer questions, boy."

"Right," Noah said with a bit of a smile. "When I brought Fletcher in for questioning, before you knew she had an alibi, did you think she could have done it?"

Jasper shifted on his feet. This was tricky. "Could she have done it? I've no doubt that she could've killed Randle—let me finish," he said when Noah straightened. "She could have killed him, but she wouldn't. Not unless she didn't have a choice, not without provocation."

"He kept her chained to a wall and branded her, for Christ's sake. If that isn't provocation…"

Jasper considered that, as he had many times before, then said, "She wanted something."

Noah's brow pinched. "What?"

"Whether she knows it or not, there was something she needed to get from him or out of him; answers is my guess. She hadn't gotten them yet, so I knew it wasn't her." Jasper looked Noah up and down. "You and everyone else done missed the most obvious thing."

"Which is?"

Jasper rubbed his hand over his whiskers. He

needed a shave, and maybe to shut his trap, but he'd let the dagnab cat out. "She could have killed that POS at any time."

Noah sat at attention. "What are you talking about?"

Hell and tarnation. "Fletch knows how to kill a man in multiple ways using multiple means. She didn't end that devil when he was hurting her up close and personal, and she coulda. But she didn't. See what I'm saying?"

The other man leaned back. "That isn't the answer I was expecting, but I'll take it."

"Sometimes the best we can do is take what we can get."

Noah sipped his beer. "Mildred Lawrence said something to me today—"

Jasper hooted. "It won't be the last time, if you haven't figured that out already."

"Seems I'm over there a couple of times a month."

"If there's any particular pastry you like, you only have to mention it once, and it will always be there whenever you're called to duty." He damn well missed his bear claws. Maybe he could mention it to Jake next time he saw the boy.

"Good to know."

Jasper stared at Noah. It was like pulling teeth. "Well, what'd she say?"

"Something along the lines of most folks being surprised you didn't pick Fletcher to take your place."

His shoulders slumped. "I didn't ask her." He hadn't had to.

"I—"

"You're my first choice, and I stick by it." Which

45

was true. Despite what he'd said this morning, the boy had proved himself on more than one occasion. And Jasper had made the right decision. He wasn't happy with Noah's actions, but Jasper was the one who had taken it personally. Made it personal, but he hoped he'd explained some of the reasons why.

Noah pursed his lips. "She wouldn't have taken it, would she?"

"Nope."

Chapter Seven

Noah stopped by the station to check in with the night crew, then headed home. It was late, and he was exhausted, but he needed to finish some paperwork before he could hit the sack. He paused when opening the front door; something was off. Drawing his weapon, he turned the knob. He'd locked the deadbolt when he'd left earlier this evening. Hadn't he?

Moving with practiced caution, he opened the door and put his back against it. Reaching with one hand, he switched on the light. He squinted at the brightness, then checked the room; there was no one there. He went through the entire house with his gun drawn, not willing to take a chance.

Once he was satisfied that he was alone, he went to his bedroom and changed into a pair of jeans, leaving his white dress shirt on but rolling up the sleeves. Barefoot, he went to his office and poured himself a scotch. He closed his eyes as the liquid traced a molten path to his stomach. Shaking it off, he sat at his desk and flicked on the TV for background noise.

On top of his stack of mail was a letter addressed to him, one that hadn't been there before. Opening the drawer to his left, he pulled out a pair of latex gloves. Using every precaution, he unsealed the envelope and dumped out the contents. He picked up the paper with his thumb and forefinger and unfolded it.

Reed around the rosy
Someone's too damn nosy
Ashes to embers
Make sure he remembers
Ashes take flight
Someone dies tonight

What the hell? Someone *had* been in his house. She'd broken in before. Hadn't she? Damn it, this had gone too far. He got a plastic baggy from the kitchen, put the note inside, slipped on his loafers, and grabbed his keys. So much for getting any sleep tonight.

****

Fletcher was in her kitchen in the main part of the cabin when some asshole started trying to punch a hole in her door. "I'm coming! Keep your damn pants on!" she shouted. She slid her gun into the back of her jeans.

She looked out the newly installed peephole and squeezed her eyes shut, then checked again. Nope, Reed was still standing there. She unlatched the door, then jumped when he shoved it open and barged past her.

"I found your fucking note, McKay! You *do* remember that threatening an officer is against the law, right?"

She shut the door. "What are you babbling about?"

He showed her a plastic baggy. "This was on my desk when I got home tonight."

"Stop waving the fucking thing in my face and let me see it." She snatched it out of his hands. Well, hell's bells. She knew that font. She handed it back. "I didn't write this, Reed. I swear. But I suggest you call in the deputies."

There was another knock at the door.

"Expecting someone?" Noah asked in the tone she deplored.

She rolled her eyes and opened the door. A young guy was standing there. "What the actual hell!"

"Ah, sorry it's so late." He pointed to his delivery truck; it was a national chain. "It took me forever to navigate the woods. Are you Fletcher McKay?"

"That's me," she said wearily. How the hell had he found her cabin? No one delivered way the fuck out here.

He stuck out a vase of white lilies. "Here you go."

It took her a minute to grasp that the flowers were for her. She took them, hoping Reed didn't notice her blush. She dug some money out of her pocket—she always kept cash for Charlie's stupid jar—and handed it to the delivery guy.

"Wow, thanks!"

"Hey, how did you find my place?" she asked before he got too far away.

The kid paused. "They sent directions with the order."

Fletcher was taken aback but waved him off before she thought better of it. She went inside, making a big production of ignoring Reed.

Noah pursed his lips. "Secret admirer?"

"Shut up!" She put the flowers on the breakfast bar, then turned to Reed. They had more important things to deal with.

Reed pointed to the crock pot. "You cook?"

"I'm multi-fucking-faceted, Reed."

Before she could say anything, he was lifting the lid. "Is it any good?"

The nerve of the man! "It's Jasper's favorite, if that means anything." Reed being in her home was making her light-headed for some reason. He filled the place with his size and heat. She shivered, then shook herself. She was pissed and needed to stay that way.

Fletcher shooed him from the kitchenette.

He grunted but moved.

"Now, like I was saying. You need to get the deputies together because last time I got a letter—ripped off from a nursery rhyme—all hell broke loose."

He rocked back on his heels. "Is that so?"

"Damn straight." She couldn't help eyeing the lilies again. "Oh, there's a card," Fletcher said, taking the small white envelope from the plastic stick. Maybe her ma or one of her sisters?

Noah crowded behind her. "Who are they from?"

She read the card, bile rising in her throat, then she threw the vase against the wall.

Reed jumped. "What the hell is with you and throwing shit?"

Fletch had thrown his own trophy at Reed once when he was being an asshat. He'd ducked. She would have smiled, but the note in her hand stopped her. *It's started again!* Patting down her pockets, she said, "Fuck, where did I put my knife?"

"McKay? What the hell's going on?"

Goose bumps rose on her arms, but she read the card to Noah. "Starlight, star bright, which McKay will die tonight? None by name and none by right, but someone's blood will spill this night."

Noah took the slip of paper from her hands and read it for himself. Then he brought out the baggy with the note left for him. "These are identical."

"No shit, Sheriff." She rubbed her hands over her face. "The fucking lurker."

"What are you going on about?"

"I found partial footprints by the window—"

"You didn't report it."

She practically growled. "There was no distinct tread pattern to the prints, and my cameras didn't catch anything but a blur."

Reed rose a dark brow. "The lurker?"

"I don't know, but it's too much of a coincidence." Fletcher glanced at the notes in his big hands. What was she doing standing here? They had viable threats—she grabbed her keys. "You coming or what?"

"Where are we going?"

"Follow me," she shouted on her way out the door.

She'd driven the path between her cabin and her parents' house countless times, but she couldn't get there fast enough. Noah's headlights were in her rearview mirror, and he kept with her insane pace. She had the absurd notion he might try to give her a ticket for reckless driving, but this was urgent—life and death.

She barely had the truck in park before she was running up the porch steps. Noah's heavy footfalls were behind her. She ran inside the house, looking for her family. She came to a halt in the kitchen where her mother stood with a cup of coffee in her hand.

"Fletcher? What's going on?" her mother asked.

"Where is everyone?" Fletcher glared back at Noah when he bumped into her.

"What's happening?" Her mother's sapphire eyes searched hers, then she shouted, "Emmit!"

"What, babe?" Pops said, coming into the room in

his pajama bottoms and T-shirt. His disheveled hair was a little more salt than pepper now.

"Where is everyone?" Fletcher asked again.

Her father looked from her to Noah. "Casey and Ryan are out of town. Alex and Jake have a guest at the B and B."

"And Charlie's at the bar with Craig. Mack's upstairs with Jebb," Savannah added, speaking of Fletcher's little brother and niece. "What's going on?"

"Someone's playing a sick joke is what it seems," Noah said.

"It's not a joke or a prank or any other bullshit. It's something horrible." She grabbed her father's arm. "It's happening again, Pops—it's started again!" She pulled the notes out of Noah's pocket before he could stop her. "Look. Someone put one in Noah's house, and someone sent me one with a bunch of lilies."

Her mother attempted to read over her father's shoulder, then looked at Fletcher. "What color lilies?"

What the hell difference did it make? "White."

"Funeral flowers," her mother whispered. "White lilies are usually what you send after someone dies."

"Well, everyone's okay, so I'll take those notes back to the station and file a report," Noah said, holding out a hand to get the notes back from Pops.

"This one says 'not by name and not by right.' " Emmit shrugged. "That excludes all of us." He handed the notes to Noah.

All the blood drained from Fletcher's face. "No!"

****

Jasper sat in his favorite recliner and cheered as "Big Dog" told everyone off. "You tell 'em!" He loved cop movies. He glanced at the clock. Maybe he could take a nap before—A knock came at the front door.

Jasper harrumphed. "Come on in, missy. You're missing the best part," he shouted. Damn girl couldn't sleep, so he couldn't sleep. And why the hell was she knocking?

He had the lights off because why watch a movie with the light on? His popcorn was hot and buttery. Thinking of that, he didn't have time to get rid of the evidence. Dagnabbit, she'd have his hide. He wiped his hands on his paper towel and went to the door. She must have forgotten the key again.

"Now don't you get snippy with me. Popcorn is an approved snack," he began as he opened the door, but it wasn't Fletcher on the other side. "Who the hell are you?" A chill crept up Jasper's spine when the dark figure moved forward. He walked backward inside the house, while he reached behind his back. His fingers grazed the butt of his gun, but he was too late. Something hit him with a mighty force, and then he didn't feel anything.

Chapter Eight

Fletcher skidded to a stop in Jasper's driveway. She didn't even take the time to get the keys out of the ignition. She ran up the porch steps; Noah's headlights illuminated her path for a moment, but she didn't stop. The door was wide open. "Jasper! Jasper Hart? You answer me now!" she shouted, running into the house. She didn't even draw her weapon.

Her steps faltered at the swath of blood on the carpet. She shouted for him again, following the trail to where he lay on the floor. "Jasper," she whispered and fell to her knees beside him. "Jasper?"

Noah came barging in with his gun out. "Holy God."

"He won't wake up." Fletcher ran a hand across Jasper's cheek, then pulled his upper body onto her lap.

Noah radioed for an ambulance. "Help's on the way," he said softly. "Fletcher, you need to let go so I can check his pulse."

"I's ain't letting go. I's ain't ever letting go. Make him wake up, Reed, please," she begged. Her speech reverted to that of her youth when she was emotional, but that was the least of her worries. She shook Jasper's limp body. "Damn it, Jasper! I said wake the fuck up, so you wake the fuck up, old man."

Noah's hand was hot against her skin as he maneuvered around her to check Jasper's throat. "It's thready, but he's still got a pulse. The ambulance is on the way. Fletcher, you have to let go."

"Don't touch me. Help him. Damn it. He can't die. Please, Noah, help me." She tightened her trembling arms around Jasper. "Please, I'll do anything if you just help us."

"I'm sorry, I've done all I can. I need to clear the scene." He drew his weapon and made his way through the house.

Fletcher held onto Jasper until sirens blared outside.

"There's no sign of anyone," Noah said, coming back into the room. "You'll need to let the paramedics do their jobs."

Fletcher stood back while the EMTs cut open Jasper's night shirt. He couldn't die. He wouldn't leave her. He wouldn't. "I want to go," she said as they pushed the gurney outside. People would be looking. Jasper would hate that; he wouldn't want anyone to see him like this.

"I'm sorry, Fletcher, there isn't any room," Noah said.

"I want to go!" What about that didn't he get?

"I'll take you," Noah told her. "Or I can call your parents."

"I'll drive my damn self!" She headed for her truck, which was still running.

****

The waiting room was as quiet as a wake, which was ridiculous because Jasper wasn't going to die. He was a fighter, like her. He wouldn't leave her.

She stared at the empty chairs. Alex and Jake couldn't desert their guest, though Jake had offered to

55

come. Charlie had gone to their parents' house to be with Jebb and Mack, while Craig finished closing the bar. She was here with her parents and Reed. Fanfuckingtastic.

"Fletcher, do you want something to drink?" her mother asked, her long honey-brown hair falling over her shoulder.

"I don't want anything," she snapped. "Sorry, Mama."

"It's okay, baby," Savannah said and reached out to squeeze Fletcher's arm.

Fletch recoiled. Her mother's fingers were icy, like Daemon's always had been. Her entire body clenched, and she took a moment to relax. She did her breathing. The last thing she needed was to go down a rabbit hole.

"Jasper's strong, Fletcher. He'll be all right," Savannah said.

"Maybe you should go home and change your clothes, Fletch," Pops suggested.

Her clothes were stained with blood. She stood to pace. "I'm not fucking leaving."

"Sweetheart, you need to calm down."

"I don't want to calm the fuck down, Ma!" She winced and was about to apologize when a nurse hustled over to them.

"Ma'am, if you don't lower your voice and keep your language clean, I'm going to have to ask you to leave."

"Fu—" Reed's big, hot hand covered her mouth.

"I'll take care of it," Noah assured the nurse, then let Fletcher go when the woman nodded and went back to her desk. Turning to Fletcher he said, "If you don't start acting like a civilized human being, I'll arrest you for inciting a riot. Now sit down and shut up!"

She shoved past him and found herself face-to-face with a woman in blue scrubs, whose name tag read Dr. Lowell.

"Are you here for Jasper Hart?" she asked.

"Yes," Fletcher said, and her parents stood behind her. "How is he?"

"I'm afraid he's in critical condition. There are some decisions to be made, but I need to speak with a family member. Are any of you immediate family?"

"Yes," Fletcher said. "I'm his daughter."

"McKay," Noah hissed and showed his badge. "I'm Sheriff Noah Reed of Blue Creek, and I know this woman is not his daughter. Jasper Hart has no children."

Fletcher turned to Reed. "Noah, please."

"You can't honestly expect me to let you commit fraud right in front of me, McKay? I'm sorry, Doctor."

"Me too. Without a family member"—Dr. Lowell shrugged—"my hands are tied."

"We are his family," Savannah said, her tone daring the doctor to say any different. And Fletcher would have cheered if her stomach wasn't in knots.

The doctor sighed. "I don't doubt that, ma'am. But without a next of kin or power of attorney, it's as I said, my hands—"

"I *am* his daughter," Fletcher said again. She would be heard, even if it killed her.

"That's enough," Emmit said.

"Fletcher, is it?" Dr. Lowell rubbed a hand through her spiky blonde hair. "I'm sorry, but this isn't helping."

Fletcher took a deep breath. "I was adopted," she

told Dr. Lowell, but her gaze never veered from her father's. "I am Jasper Hart's daughter; the paternity test was done at this hospital. The results should be in your system, and if that's not enough, I have his power of attorney. His medical directives should also be on file. Why don't you go check?" Why hadn't she said that in the first fucking place?

"I—" The doctor's gaze darted amongst them. "I'll just be a minute."

Fletcher turned to her parents. "I didn't want to tell anybody. Jasper always wanted to. He thought we should but"—she lifted her shoulder—"I's didn't want to hurt you. I'm sorry for the subterfuge," she whispered, then ran to the bathroom. Chickenshit that she was.

She did her breathing, then splashed water over her face several times and grabbed a few paper towels to mop up the mess. Jasper's blood was smeared across her face. She tried to wipe it off and jumped when the door opened. "This is the ladies' room, Reed," she said and tossed the paper towels in the trash.

"It's true, isn't it? About Jasper?"

She looked into silver eyes. "Yes." She slid to the hard floor and rested her head in her hands.

"I can see it now. See you in him or him in you. The eyes," he said, motioning to his own.

"Get my height from him too." She grinned, then sobered. "I just crushed my parents." That was putting it mildly. She could almost hear Jasper say, *See what keeping secrets gets ya, missy?*

"They'll understand," Noah said and sat on the floor next to her. "What choice do they have?"

"These are the McKays you're talking about. Trust

me, I'm royally fucked." She looked over at him. "Jasper wanted to get the truth out in the open so bad. Warned me it would come back to bite me in the ass. He was right…as usual."

Noah shook his head. "You love him."

"Of course I love him." She stared at her hands. "I love Pops too. I love being a McKay, and I was never willing to give that up. Jasper respected my decision. If he dies, I don't know what I'm going to do."

"You'll get through it. I'm not saying you won't be in a world of pain—you will—but that lessens with time. Besides, if I know anything about you, it's that you're a survivor," Noah said and bumped her shoulder with his. "I think this is the first conversation we've had in years where you weren't calling me an asshole."

"The night's still young, Reed," she said and stood. "I've got a lot of explaining to do." She sighed. This was so going to suck, but she would suffer the hounds of hell for Jasper.

He got to his feet and dusted off his pants. "If you need any help…"

She snorted. "Don't worry, I'll call someone else. What?" she asked when he took hold of her arm.

"Give me your phone."

Fletcher scrunched her brows but unlocked her cell and handed it to him. He pressed in some numbers, and the phone in his pocket rang. She smirked when he handed it back to her. "Thanks," she said. There was no way in hell.

"It's my new number; call if you need me."

Yeah, right. She straightened her shoulders and took a deep breath, but it shuddered in her chest, and a fresh wave of tears began. Aw, fuck, she didn't want

Reed to see her cry. She couldn't afford to be weak around him.

He took her arm again and led her to the sinks.

"You're awful grabby tonight, Reed." She sniffed.

"Shh, let me." He got a couple of paper towels, wet one, moved her braid over her shoulder, and placed the wet towel on her neck. He used the others to dry her tears.

Fletcher sighed. She would never admit it was nice. And she would cut out her tongue before she ever told anyone being next to him quieted the chaos within her. It's like he was so freaking huge, he blocked whatever negative waves were on the offensive. She hated that Reed was the only person she had ever experienced the sensation with. It was some sort of trickery, and she couldn't figure it out. He made her feel safe, when history proved she was anything but safe with Reed. He was a danger to her on multiple levels, and she needed to get the fuck away from him.

He put the towels in the trash, then stood in front of her again. His silver gaze was intense, and she swayed toward him. Drawn to him. "There's something I've wanted—"

She sucked in a breath. "It's a bad idea." Fletch wanted it too. Had wanted it for so long, denied it. Hated him more for being able to make her want it.

He cupped her cheek. "Shut up, McKay," Reed said, and before she could snap back with something snarky, he kissed her.

Fletcher kept her eyes open for a good two seconds, then she let herself indulge in Noah's lips and scruffy stubble. In one deft move, he picked her up and set her on the edge of one of the sinks. She wrapped her arms around his neck and sought entrance into his mouth.

Noah tilted his head; he tasted like coffee and scotch and, hell's bells, the heat. His hard body was scorching against hers. She wanted to entomb herself in him, become one with him. From the first time she'd seen him… Those thoughts scared her, reminded her, and she stiffened. Noah must have realized what they were doing too, because he brushed his lips against her jaw line, then took a step back.

Fletcher hopped off the sink, resisting the overwhelming urge to touch her lips. She almost made it to the door without looking at him. Shame swathed her. She'd given in to it. In to him. It had been brief, but hell's bells—

"McKay?"

She stopped but refused to make eye contact. "Yeah?"

"Was that a mistake?"

"We're enemies, Reed. With a capital E." She licked her lips. "To say this was a moment of weakness is an understatement."

Her parents were still in the waiting room. She took a breath. *Here we go.* She had almost come within their line of sight when Dr. Lowell stopped her. That got her parents' attention too.

"Ms. McKay? Fletcher?"

"Yeah?" Her parents were behind her.

"I found the files, and I need you to sign a few things so we can get your father situated."

"Can you give me a sec?"

Dr. Lowell looked past Fletcher's head, at her parents. "Of course. I'll wait right here."

Fletcher nodded. She motioned her parents farther into a more private corner of the waiting room. "I'm sorry I didn't tell you."

"You're always sorry you didn't tell us something," her father snapped, his blue-gray gaze cold.

"Emmit, let her finish," Savannah said with tears in her eyes.

"I'm sorry, Pops," she croaked out. "This is why I—I didn't want to hurt you."

"Go take care of Jasper, and I'll talk to you later," he said and moved to leave, then turned back. "And, Fletcher, I'll call you. Don't call me."

"He doesn't mean that, baby. He's upset. You do what you need to and call me later, okay?" her mother said; then her gaze went to the door as it slammed shut behind Pops. "Maybe you shouldn't come by the house until he's had some time. I love you, Fletcher, and none of this changes that."

"Okay, Ma," Fletcher said around the lump in her throat.

****

Dawn was breaking by the time she reached her cabin. Walking inside, she bypassed the kitchen where Jasper's chili still simmered in the crock pot. She ignored the wilted flowers and broken glass and headed straight for her underground lair. Once in the second tunnel, she let the tears come again. By the time she got to the main bunker, she was sobbing.

She had sat with Jasper's unconscious body for hours, listening to the steady beeps of the machines that were keeping him alive. There had been an issue during surgery. One of the two gunshot wounds had done its job, and Jasper had flatlined; the trauma surgeons had resuscitated him, but he slipped into a coma. Fletcher had asked Dr. Lowell if there was a chance he'd recover. Slim, the doc had said. But a chance was a chance, and Fletcher would risk it until she felt otherwise. She wasn't a quitter, and neither was Jasper.

She turned the shower on, undid her braid, then took off her bloodstained clothes. Once steam was rolling across the top of the stall, she stepped under the spray. She glanced at her feet; traces of Jasper's blood slid down the drain. Fletcher covered her mouth to stifle the sob.

Life as she knew it was over. Her secret was out, and it was time to pay the piper. Pops had been distraught, and her sisters had already texted her multiple times. They were upset about the situation too, but they'd all have to wait. Right now, she had to bring Jasper justice. Carrying on like a sissy crybaby wouldn't accomplish anything.

Fletch washed her hair twice, then scrubbed her body until it was pink—until she was clean again. It had taken her four showers a day for two months to feel unsullied after Daemon had taken her hostage. Everyone had thought Daemon had raped her while she was his captive, but his psychosis had left him blessedly impotent. Of course, in his twisted mind, he thought he had gotten her pregnant, and she had let him believe what he wanted. But it took sperm to make a baby, and there wasn't any exchange. Fletcher was beyond thankful for that. There had been kissing, but—she gagged and scrubbed her face again, not wanting to go down any rabbit holes.

The water turned cold, so she shut it off, patted

herself dry, then wrapped the towel around her head. She went bare-assed to the kitchen and put on a pot of coffee. There was no way in hell she was going to sleep.

She slipped on her underwear and with loathing put on her bra. She wore a C cup, which would be all right if she wasn't vertically challenged and small-boned. She looked top-heavy. She shook her head at her reflection, then trapped her hair in another long french braid.

She pulled on a pair of jeans, one of her nicer tops, and studied herself in the mirror. Not too shabby. Not that she was a prissy pants or anything, but people generally believed what was in front of them, and if they saw a determined woman, then that's how she wanted to be perceived.

She was pouring a cup of coffee when the bunker shook. Dirt sprayed through the slats of the ceiling. She rolled her eyes, then grabbed a travel mug and switched her coffee into that. She wet a dishtowel, snagged her cell from the bed, then crawled under her desk and hit redial.

"Reed."

She looked at the phone. Hadn't her parents been her last call? Yes, but Reed had put his number in her phone after. Some of the ceiling fell on the floor in chunks. Fuck it. She cleared her throat and practically purred, "Hi, Noah."

"McKay?"

"Were you sleeping?" Should she get a breakfast bar? Making a mad dash, she grabbed the box, an apple, and a bottle of water.

"Trying to."

"You sound sexy on the phone," she said, taking a bite out of her apple. "Did I ever tell you that?" They'd spent hours on the phone once upon a time.

There was a long pause. "No."

"Oh, well, you do." She chewed. He was sexy. She hated him for that. She hated everything about him. The bastard.

"Is something wrong?"

"I forgot you put your number in my phone, and I hit redial." The overhead light crashed to the floor, and she growled. It had taken her forever to find that fucking fixture.

"What's all that damn noise? Where the hell are you?"

"I'm at my cabin in my bunker."

"You have a bunker under your cabin?"

"Yep." She finished the fruit, then threw the core out on the floor. It didn't matter now.

"What is that noise?"

"Well, did we have an earthquake?" She took a sip of her water.

"No. What kind of question is that?" His voice had gone deep and growly. Was she annoying him? Good.

Puffs of debris formed. "If we didn't have an earthquake, then you need to come get me."

"What are you talking about?"

"Someone blew up my cabin." She shook her head as more crap rained down. Motherfu—

"What?"

"Someone put what I'm assuming was an explosive device in my cabin, and it went boom."

"Are you fucking serious?"

"Unfortunately. I forgot to do a perimeter check

before I came inside," Fletcher admitted. She'd been too distracted. Stupid, stupid mistake. Like not making a direct exit out of this bunker. Fucking idiot.

"The lurker?"

"That's my guess… Now, if you could hurry the hell up, I'd appreciate it. I've got about a two-day oxygen supply in here, but the aftershocks are strong enough to cut that off, which would give me about two hours of air. But if any flames reach the oxygen stores…there'll be a much bigger boom. So, if you could call some people and come get me the hell out of here, that'd be great." She smiled. He must have dropped the phone because there were fumbling noises, and then some colorful language. The latter impressed the hell out of her.

"I'll call Todd Mae and get help out there. Do you want me to call your family? Wait, how the hell are you talking to me?"

"Cell phones are great, aren't they?"

"They aren't that good."

Fletcher snorted. "Well, when you rig a signal so it's right above your house, connections are generally consistent."

"Fine, I'm on my way."

"I'll be here," she said around a mouthful of the breakfast bar.

"Do you want to stay on the line?"

"Nah, I'll see you soon enough." Turning off her phone, she got comfortable and rested her head against the back of the desk. Would her parents come to investigate if they heard the boom? Would Pops show? Fletcher pursed her lips. It was safer not to dwell on it.

Better to figure out a way to make someone pay for all this fuckery.

Chapter Nine

The firetrucks were there when Noah arrived. They had the fire over 60 percent contained. He waved to the fire chief, Todd Mae. The sheriff's department didn't have funding for a bomb squad like the city police, but Todd had made sure his guys were certified. Noah took in the destruction and closed his eyes. If she hadn't been in her bunker, she'd be dead. Who the hell built a bunker in their home anyway? Fletcher J. McKay, that's who, thank God.

When he'd answered his phone and heard her loud mouth, Noah figured she'd remembered he'd kissed her and was calling to tell him to go to hell. He couldn't blame her; it had been a moment of pure insanity, hadn't it? But…she had been flirting, right? With Fletcher, one was never sure, and then she'd said someone blew up her cabin. He shook his head.

Emmit came running down the path shouting at Noah. "Is she in there?"

He grabbed Emmit's shoulders. "She called me from her bunker. She's fine for now."

"What the hell happened?"

Noah filled the other man in.

Emmit shifted from foot to foot, not taking his eyes from the rubble. "Do they know where she is?"

Noah nodded. "I talked to Todd on my way over here." The firefighters turned off their hoses and started to dig through what was left of Fletcher's home.

"Found the timer," the fire chief called out.

"I've got to check that out," he told Emmit. Noah went over to where Todd Mae was standing. "Professional?"

"Nah, it's the kind of thing anyone can find online," Todd said.

"Did the job, though." Noah examined the burnt piece of plastic, then glanced at Todd; the older man looked pained. The fire chief was in his fifties with salt-and-pepper hair and hard, dark eyes. He was one of the good guys in and outside of the job.

"We're looking for a way to get in the bunker." He rocked back on his heels and shook his head. "Nothing normal about that girl. Heard about Jasper. How's he holding up?"

"He's in a coma. It's wait and pray right now."

"You make sure you get the son of a bitch." Todd spoke into his headset and looked at Noah. "We found it. You want to get her? We've got extra gear."

Noah grinned. "Love to."

****

Fletcher held the wet towel to her face and tapped the foot that was going numb. What was taking so damn long? There was a lot of commotion going on above her, and she had to pee. A shaft of light broke through the darkness. She dropped the towel. "It's about time!"

"McKay?"

"Reed?" What in the actual—

"Come on, McKay, where are you?" Noah asked, the beam of his flashlight bouncing off the wreckage.

"Glad you could make it. Now get that light out of

my eyes, and get me the hell out of here," she said, flinching when he lifted her desk and tossed it aside. "I liked that desk."

"Shut up and give me your hand." When she hesitated, he bent and lifted her in a fireman's hold.

"Take it easy, would you? I have to pee so bad it's not even funny." She was not amused when he smacked her butt.

It took two firemen to help them out of the bunker. Once Noah put her down, she ran behind a tree. When she came back out, everyone was staring at her.

"What? None of you have ever had to relieve yourselves before? Didn't think so." She waved at her father and would have started toward him, but he turned on his heel and walked away. The tears in her eyes were from the smoke, not because her father turned his back on her.

"You okay?" Todd asked and gave her a one-armed hug.

"About as good as I can be. My cabin's not doing so hot though." She went through the events of the morning with the fire chief.

"All right, call your insurance company, and I'll talk to you later," Todd said, then made a circle with his finger telling his men to come together for a briefing.

Noah walked over to her. "Do you need me to take you somewhere?"

"Nah, my truck's right over there." She pointed to her vehicle, thankful it was okay, just covered with a thick coating of dust.

"Where are you going to stay?"

That was a damn good question. "I'll find a place. Have the guys cleared Jasper's house yet?"

"I can't give you information on an ongoing investigation," Noah reminded her.

"Seriously? Get the stick from out of your ass, Reed. I'm the victim's daughter and have the right to know what's going on concerning his case."

"Do you really want to go that route? If you do, the entire town will know the truth."

Anger curled in her belly. "Don't fuck with me, Reed," she warned and fished her keys out of her pocket. "You have a choice. We can join forces or—"

"You're not a deputy anymore, McKay."

"Yeah, well, I have a PI license, so I'll hire myself to find out who tried to kill Jasper and me. See, Reed, I don't need you. Can you say the same?" Fletcher raised a brow, then headed to her truck. She started the engine and gave Noah the one-finger salute as she drove past him.

****

Fletcher opened the door of the diner. It was before lunch, so the place wasn't crowded. She stopped midstride when Charlie called her name and ran her way. Fletcher let her sister hug her and even hugged her back.

"I just got off the phone with Alex; she told me what happened. My God, Fletcher!" Charlie shook her head and hugged her again. "You could have been killed!"

"I'm fine," Fletcher said. "I could use some coffee though." She was relieved when Charlie pulled her toward a stool.

"Sit. Are you hungry?"

Fletcher pointed to the machine on the counter. "I'll take that pot of coffee and a straw."

Charlie let out a huffed laugh but hurried around the counter and poured Fletcher a mug of coffee. "Drink up."

Fletcher pulled twenty bucks from her pocket and placed it in front of her sister. "For the jar."

Charlie hesitated. "You've been through a trauma—"

"May as well cover my ass," Fletcher said with a smirk. Knowing the "ass" was all it would take.

Charlie rolled her eyes. "If you're going to be like that…" She snatched up the bill and put it in the Pay for Profanity jar.

Fletcher gave her sister a small smile, then fixed her coffee to her liking. Before she'd even brought the cup to her lips, she was out of her stool and being hugged by Tiny. She patted his big shoulder. If he kept this up, she'd start crying like a sissy.

"Oh, shug," he whispered and squeezed.

"Damn it." The tears started. Tiny set her down and grabbed a napkin to dry her eyes. She snatched it from him. "You being sweet to me is making it worse, Tiny." She turned into a silly puddle of mush anytime the man was affectionate with her. He was her coach; he was supposed to be a hard-ass—

"Should I call Julia?" Tiny looked at Charlie, then back at Fletch.

What little heat she had in her body flooded to Fletcher's cheeks. Julia was Tiny's wife and a renowned head shrinker. People literally lined up to talk to her whenever she visited Tiny at the diner. She was wicked smart, beautiful, and everyone wanted a moment with her. Fletcher had spent an unprecedented amount of time in her youth bombarding the woman with questions about psychology. So much so, Julia implemented the rule about never taking any of her neighbors as clients, especially the McKays.

Fletcher glared at him and pointed to the two customers sitting in the back booth. They seemed a safe distance away, but even the napkin holders had ears in Blue Creek. If she was going to seek assistance on matters of mental health, that was her business. She leaned closer to Tiny, and the big man bent. "I may or may not have already spoken with Julia." Tiny was one of the few people who knew certain things about where Fletch had gone on her "vacations."

Tiny straightened with a nod. "I gotcha, shug." His gold tooth flashed, and he gave her another squeeze. "Hungry?"

She shrugged. "I don't rightly know how I feel." Somewhere between amped on adrenaline and the crash that came after.

"I'll make some sandwiches, see how that does," he said and gave Charlie some kind of signal, which her sister returned.

"It's most appreciated, Tiny," Fletcher said before the swinging door closed. She sipped her coffee and sighed. "What?" Charlie was staring at her in that weird mother way she had that made Fletcher's scalp prickle.

"Why didn't you tell anyone about Jasper?"

Fletch winced. "Won't no one's business. Now keep your damn voice down."

"Fine, don't tell me; maybe you'll talk to them." Charlie smirked and pointed to where Jebb and Jake walked in.

"Kid!" Jake picked Fletcher up from her stool, swung her around, and then held her tight. "You're trying to make my hair fall out, aren't you?"

Fletcher rolled her eyes and accepted Jake's hug. "It's not like I set the explosives myself." No, the lurker had done it. Her surveillance was saved online, so Fletch had looked at the footage from the night before.

"My turn," Jebb said and picked her up.

"Put me down, bullfrog!" Fletcher kissed her brother's cheek when he did. He looked so much like Pops it was almost painful. But his sapphire-blue eyes were shiny with tears, and Fletcher couldn't do anything but try to comfort him. "Don't get yourself all worked up, okay," she said, then asked Charlie what in the world she was doing. She had boxed her other customer's meals and shooed them away.

"We're closing for a private event. Tiny and I will fix some sandwiches, and we'll talk about things."

"All that hard work," Jebb said shaking his head. "And boom, it's gone."

"Do you think the same person who attacked Jasper bombed your house?" Tiny asked as he and Charlie handed out sandwiches and chips.

"I won't discount the likelihood of that," Fletcher said. As they ate, she explained about her uninvited guest.

"You couldn't get any decent footage?" Jebb asked with his mouth full.

She shook her head. "Just a dark, lurking shadow moving around the cabin. My guess is they were placing explosives. They knew I wasn't there."

Jake rubbed his beard. "Maybe they set it up so you wouldn't be there?"

"Exactly." She sipped her coffee. "And if that's not enough, I went to Jasper's before I came here and found these in his office safe." She pulled a plastic baggy from her back pocket. The bag contained several notes, all in the same style of writing as the notes left for her and Noah. She told the table that.

"What do they say?" Jebb asked.

Fletcher glanced at the others. "They're warnings. Telling Jasper to watch his back. He should have fucking listened or told me about it."

"You can't be pissed at him, kid," Jake said. "You did the same thing."

"Yeah," Charlie agreed. "Why would Jasper be any different?"

"He's recovering from heart surgery. He didn't need to keep this to himself and add more strain." Not that it mattered now; she ducked her head.

Tiny reached over and gave her shoulder a squeeze. She met his gaze, patted his hand, and mumbled, "Stop being sweet to me." Tiny's gold tooth flashed.

"Dad doesn't want anyone near either of you," Jebb said with a surprising amount of bitterness.

"Bullfrog, don't you be getting in the middle of this. You understand me? What's happening with Pops is between him and me. There's no need for you to be going to bat for me and pissing him off. I appreciate it, but stop." She didn't want her brother joining her on their father's shit list.

"Someone's gotta do something. He and Mama got into a huge argument this morning. She couldn't believe he left your cabin without asking you if you were okay. She was really upset." Jebb leaned closer to her. "There were tears."

"I'll talk to Ma." Fletcher spoke to the entire group. "And when the time's right, I'll talk to Pops too."

Charlie topped off Fletcher's coffee. "You can talk to our parents at your own pace."

Fletcher toasted her with her mug.

"What's the latest on Jasper?" Tiny asked.

"Doctor said there was a slim chance he'd come out of the coma, and I should start making preparations." Fletcher fiddled with her unused utensils. She wouldn't make arrangements. Couldn't. "Said the machines are keeping him going right now."

"Jasper Hart is too damn stubborn to give up. He'll be fine," Jake decreed.

"Damn straight. Jasper ain't ever let anyone bring him down. That's not going to change." Fletcher hoped.

"What I want to know is whether or not you're planning on showing Noah the letters?"

"Be serious, Charlie!" Jake shook his head. "She took those out of Jasper's house. She fucked with the crime scene."

"I called one of the deputies to make sure they were done going over the property. It's not my fault they didn't find Jasper's safe," Fletcher assured them. If Reed wouldn't keep her informed, someone would.

"But still." Charlie worried her lower lip. "Noah could get you on breaking and entering, couldn't he?"

"Can't break into your own house," Fletcher murmured, halfway hoping Reed would try.

Tiny paused from gathering empty plates. "What are you talking about, shug?"

Fletcher sighed. "After Laura died, Jasper signed the deed for the house over to me." Laura had known the truth about Fletcher and had welcomed her into their lives like the daughter she'd never been able to have. She had kept their secret and never treated Fletch with anything but love and kindness.

Charlie sucked in a breath. "He did?"

"He was depressed. I said I didn't want his stupid-ass old house, but he said he wanted me to shut my damn mouth and take it." She shrugged, then grinned. "Whenever something goes wrong, he bitches to me about how his landlord needs to fix it." Everyone laughed. Jasper did that, made you laugh. Made your heart lighter.

"What are you going to do now?" Tiny asked when everyone had fallen silent.

"I'm gonna find this lurker wannabe-lyricist."

"Then what?" Jake asked with narrowed eyes.

She brought her mug to her lips. "Then I'm gonna get justice."

Chapter Ten

Noah sat behind his desk at the station. People had been coming in and out all day to see if the rumors about Jasper were true. He sympathized with their concern, but he didn't want to be asked what he was doing about it. His damn job, that's what.

He looked up when there was a knock. "Come in."

"Noah?" Craig shut the door and took a seat. Noah's cousin was a few inches shorter than him, but the other man was built like a tank with reddish-brown hair and blue eyes. They'd been close as children and lived together in college, but Noah wasn't sure which family Craig was representing on this visit. "How's your day been?"

Noah leaned back in his chair. "I'm sure news has broken out at the McKay camp. In fact, you probably know more than I do."

"Probably." Craig pulled out a plastic baggy.

"What's this?" Noah grabbed a pair of latex gloves when Craig explained. He took the bag. "Did you inform Ms. McKay that breaking and entering is a crime?"

"One of your deputies gave her the all clear, said y'all were done collecting evidence, and…it's her house." Craig grinned when Noah cursed under his breath.

"I should have known. Was she aware of these?"

There were seven notes in total, and Noah read through each one. Jasper should have trusted him.

"No. She was pissed, but that's nothing new for her. You find anything? Don't look at me like that. We'll find out one way or another."

Noah rose a brow. "We? As in the McKays?"

"Charlie may have taken my last name, but it probably should have been the other way around. I swear it's like a sickness. The McKays surround you until you're one of them. Like mind control or something. Even Mack. In fact, I think she's the best one of them all."

Noah couldn't help but smile. The little girl was a charmer, and he was glad his cousin had finally found happiness. "I'll give you this; the person who sent the flowers to Fletcher sent the florist a money order which included a hefty tip, a note with directions to Fletcher's cabin, and a personal letter for the recipient."

"Not traceable?"

Noah shook his head. "That bit of information is free, and I'll remind you civilian intrusion in police matters is a no-no."

" 'Course not. I'm working with a group of private investigators. They need my skills, and I'm willing to do it, seeing as how they're family."

"The Kellers?" Was he surprised they were butting in? Nope.

"Right you are," Craig said, grinning. "My cousin, so smart."

"This is a bloody mess, Craig." Noah sighed.

"No shit. With everything that's going on and then add Emmit not speaking to Fletcher, Charlie's going berserk. She likes everything nice and peaceful in the family."

"I wondered about that this morning when Emmit left the scene." Noah shook his head and thought of what he and Emmit had discussed the day before. Had it only been a day?

"I love Emmit like a second father. He's always been good to me and accepting of me. But this turning his back on Fletcher shit has stumped all of us. Pissed most of us off."

"He's having a rough time. Emmit felt like there was a disconnect between him and Fletcher before all this. He perceived Jasper as competing for his daughter's attention, only to discover his competitor was Fletcher's birth father. Be honest, Craig, how would you feel?"

His cousin rocked back on his heels. "Like someone sucker punched me."

"Exactly. Instead of talking to Fletcher, he's keeping silent. He's petrified she wouldn't choose him if it came down to it. He's pushing her away to protect himself."

"Damn."

"I'll find whoever hurt Jasper and blew up Fletcher's cabin. Tell your brothers-in-law to keep their noses out of it."

Craig laughed. "Noah, when are you going to learn? Nothing is ever that simple. You do your part, and we'll do ours. Hopefully, we'll all come to the same conclusion or meet in the middle."

"Fine. But I will arrest anyone who gets in my way." It was an empty threat, and they both knew it.

"Duly noted. And, hey, don't take for granted what it took for me to get those from Fletcher."

"She didn't want me to have them?" Noah wasn't surprised. He had brushed her off this morning.

Craig went to the door. "Let's just say, you owe Tiny a beer…or a twelve pack."

"Noted," Noah said, returning his cousin's phrase. Craig nodded, then left.

Noah sighed and took another look at the letters Jasper had received. There had been no sign of forced entry, no fingerprints, and no leads. But someone had been watching Jasper. Someone…he paused. What had Craig said? Going through his folders, Noah found the note sent with Fletcher's flowers. Craig had mentioned something about the McKays sucking you in until you were one of them. Noah read the note out loud. "None by name and none by right." The daughters all had the McKay name. But their husbands were McKays by marriage.

Jasper was close enough to the McKays to be considered one of them. Noah flipped through Jasper's stack and at the one letter that didn't mimic a nursery rhyme.

Sheriff, I'm disappointed, I confess
Here you're drowning in her mess
Every word she says is a lie
Do you ever ask her why?
Interesting choice to take your place
Everyone will see her disgrace
Simply a pawn in this game—for shame, for shame.

Why was this note different? He went back over it a few times. The last couplet was on one line instead of two. Why? It was obvious they were talking about

Fletcher and him. Someone expected Noah to "disgrace" Fletcher. By arresting her for Daemon's murder?

Turning in his chair, he took the note and made a copy. He circled the first letter of each line with a marker. Then he wrote the letters in order at the bottom of the page.

"Son of a bitch," he hissed. The letters spelled out: She Dies. Fletcher was the target.

He snagged his keys and headed out of the office. He told his deputies to call him if there were any problems. It didn't take long to get to the McKay home. Fletcher wouldn't be there, but Noah could update Emmit of the latest under that guise. Keeping the older man informed was the least Noah could do, considering Emmit had taken him into his confidence.

He knocked on the door and waited. Maybe he should have gone to the hardware store, but Ryan had taken over for the most part, and Noah hadn't wanted to waste time. Or butt heads with Keller. Though he got along well with Ryan. But wait…Ryan and Casey were out of town, weren't they? Damn, he should have—

The door opened, and Savanah said, "Noah, should I take it by your uniform that something else has happened?"

"No, ma'am. I was looking for Fletcher."

She looked him up and down. "She's not here."

Noah nodded. "I don't suppose Mr. McKay's home?"

"Go around back. He's in his workshop brooding like he's been doing all afternoon!" She shut the door in his face.

The rotary saw's roar intensified the closer Noah

got to Emmit's workshop. He stopped in the doorway and waited for the other man to notice him.

"Noah," Emmit said after he shut off the machine. He opened the mini fridge and offered Noah a beverage.

"I'll take the tea, thanks."

"Here you go." Emmit took a water for himself.

Noah popped the top of the can. "What are you working on?"

"A few custom orders I had at the store."

"You closed early today?"

"Yeah, Ryan's out of town." Emmit cocked his head to the side. "What brings you out this way?"

"I found evidence that may shed light on why Jasper was shot."

Emmit hopped up on his workbench. "What kind of evidence?"

Noah told him about the letters. "They tried to kill him to get to her. To make her suffer first. I don't think they'll come after any of y'all."

Emmit rubbed his stomach. "Why not?"

"Because others have tried and failed, and this feels like a personal vendetta against Fletcher. They went after Jasper because she made him part of your family. Everyone in Blue Creek knows how close they are. The perfect pawn."

"They tried to kill Jasper to hurt Fletcher."

"This isn't about the McKays *or* Jasper, it's about her." He'd bet his badge on it.

"She's in danger. I guess that's obvious with the bombing of her cabin."

Noah pinched his bridge of his nose. "That's the thing; it's too soon."

"What do you mean?"

"When a cat gets a mouse, they play with it for a while before they kill it. They weren't trying to kill her this morning." That was Noah's theory.

"What?" Emmit shifted on the workbench. "This morning was some kind of miscalculation?"

"I believe so. The detonator was on a timer, not a sensory trigger. Whoever did this rigged the place while Fletcher was at the hospital. They weren't expecting her to return." He had to be missing something, but Noah couldn't put his finger on it. The person who Fletcher called "the lurker" had to be involved. It was too much of a coincidence.

Emmit took off his cap, scratched his head, then replaced the hat. "This isn't over."

"No," Noah said and took a long, hard look at Emmit. "I think it's resurfacing."

"Resurfacing?" Emmit grimaced.

"When Fletcher was getting drugged, she was the first one to suffer. The notes she received then are almost identical to the note she received the other night." The lurker again? Fletcher had claimed there had been someone hanging around her cabin when she'd been drugged. With the induced psychosis, people had doubted her. But now...

Emmit shook his head. "But we got the persons responsible."

"Did you? Think about it, Emmit. Someone killed the primary suspect, and the only people who would know about it are dead."

"Someone murdered Daemon Randle before he could, what? Talk?" Emmit hopped off the workbench and paced.

"They intended to kill two birds with one stone."

"How do you mean?"

Noah shrugged. "By taking Randle out, not only did they get rid of what we can only assume was an accomplice, but they framed Fletcher too, not knowing she would have a world-class alibi."

"But who could it be?"

Noah pulled out his keys. "That's what I'm going to find out."

Emmit nodded, then kicked at the dirt with his shoe. "Have you stuck a guard at Jasper's door?"

"I have." Noah was about to leave but decided to say one more thing. "Emmit?"

"Yeah?"

"I want you to think something over for me."

"What's that?"

"Fletcher said Jasper wanted the truth out, didn't want to hide their relationship from you or anyone. She loves Jasper, and everyone knows she'd do anything for him."

Emmit looked away, swallowed, then met Noah's eyes. "Go on."

"But she wouldn't do this for him, denied him the one thing he wanted most. Ask yourself why. Who was Fletcher protecting by keeping this secret?"

Chapter Eleven

Fletcher hefted the overflowing laundry basket on her hip and walked across the parking lot of Granny Vaughn's toward the apartment above the unattached garage. It was late, and she was exhausted. She had stayed at the B and B the night before, and Alexandra had offered use of the place until Fletcher either found somewhere else to stay or rebuilt her cabin.

Shifting the basket to rest on her thigh, Fletcher pulled the key from her pocket and unlocked the door. The small apartment was still furnished from when Alex had rented it to Craig. It was set up with the basic amenities: water, electric, Wi-Fi, and internet access. Not to mention Alex had already stocked the fridge and put fresh sheets on the bed. Who could ask for more?

Fletcher had gone by the hospital earlier in the afternoon to check on Jasper and found Pops there. He hadn't seen her; she had stood outside the door while he spoke to Jasper's unconscious form. She had listened for a few minutes but left when Pops started going on about how he couldn't look at her. Pops wasn't her favorite person right now either, but she was squashing those feelings down deep.

Fletcher shook her head. Better not to think about that. She went into the bedroom and plopped the basket down on the mattress. She had come back to the B and B from the hospital and been besieged by the women in her family. They'd insisted on taking her out to replace some things she'd lost.

She thanked the good Lord again that she had left her bag in her truck the morning of the explosion. Sure, it had been pure laziness on her part, leaving her bag under the front seat of her truck instead of bringing it inside, but she was thankful anyway. She wouldn't need to replace her license, permits, or credit cards.

But she had had to replace a bunch of crap which meant going stupid shopping. She'd been poked and measured. Prodded and color coordinated. Except for when they had gone to the hunting store and bought a new knife, Fletcher had been miserable.

Her mother and Charlie made sure she got the basic necessities. But none of it made up for the fact that she had to be shopping for over four hours. Not to mention another two hours of girl talk while she washed her purchases at the B and B.

Sighing, she put away her new threads. She'd bought a bunch of clothes and a couple pairs of shoes. Then there had been the underwear…Alex hadn't only made her match all her bras and panties, but she'd also insisted Fletch buy some frilly, lacey, fancy crap. Fletch had gone along with whatever her sister suggested to hasten their exit from the lingerie store. She rolled her eyes. Like anyone was gonna care what she wore under her clothes. "Waste of money," she said to the garments as she shoved them in the drawer.

She had a few things at her parents' house and Jasper's, plus a storage locker with spare clothes and supplies, but Fletcher didn't want to use her backups. Though she might go there to get some security cameras. Craig had outfitted the B and B with a top-of-the-line system, but he hadn't gotten around to the apartment yet. She would add it to her list of things to do.

After she took a shower, she put on some undies and a sports bra, then brushed out her long, wet hair and let it hang loose. While she was looking at her reflection, she grabbed a smaller mirror and inspected the damage. Would the scars ever fade?

Turning, she examined her front. There weren't too many scars on her belly, but her back had taken a good lashing or five. Maybe she should get a full body tattoo. Nah, she wouldn't, but it would shut everyone up. She put on her new, clean jammies, then went to the kitchen and started a pot of coffee.

She pulled her favorite show up on her tablet and set it aside. The file boxes she'd taken from Jasper's house were stacked on the kitchen table, so she began sorting through them. When Jasper was sheriff, he'd kept personal records on every citizen of Blue Creek. He knew everything about everyone, and Fletcher was going to too. Despite popular belief, Jasper did not reveal his secrets to her; the man was an enigma.

She was a quarter of the way through her first stack when she came across a name she recognized, not because they were from Blue Creek but because they weren't. She read and reread the file, her stomach churning. The date was wrong, the—the death was wrong. Without a second thought, she grabbed her keys and rushed out the door.

She arrived at the hospital barefoot and had to buy flip-flops from the gift shop before she could go any farther. Visiting hours were over, but she didn't care. She had clearance with Dr. Lowell. She gave a nod to

Deputy Hewitt, who Noah had put on guard duty. Hewitt would no doubt fill Noah in on her presence; the man was a tattletale. She went into Jasper's room, stared at the monitors, then looked at him.

"How could you lie to my face all these years?"

"McKay?" Noah said coming into the room. "You planning on staying the night?"

"Bite me, Reed," she sneered, then looked at Jasper. "You better wake up, old man, because when you do, we're gonna have the biggest quarrel of 'em all!"

Noah pointed to her shoulder. "What's that?"

She glanced at her tattoo. "A peony, you know, the flower?"

"Peony?" Noah murmured and leaned closer.

His body heat was intense and inviting. She steeled herself. "I've got 'em on my back too. Entry and exit wounds. See?" She turned this way and that.

His steely gaze met hers. "Nice."

She shrugged. "Thanks."

"Why are you upset with Jasper?" he asked, motioning to the bed.

"None of your business," she said and headed for the door. "I'll be out of town for a day, maybe two, so if anything should happen, anything at all, call me." She didn't wait for an answer.

Chapter Twelve

She left the apartment not long after having brunch with Jake and Alex. It was about a two-hour drive to get where she was going. If you wanted the facts, you needed to go straight to the source. The truth she had found years ago was only what Jasper had conjured up. The nerve of the man!

Walking to the courthouse, she tightened the strap of her messenger bag and straightened her suit jacket. If Alex had taught her anything, it was that how you dressed in business situations spoke volumes; know your audience. Under normal circumstances, Fletcher couldn't give a rip. Her uniform, her gun, had always spoken for her, but those days were gone.

Fletcher found the clerk of courts office, went to the big wooden desk, and pressed the bell labeled Ring for Service. A young guy with blond hair and blue eyes came out from the back and asked what he could do for her. Fletcher gave him her best smile and handed him the slip of paper where she'd written the case file number from Jasper's notes.

"No problem," he said and began typing. "Uh-oh."

She stepped closer. "Is something wrong?"

"Oh, no. That was the sound I make whenever I have to send someone to the chamber." He bobbed his eyebrows.

She couldn't help but smile. "What's 'the

chamber'?"

"The no-man's-land of lost and forgotten files. They're organized, but it's dark and dank down there. What's even stranger is that, given this date, these should be electronic, not paper. Certainly not in the chamber. It's almost as if someone—"

"Someone what?" She eyed him.

He pursed his lips. "Nothing. It's probably an error. Anyway, it's a pain in the butt to find things. Organized or not. Are you sure you want to look?"

"Positive." She didn't want to, she had to.

She followed the guy, whose name was Taft, named after his stoner mother's favorite president, or so he told her. But really, whose favorite president was Taft? This Taft was a criminal justice student, and he was her age. He was pretty cute in a bookworm sort of way, and he wasn't that much taller than her, which was a bonus. She should think about men like him, not big brutes like—

"This is it." Taft flipped the lights on.

"Nice." The room was exactly as he'd described. It kind of reminded her of a closet, which was fitting, but it sucked just the same.

"Do you want me to help?"

"No, thank you." She gave him a small smile. Why wasn't he scurrying away?

Taft shuffled his feet. "If this is going to take you a while, would you want to grab a bite to eat? I get off in a few hours."

"We could grab a beer." She was no doubt going to need one. And Taft was an interesting guy.

"Really?"

She rubbed her nose. "Why ask if you weren't sure

I'd say yes?" Why did men have to be so confusing? The guys she was usually attracted to turned out to be gay, disturbed, or assholes. Taft seemed safe.

"I was hoping you'd say yes, and you did, so I'll come and get you if you're not finished when I get off work," he said quickly and left.

She stared after him for a moment, then shrugged and started her search. She went through row after row of boxes. This place had probably been organized once, but they'd long since given up on keeping it that way. She snorted. The chamber of lost shit was what it was.

Fletcher let out a heavy groan. She'd been at it for almost two hours with no results. After scrounging up a cup of coffee from a vending machine, she went back to work and found a group of boxes that weren't labeled on the side but on the top. Several in, she came across one marked with the case number she'd found in Jasper's files.

She carried the box to the one rickety table and set it down. She lifted the lid and sucked in a breath at the name on the file. "Wayne." That had been her last name at some point: Jamie Wayne. What mattered in this moment was that it was her birth mother's last name. Greta Wayne, AKA Mommy Demented.

Her eyes widened. There was more than one "Wayne" folder. That wasn't right. They should be filed separately, shouldn't they? She shook off the chill, pulled out the one with the oldest date, and sat in the wobbly chair. Greta Wayne, twenty-eight, was admitted to the emergency room at seven p.m. with internal injuries. The child, Jamie Wayne, two years old, in the care of Ms. Wayne, was put into a foster home upon social services' request. The dossier also contained a waiver of parental rights.

A picture of Greta was paperclipped to the file, and bile rose in Fletcher's throat. "You should have died that day," she said to the photo. Fletcher never had cause to doubt the evil woman was dead. The memories, which plagued her dreams, were clear. If she made a big enough noise, the woman would come. Fletch had been two, but smart enough to put a bunch of crap at the top of the landing; then she'd broken a vase or something, and down the steps Mommy Demented had fallen, like Humpty fucking Dumpty. She'd had enough time to lock Fletcher in the closet; then she died, or so Fletch had thought. But that wasn't what happened.

She set the file aside and grabbed the other. Her gaze froze on a name. What in the…? Greta Wayne, thirty-nine, was pronounced dead upon arrival. Blunt force trauma to the cerebral cortex. The assailant Laura Hart, forty-five, of Blue Creek, North Carolina.

"Oh God, Jasper, why didn't you ever tell me?" Fletcher blinked back the flood of tears. Laura, sweet, compassionate Laura. The woman who had forgiven her husband and had loved the product of his mistake anyway. Fletcher closed her eyes. Laura had known the truth about Fletcher's origins and the circumstances surrounding her arrival at the orphanage. She must have gone to confront Greta when Laura realized the woman was alive.

She flipped to the transcripts of the trial. Short version: Laura had gone to see Greta, and Mommy Demented attacked—big surprise. In an effort to defend herself, Laura had struck Greta, who fell and hit her head. Laura called for an ambulance, but Greta was dead on arrival. They charged Laura with involuntary manslaughter. They'd opted for a bench trial and pleaded not guilty due to self-defense. The prosecution couldn't prove otherwise, and the judge came to a quick "not guilty" verdict.

Fletcher squeezed her eyes shut. She understood Laura's last words. "I don't regret anything I've done for you." Fletcher had always thought it was Laura's way of saying she didn't regret welcoming Fletcher into their home, their lives, and their love.

Jasper must have promised Laura he would keep her secret. Fletcher wanted to be mad at him, but she couldn't. He was protecting Laura. She would have done the same.

She went through each folder twice. She could pay to get copies of the files—they were public record after all—or take photos with her phone, but she didn't want to have them. Some pasts should not be unearthed.

"Right where I left you?"

Fletcher started, then smiled at Taft. "Yep." She stretched and glanced at her phone. Hell's bells, she'd been down here for hours.

"You still wanna get that beer?"

"Absolutely."

Fletcher found herself in what Alexandra would call a kitschy local bar listening to Taft go on and on about his life. Some people were like that. Not that she was paying attention to what he saying, but he was oblivious. "Excuse me," she said when her cell phone rang. Her heart jumped to her throat. It was Reed. "Did something happen?"

"Where are you?" Noah asked.

"In a bar with a cute guy."

"Funny. Be serious," Noah growled.

She put a finger to her other ear to muffle the crowd. "Did something happen or not?"

"No. I wanted to make sure you were staying out of trouble."

"I'm staying out of trouble. I'm at a bar with a cute guy." She winked at Taft. Fletcher hadn't understood the concept of flirting until she'd met Craig. Her brother-in-law was a born flirt, and he'd taught her a lot.

"You're hilarious."

"I'm serious. Here, you can talk to him." She handed the phone to Taft. "Don't be scared."

He gave her a curious look. "This is Taft. No, that's my real name. Who's this? Oh." Taft's voice went up an octave. "Um, we're…"

Fletcher sipped her beer and winced when Taft told Noah their location.

"She's fine, buddy, I swear. He wants to talk to you again." Taft handed her the phone, then gulped his beer.

"Yeah?" It was a good thing Taft wasn't face-to-face with Reed; poor guy would probably shit himself. That's probably why she didn't mind flirting with him; Taft wasn't a threat.

"What's the big idea hanging out with some kid?"

She snorted. "He's my age, Reed; not all of us are as ancient as you."

"I'm not old."

"Bully for you," she said and winked at Taft again, but he didn't get her joke. She shrugged. "Call me if anything really happens." She ended the conversation and slipped her phone in her pocket.

"That wasn't a boyfriend, was it?" Taft asked.

Fletcher burst out laughing. "Hell, no."

Taft grinned and signaled to the waiter. "How about we get some food then?"

****

He was losing his mind. Noah turned off the exit and followed the directions his phone chirped out. Why was he doing this? Why was he coming out here? He could say it was because she was in danger, which, technically, wasn't a lie. Fletcher was at risk. But the truth was worse than that. Much worse.

He'd had a taste of her—one taste—and he wanted more. She'd let him in, kissed him back, and, despite his efforts to stay away, Noah couldn't let this opportunity pass him by. The idea of her flirting with someone else, kissing someone else after their... Noah rolled his neck. She was forbidden fruit, and he craved her with an irrational intensity. What else would bring him out here?

He pulled in next to her truck, annoyed she hadn't parked in a well-lit area. She knew better. Luckily, he didn't have to wait long. Fletcher came down the street with a younger guy. Noah got out of his vehicle and put his hands in his back pockets.

They hadn't seen him yet, and he would have waited until lover boy had left before making his presence known. But the kid, Taft, or whatever the hell his name was, kissed her.

Noah stepped around his vehicle and growled. "You should learn to keep your hands to yourself."

Taft jumped maybe ten feet in the air. "Holy shit!"

"Reed! What in the hell are you doing here?" Fletcher glared at him. "We were ending our date."

Taft pointed to Noah. "This is the guy I was talking

96

to earlier?"

Noah grinned.

Fletcher rolled her eyes. "Yes, this is the asshat you spoke with."

"Now, Fletcher, honey, you don't mean that." Noah looked pointedly at Taft. "She doesn't mean that. Do you, cupcake?"

Fletcher circled around. "Who in the hell are you calling 'cupcake'?"

"Look, buddy," Taft began, his hands raised in mock surrender. "I don't want any trouble. She said she didn't have a boyfriend."

Fletcher glared at Noah. "Taft, he's messing with you. He sure as hell isn't my boyfriend."

"Is that a chance you're willing to take, *boy*?" Noah stretched. The short sleeves of his gray polo shirt rode up and tightened across his chest as he lifted his arms above his head. He took his time about it, flexing.

"Gotta go," Taft said and hauled ass down the street.

Noah laughed.

"What was that about? And why in the hell did you drive two hours to—to do whatever it is you just did?" Fletcher stomped her foot on the last word. "I liked him."

"Be serious, McKay. He's puny. Hell, you'd crush him."

"At least he's not some testosterone junkie. Big as a freaking oak tree." Fletcher turned and unlocked her door. She threw in her bag and jacket.

"You can't honestly expect me to believe you got hot and bothered kissing that guy?" Noah asked, turning her around.

"I never said I did," she told him. He boxed her in, and she snorted. "Reed, I could take you too."

He had lost his ever-loving mind because the idea of her taking him made him hard. "Take me where?"

Fletcher poked a finger at him. "Stop being weird."

He rose a brow. "I'm weird?"

"Well." She rubbed her nose. "You're freaking me the fuck out."

He reached up and let her long, tawny hair down, then ran his fingers through it. He loved her hair.

Fletcher swatted at his hands. "It took me forever to trap all of that."

He smirked. He'd learned a long time ago that "trapping" hair meant putting it up. "I like it down," he said as he brought a couple strands to his nose. "I like the way it smells too." Noah shivered. He could eat her alive.

"It's my shampoo." She told him the brand. "You can buy it and smell it all damn day. Squirt it up your fucking nose for all I care."

"Don't be like that," Noah said and bent until he was nose to nose with her. He leaned in and...she bit him. "Damn it!"

"I'm mad at you! There's no blood. Come 'ere, you big baby," she said and tugged his lip. "Oh."

"I told you." He sucked on the wound. She was staring at his mouth, and he grew harder in his jeans, if that was possible. Her gaze met his; it was green right now.

She pulled on the collar of his shirt, and he bent to her level. Their eyes held as she brought her lips to his, then laved the cut with her tongue. He growled.

Noah lifted her up, put her on the driver's seat of

her truck, and deepened the kiss. He stepped between her thighs, sliding his hands through her hair, and groaning when she wrapped her legs around his waist. He swiveled his hips, and she sucked on his tongue.

Her fingers were roaming over his chest, trying to get to his skin, but Noah stilled her hands and ripped open her shirt, making her gasp. Buttons flew in every direction. She lay back against the bench seats, giving him access, and he licked her from navel to neck.

Noah turned off the cab light, then brought his hands to her breasts. He slid his fingers inside the lacy material and plucked her hardened nipples. He pulled one cup down and latched his mouth on a taut peak. Rubbing his face against her skin, he breathed in her soft, powdery scent.

Fletcher pulled at his shirt, and Noah obliged by divesting himself of the garment. Her fingers stroked his chest again and again; Noah squeezed his eyes shut. Her lips touched his, and he succumbed to her kiss. She nibbled on his top lip, making him nuts, before bringing her tongue back to mate with his.

Using her preoccupation with his mouth, he relieved her of the rest of her top, leaving her in the lacy bra. He ravished her breasts, tasted her skin, and kissed her again.

He moved so their lower bodies were aligned and her nipples grazed his chest through the lace. Her sexy moans made him desperate. His erection strained against the teeth of his zipper. She pressed herself tighter against him and brought her legs higher on his back, increasing the friction between the material of their clothes and heated flesh. Noah caught the sound of her orgasm against his mouth, and unable to control himself, he went with her over the edge.

The last time he'd come in his pants, he'd been a teenager. But he didn't care about that. Or the fact they'd committed an act of public indecency.

Fletcher slowed the kiss, then pushed against his shoulder. He straightened, then grunted when she flung a towel at him.

He cleaned himself up. When he turned back around, she'd put herself to rights. Her shirt was screwed. He apologized, but she shrugged and tied the ends together.

"You might need this." She tossed him his shirt.

He slipped it over his head and straightened the collar. Her lips were swollen and pink. And all he wanted to do was bury himself inside her. He stepped forward.

"Just so you know, this"—she pointed between the two of them—"isn't gonna happen again."

He stared at her, incredulous. "You can't be serious?"

"Are you out of your mind? Of course, I'm serious. We're enemies, Reed. With a capital fucking E. Get it?"

He narrowed his eyes. "I'm sorry. Was I the only one present in your truck?"

"That's not the point. I'm Fletcher and you're— you're you." She pulled a hair tie from the gearshift and put her hair in a sloppy bun. "This was not supposed to happen."

He crossed his arms. "Well, it did."

"No shit!" She shoved him, then gagged. "I had Marylou's sloppy seconds."

Noah's entire body flushed. Could he, should he, admit the truth? He looked her up and down. "I never slept with Marylou."

She guffawed. "Bullshit! Like I'm gonna believe that."

He rolled his neck. "It's true."

Her eyebrows bunched. "I don't understand."

"We weren't together that long," he began, using the first excuses that came to mind. He couldn't admit all of it. Not now.

She stared at him, then threw her hands in the air. "It doesn't matter. We can't do this again. Never, ever."

"You expect me to pretend like none of this—"

"I'll make it easy. Say something to remind me why I hate you."

Noah rubbed his hands over his face. "This is ridiculous, Fletcher."

"My request is not only rational but also vital to the balance of this existence."

Noah shook his head. "You're talking crazy."

"Thanks," she said putting on her seatbelt. "I'm not crazy!"

He stopped her from shutting the door. "Wait, what?"

"I am not insane. I do not lack either intelligence or my grasp on reality. But thank you for reminding me what an asshat you are and why I can't stand you." She slammed the door shut.

Noah could only stand there with what had to be a stupid look on his face. She drove away with one finger in the air.

Chapter Thirteen

Fletcher did the speed limit all entire ride home. Well, most of the way. If Reed was behind her, she didn't want to give him a reason to pull her over. Reed…she shook her head. Had he driven to the city to check on her? To—to make out with her?

Had he been jealous of some guy she'd never see again? Reed jealous? Because of her? She couldn't wrap her head around it. Or the fact he hadn't slept with Marylou. Did she believe him?

Marylou was noxious, but if you didn't know her, you'd probably think she was hot. Guys wanted to get it on with hot chicks. Hell's bells, a lot of men had gotten it on with Marylou. Fletch didn't judge. More power to women who went after what they wanted. But Marylou had cheated, and Fletcher had delighted in leaving the photographic evidence of the multiple affairs for Reed to find.

Had not consummating the relationship been Marylou's choice? Had she played hard to get and bored Reed to tears? How had she not tried Reed on for size? He dripped sex. Compared to the other men Marylou had slept with, Reed was top shelf, but the woman was an airhead.

Hell, Reed had given Fletch an orgasm through her clothes. She bit her lip. She didn't have a lot of experience, and she had heard of heavy petting or whatever, but what they'd done…done right here in her truck…Fletch was baffled. What was worse, she wanted more. She wanted him. It was carnal, chemical—he did something to her. The first time she'd come face-to-face with him, everything in her body had turned on. Like, every-fucking-thing.

She had never reacted to anyone that way before or since. She'd been attracted to the danger of Daemon, but she hadn't craved him the way she did Reed. He had wronged her; he was the enemy, and yet she had never stopped wanting him. It was pure unadulterated lust with Reed. And that's why lust was one of the deadlies. She needed to get that tattooed on the inside of her fucking eyelids.

Fletcher straightened her shoulders and pulled into Granny Vaughn's. She wouldn't give in to temptation again. Reed was her opponent. Yeah, so he wanted her, but he wouldn't hesitate to snuff her out if it was in his best interest. He'd done it before, and she couldn't forget that.

She yawned and headed upstairs to her apartment. It was either really late or really early depending on how you wanted to look at it. It had been a long day, and maybe she could get some dreamless sleep. She hoped she hadn't woken anyone when she pulled in. Alex had a sixth sense about people driving into the B and B parking lot. Granny Vaughn had said it was a sign of a wonderful hostess, not only to sense when guests arrived, but to be prepared for them. Alexandra was the fucking empress of hostesses.

Fletch unlocked the door and flicked on the light switch. She took in the state of the room, then closed the door and went back down the stairs. She sat on the bottom step and fiddled with her locket.

Fletch could go and try to figure it out, or she could sit here until someone came by to do it for her. Then, when they called the sheriff, *they* could deal with Reed. Thinking of him, she glanced at her shirt; she needed a different one. She could go grab one of Jake's shirts; he wouldn't mind. What she wouldn't do was go down any rabbit holes. Nope!

She almost smiled when Reed pulled in right in front of her. He stalked out of his truck to hover over her like a boulder. "You better not have woken Jake up!"

"What in the hell are you doing out here?" Reed asked.

She looked on either side of herself. "I'm sitting." Duh!

He closed his eyes. "Why?"

"Because someone broke into the apartment and posted pictures of Daemon on every available surface." She shifted out of his way when he ran up the steps. See? Wait long enough and someone would get all upset and pissy for her. If she had installed those cameras she'd talked to Alex about, this wouldn't be an issue. But she had put it off. She rested her chin on her hands and shifted again for Noah.

"You're coming with me."

Fletcher evaded his grasp. "Been there, done that." She laughed, then covered her mouth. There was no way in hell Alex wasn't awake.

"Funny." Noah stared at her. "I'm taking you into protective custody."

She snorted. "Like hell you are."

"I'm the sheriff, and you are going into protective

custody."

"Ha!" She hopped to her feet, dodged him, and ran up the steps.

Fletcher rushed into the apartment and threw papers into one of the boxes she'd brought from Jasper's house. Whoever had been here wasn't a professional. She'd had all of Jasper's notes, and they hadn't touched them. Amateurs.

She hurried to her room and stripped out of her clothes. She ignored Reed, who was leaning against the doorframe. Let him look; she was a Jackson freaking Pollock. She put on jeans, a McKays Diner sweatshirt, socks, and sneakers. She shoved some things into the duffel bag she'd bought. "Excuse me," she said when she tried to pass him.

"You're coming with me, McKay."

"No," Fletcher began, "I am not. I hate you. What don't you comprehend about that statement? I loathe you, despise you, I—" He cut her off with a kiss.

She put her knife against his throat. Reed sighed. "You don't want to do that, cupcake. Or maybe you should, so I could arrest you for assaulting an officer."

"I'm not your fucking cupcake," she said, then head-butted him, which threw him off guard giving her time to punch him in the solar plexus. While he tried to catch his breath, she grabbed the box and hauled ass out of the apartment. She ran down the steps and into Jake, who was by her truck. "Hey, Jake, sorry if I woke you and Alex. Um?" She glanced up; Reed was holding his stomach and heading her way. "Reed wants to arrest me for assaulting an officer. Talk him out of it, okay?" She kissed Jake's cheek, then jumped into her vehicle, wincing when the gravel spewed up.

****

"You should have told me the woman was alive, and I would have taken care of it." Fletcher squeezed Jasper's hand.

"But no. You didn't do that. I can dirty my own hands, Jasper Hart. You don't need to be doing that for me. And neither did Laura. God, it must have torn her up inside." She couldn't imagine what it had been like for them. She remembered the couple going out of town for a few weeks once; it must have been to go to court. Laura would have been terrified. Jasper too. What hoops had he jumped through to keep it secret?

She took a can of shaving cream out of her duffle, got a washcloth from the nurse, wet and lathered his face, working around the tubes. She took out Jasper's straight razor and began to shave off his gray beard. After each stroke, she wiped the blade clean, then she used the cloth to get any remaining lather.

"Now you look presentable. Diaz told me people have been trying to get in to see you all day. That's nice, huh? They don't know what an ass you can be. Don't think I'm letting you off the hook 'cause you're in a coma!" She kissed his soft cheek and scooted her chair closer to the bed.

She grabbed the locket from around her throat and fiddled with it. She'd been nine when her mother had given her this locket; hell, Savannah hadn't even been her ma yet. Fletcher had stared at the small, wrapped gift in her hands, not wanting to open it. Van, as she'd called her mother then, had gotten all her sisters jewelry for Christmas, so Fletcher had known she would find some kind of girly thing in her box.

She had hesitated, not because she didn't want the

present, but because she hadn't cared what it was; she had wanted it more than anything *ever*. When she'd finally opened the box and pulled out the locket, tears had misted her eyes. Then she had turned it over; Van had had it inscribed. Her sisters hadn't said anything about inscriptions, so hers must have been the only one. It read *lovely girl*. After Savannah had become her mother, she'd added "my" to the inscription. It was one of Fletcher's most prized possessions, and it didn't leave her neck without reason.

She gripped both the locket and Jasper's hand tighter. She needed to hold on for whatever came next. Fletcher rested her head on Jasper's shoulder and fell asleep.

****

It was late afternoon before Fletcher was walking in the woods with her duffel bag and a box of Jasper's files. The bag held some clothes and some electronics. After leaving the hospital, she stopped by the storage facility. She had raided her stash of surveillance equipment, grabbed a backup laptop, and an array of tools. Fletch had parked her truck next to the ruins of her cabin and headed out on foot. When she got to her destination, she set her things beside a tree and got out her laptop.

She had broken into this particular place before and was familiar with the security system. But people changed security codes all the time, so it was better to be safe than sorry. It took her a moment to log onto the Wi-Fi; that password hadn't changed. Through the Wi-Fi, she accessed the connection to the alarm system and cameras, then shut them all off.

With a smirk, she grabbed her stuff and headed for

the back door. She knelt on the porch and pulled out a small picklock kit. It took her less than ten seconds to open the door. After waiting a beat for the house to settle, she made her way to the kitchen to get supplies. She turned on the coffee pot and pulled her thermos out of her bag. While the coffee was brewing, she went to the pantry and filled her duffel with a few bottles of water and nonperishables. Fletch even made a couple of peanut butter and jelly sandwiches.

She went into the garage, found a big bucket, and grabbed an extension cord. There was an old fleece blanket neatly folded on a shelf, and she took that too. She carried most of her supplies upstairs and set them by the landing, then went back down to the kitchen.

Fletcher pursed her chapped lips at the landline. Few people still kept a landline, but she would use it to her advantage. She dug through her things and took out the case with her recording equipment. She placed taps on the phone and small video surveillance cameras throughout the house.

By the time she returned to the kitchen, the coffee was ready. Fletcher filled her heavy-duty thermos with the hot liquid, then went to the fridge to add cream. That done, she cleaned up any evidence of her presence and headed for the second floor. She went into a spare bedroom, through to the walk-in closet, and opened the door that led to the third-floor attic.

Fletch slung her duffel over her shoulder, put the flashlight on her phone, and headed up. The steps creaked under her feet; she winced but continued. She dumped the bag, then went down to collect the rest of her things. She did one more check to make sure she hadn't left any sign of herself, then shut the attic door behind her.

There was a light switch up here and an outlet too. It only took her a minute to locate the switch. After a little debate, she decided shining a light on the subject was called for. Her jaw dropped; the place was packed. Fletcher grinned; she hadn't expected to find any furniture, but it was a regular showroom. There was even a mattress.

She took Jasper's files out of the box and set them on the old cherrywood table. She unpacked her supplies and got herself situated. After several minutes of shifting furniture, she found the outlet and plugged her laptop into the extension cord. Why drain the battery when you had access to power?

She grabbed an apple and booted up her computer. She used the Wi-Fi to connect to the surveillance equipment, then loaded the program. Several video boxes appeared on the screen. They were a go!

With the connections running, she reset the alarm. She took out her tablet and pulled up her favorite show; then it was time to go through more of Jasper's files. Fletch didn't know what else she would find, but she had to take the chance. She poured a cup of coffee from her thermos and sat to read.

Almost two hours later, a truck pulled into the driveway. She rushed to shut off the light and closed her tablet. The best place to hide was in plain sight, or so Fletcher had always thought. That being the case, where better to hide than over the head of the man looking for her. She grinned. Noah would piss his pants if he found out she was right under his nose, or above it, if you wanted to get technical.

Fletcher went to her laptop and tapped on the video

for the front door. Deciding sound was a good thing, she put in her headphones. If she'd noticed anything about Noah, it was his constant need to hear to his own voice.

****

Noah slapped together a sandwich, grabbed a beer from the fridge. He paused when putting the bread back. Had his housekeeper come today? Noah didn't think so, but...he shook his head. The days were bleeding into each other. He needed to make a grocery list, but that could wait. Once he was seated at his office desk, he grabbed a sheet of paper to use as a plate and turned on his computer. The home screen popped up, and he sipped his beer.

He hit a few buttons and logged on to his system at the station. He'd had a shitty day. There was a group of kids running around destroying people's property, and the folks of Blue Creek wanted them found and dealt with. Petty vandalism was a crime, and he was the law in town now.

Not to mention word was out that he was planning on taking Fletcher into protective custody, and anyone who had any information as to her whereabouts was to contact him immediately. Anyone caught hiding her would be charged with interfering in a police investigation. Jasper had told him not to go after the McKays, but Noah had been pissed. He and Jake had gotten into a row, and his annoyance with Keller had overrode his memory.

Deputy Diaz had told him Fletcher had been at the hospital, but she had given him the slip. Yeah, right. "Damn it, Fletcher, when I get my hands on you." He took another bite of his sandwich.

Swallowing, he closed his eyes. Last night… He'd never experienced anything like her. She was so fucking responsive. He would swear he could still smell her on him, in his house…everywhere.

He downed the rest of his meal and attempted to get some work done when the phone rang. "Reed."

"Noah?" said the saccharine sweet voice on the other end.

"Marylou," Noah said, lip curling. "I told you not to call me. Remember?"

"You can't still be mad at me, big boy," Marylou purred.

He stretched his neck. "Must I remind you, I hate that name, and I still suspect you of illegal activities." She was guilty as hell, but he didn't have anything solid enough for the DA.

"You don't have any proof," she hissed.

"Not yet." But he was working on it.

Her laugh echoed in the receiver. "You don't have any proof because there isn't any, Noah. Be realistic. Don't you miss me even the teeniest bit?"

"No. Hell, I don't want anything to do with you." Other than locking her up, that is. Which he would do as soon as he had sufficient evidence.

"I called because I miss you, and I wish we were enjoying each other's company. I'm sure you regret we didn't consummate our relationship. The things I could do to you—"

"What part of me not wanting anything to do with you don't you understand? Frankly, I'd rather stick my dick in an electrical socket." He slammed the phone down, then glared at it when it rang again.

What had he been thinking dating that woman? She

was a crook and a cheat, but he hadn't known that in the beginning. All he'd known was that the McKays despised her and vice versa.

Hell, if Marylou were in the country, she'd be his number one suspect. But she wasn't here, and he had no suspects, no clues. "Zilch!" he said to the empty study. He downed the beer and went back to work.

Around midnight, he shut everything off and headed upstairs. He unbuttoned his shirt, leaving it to hang open, and entered his bedroom. Instead of turning on the light on his nightstand, he went to the adjoining master bath and hit the switch. The king-sized bed dipped when he lay back against the mattress. He rubbed a hand over his chest and closed his eyes. He could still see her: Fletcher's sexy hair tumbling into his hands, her bow mouth hot against his. Noah groaned. She'd touched him. She'd wanted him. He hardened against his zipper. She might deny it, but it was true.

He couldn't blame her, could he? She was right; they had been enemies for years. It may have stopped her from thinking of him in a physical sense, but it had never stopped him. Never. It twisted him up inside. How could he loathe and want someone with equal fervor? The power she had over him made Noah resent her all the more.

Once, when Charlie had been missing, Fletcher had confronted him at his office in the city. She had been pissed, wanting him to help her, and he had been difficult on purpose. She had swept everything off his desk in a fit of rage. If they had been alone, he may have scooped her up, put her on said desk, and had her right there, but they hadn't been alone. He had been thankful for that.

With a grunt, he stood, went into the bathroom, and turned on the shower. He'd had the bathroom renovated when he moved in. The original stall had been too small for him, so he'd put in a spa with two showerheads and two seats built into the far corners. Plus, a soaking tub big enough to fit him. He couldn't help wanting a little luxury.

He shucked off his clothes and got under the hot spray. Closing his eyes, he remembered the feel of her hands on him. The taste of her still lingered on his tongue. Leaning against the cold tile, he rubbed a hand down his stomach and let himself revel in the memory of Fletcher McKay.

****

Fletcher closed the laptop and blew out a breath. She hadn't put any surveillance equipment in the bathrooms—she wasn't a perve. But she'd still been able to make out some of what he said in the shower. And if she wasn't mistaken, it had been her name. She shivered. Her cell vibrated on the table, and she snatched it up. "What?"

"That's how you answer your phone?"

"Sorry. Hello, Casey, how are you doing? Is that better?" Fletcher tiptoed across the attic to put more space between her and Noah.

Her sister's snort echoed on the phone. "Much. Where are you hiding?"

"If I told you, I wouldn't be hiding."

"Are you still in Blue Creek?"

She chuckled. "I'm in the last place on Earth Reed would ever think to look."

"That's good then." Casey waited a beat. "Find out

anything yet?"

"A few things that I'll be needing to talk with Jasper about when he wakes up."

"He might not wake up, Fletch," Casey mumbled. "You still there?"

"I'm here." But she wouldn't be going down that particular rabbit hole anytime soon.

"Pops said Noah told him that whoever's behind all this wasn't fixated on Jasper."

"They shot him." Fletcher opened a bottle of water. Reed had been talking to Pops?

"To get to you."

"That makes sense," she said after a minute.

"You took that entirely too well."

Fletcher smirked. "I'm in the first stages of denial."

"I thought the first stage was to deny you're in denial."

"It is. But I tweaked it." Fletcher opened her laptop again. She couldn't help herself. "Damn." He's in bed.

"What?"

She blushed. "I, uh, stubbed my toe."

"That hurts like a bitch."

"Tell me about it."

"Do you need anything? Ryan and I can come back earlier than planned—be all secretive and shit. Covert ops, remember?"

"Like when we were kids?" Fletcher grinned. Those had been the best days.

"Yeah. Ryan and I discussed a few strategies…"

She nodded even though no one could see her. Casey said they would pick her up and take her to Alexandra's. Then Fletcher could hide out in the secret passageways. "I'm good where I'm at right now. You guys stay there and enjoy your babymoon."

Chapter Fourteen

Two days and no leads later, Fletcher decided it was time to get out of the house.

Noah left at the ass crack of dawn most days, so she had been lucky. She hurried down from the attic stairs and made use of his bathroom. She was sick of doing her business in a bucket at night and cleaning it up the next morning. Nasty.

Yesterday she'd almost given in and taken a soak in his big-ass bathtub. Noah had renovated a lot of the judge's estate after he bought it, and the tub was the best addition, if you asked her. If his housekeeper hadn't shown up when she did, Fletch would have indulged.

After she took a shower and put her hair in a braided bun, she pulled on a pair of jeans and a sweatshirt. Wiping the shower, she ran the towel through the dryer, then put it back on the shelf. That done, she made some coffee and a call.

She waited for her ride at the end of the drive. Her brother's pickup truck pulled in next to her. She waved and hopped in when he stopped.

"You sure do have brass balls, Fletch," Jebb said and put the vehicle in reverse. "I mean, damn, you're staying in Noah's attic."

She nodded and put on her sunglasses. "Always hide in plain sight."

"I have an hour before I have to be back in class. Where are we going?"

"I want to see Jasper." She needed to check on him. Dr. Lowell and her mother had kept her informed. Nothing had changed, but she wanted to see for herself. "What?" she asked when he got broody. Their dad did that too.

"He ain't gonna make it, Fletch," Jebb choked out.

She turned in her seat. "Who's been feeding you that shit?"

"Everybody's saying it. Everyone," Jebb said and made the turn toward the hospital.

Fletcher snorted. "Well, there you go."

"What?"

"Jasper's a stubborn cuss, so if everyone's saying it about him, he won't do it."

"Do you really believe that?"

"Yep!" She had to.

As they headed to the hospital, Jebb filled Fletcher in on what was going on at home. Pops and Ma were still at odds, but better today than yesterday. He talked about their sisters and puffed his chest out because Fletcher had chosen him for this mission. When they pulled into the hospital parking lot, she asked, "Did you bring me the beanie and sweatshirt?"

Jebb pointed behind him. "Do you think you'll pass as a boy?"

Fletcher laughed and climbed in the backseat. "I've been passing for a boy most of my life." She replaced her sweatshirt with his. It swallowed her up, which had been the point. Then she put the beanie on, covering her bun. Maybe she should wear her sunglasses too.

"Hey, Fletch?"

She shut the back door and went to the passenger side. "What is it, bullfrog?"

"Keep me in the loop, okay? Text me."

She reached across the seat and squeezed his hand. "I'll do my best."

She waited until he was out of view to head into the hospital. She hoped she hadn't made a mistake by calling him. Part of her wanted to make sure Jebb didn't feel excluded in the real goings on, but the other part of her didn't want to put her baby brother in any danger.

It didn't take much to get to Jasper's floor; in fact, the lack of trouble made her wary. She turned the corner to go to his room and was jarred by the blaring noise. It was a code blue. She rushed to Jasper's room and ran right into her father. "Pops?"

He closed the door and shook his head. "I'm sorry, sweetheart."

Swallowing was a problem…breathing was difficult. The alarms going off in the corridor had nothing on the ones blaring in her head. She tried to dodge him, to get into Jasper's room, but he wouldn't budge. "Let me fucking in!" The words screamed in her head but only came out as a whimper. Tears blurred her vision.

Pops bowed his head. "You don't want to see him like that." He gave her a little shake. "You don't want to go in there."

She *did* want to, didn't she? No. She wanted to melt into the floor and die. She pulled herself from her father's grip and stared at him. Tears tracked his cheeks, and her entire body shook. "He's gone?"

He moved to touch her but dropped his hand. "I'm sorry, sweetheart."

Pain gripped her in a vise. She turned on her heel and ran for the elevator. Chickenshit that she was. As if expecting her, the doors slid open, and there stood Noah. She tried to blink back the flood of tears, but there were too many.

"He—" She couldn't get the words past her throat. But Noah understood. He lifted her in his arms and held her. She buried her face in his neck, letting his heat chase away the all-consuming chill. His calm quieted her chaos.

It took her a moment to realize Noah had sat her in his truck. She was vaguely aware of him saying he'd be right back. She waved him off. Thoughts spun in her head, swept up in the storm of grief and fury. Jasper had left her.

She didn't know how long Noah was gone, but at some point, he got behind the wheel and started the engine. "Why did he quit on me?"

"He—"

She put her hands over her ears. "Let's go. You can take me wherever, okay? I don't care anymore."

****

Noah brought her back to his house. If she'd been feeling herself, Fletcher would have found it hilarious. He'd been kind to her, tender even, and she was having trouble processing it. Processing him. She shook her head and turned on the shower.

Noah had offered her one of the guest rooms and a chance to clean herself up. He was being a good host, but it was weird. Though it did take her mind off the other things.

Fletcher checked the temperature of the water, then took off her clothes. She didn't know how long she stood under the spray, but it was long enough that Noah had knocked on the door to make sure she hadn't drowned. She'd assured him she was okay, though she was far from it, and he'd suggested she try to take a nap.

Sleep hadn't been kind to her, but she put on the T-shirt Noah had left for her and crawled between the sheets. Pulling the covers over her head, she closed her eyes. She was so tired—body, mind, and heart.

The room was darker when she woke up. The truth of the day rushed to greet her, but Fletcher pushed the thoughts aside. She put her clothes on and went in search of coffee.

She took the back steps to the kitchen, surprised to find a carafe already brewed. Fletcher poured herself a cup. She put in some cream and sipped, letting the hot liquid soothe her. Noah's coffee was about like hers, not as good as either Charlie's or Alex's, but drinkable.

The caffeine hit her system, and voices carried from the next room. She was outside the door when Pops said, "If you think she's mad now, wait until she finds out what we've done."

What had they done?

"What *I'm* doing," Noah said.

Deciding against stealth, Fletcher burst into the office. "And what have you done?"

Her father rose from the leather couch.

"Pops?" She eyed his ruddy cheeks from over the rim of her mug.

Noah stood. "I've officially put you in protective custody or house arrest."

She rose a brow. "This house?"

"Yes." Noah walked around his desk. "How did

you sleep?"

Fletcher cocked her head to the side. She would go where she pleased, but let him believe whatever. "Better than expected."

Noah nodded. "I'll give you two some privacy."

Her gaze tracked Reed's movements across the room, and his silver eyes met hers for a moment before he shut the door. She shivered. There was no denying the pull he had on her. Lust *was* one of the deadlies, remember? She shook her head and turned to her father.

"Your mother wanted to come, but Jebb was—"

She raised a hand. "No need to explain." She was weary of him. He'd shut the door between her and Jasper, and that…that had done something inside her. Part of her, the rational part, understood. Pops had been protecting her from seeing Jasper's death. But the other part of her…he'd denied both Jasper and herself their final good-bye.

He pointed to a small bag on the sofa. "She fixed you a bag with some clothes and toiletries."

Fletcher glanced at the bag, then turned back to him.

Pops squirmed. "Do you want to talk?"

"What's to talk about? He gave up on me."

His eyes widened. "I—"

"I can't fucking breathe," she said and set her mug on the coffee table. She put her hand on her chest. "I don't know how my heart's beating because it was ripped from my body. And you know what? It's my own fault."

Pops shook his head. "The person who shot Jasper—"

"But it *is* my fault." She paced. "Everything

Jasper's done has been for me. All his secrets and all his worries belong right here." She put her hands on her shoulders.

"Jasper's his own man. He did what he wanted the way he wanted."

Tears fell from her eyes. "I didn't kill her."

Pops stared at her for a moment. "Who?"

"My birth mother, Greta fucking Wayne. I didn't kill her." It had been a shock to see those papers. A shock, a betrayal, a kindness? She wasn't sure; the feelings were a collage of horror.

"What?" Pops whispered.

"She survived the fall down the stairs. She was unconscious when they found her. There was some internal bleeding, but she survived. She signed away all rights to me. And he never fucking told me."

Pops pinched the bridge of his nose. "Jasper knew?"

She walked closer to him. "Not only did Jasper know, but Laura did too. She, she—"

Emmit sat and put his head in his hands. "Laura?"

Fletcher dashed tears from her cheeks and nodded. "I went to the city, to the clerk of courts, and found everything. Laura confronted Greta, and the psycho attacked her. Laura fought back and killed Greta in self-defense. There was a trial and everything. Jasper never told me."

"I don't know what to say." Pops rubbed his jaw. "There had to be a reason Jasper kept this from us."

"What fucking reason would that be?" But she knew, didn't she? He had been protecting Laura. Protecting Fletch. As always.

Pops stared at her. "Maybe you should go lie

down."

"Why is it when a body's shit deep in emotional agony, everyone tells them to 'lie down'? I rested enough. Hell, I'd rather be out of my mind again." It hadn't hurt this much.

"Don't talk like that." Emmit stood. "Don't say things you don't mean."

Fletcher looked at her hands, then her arms. She had scars everywhere, and now she had another one deep inside. What happened when all you were was a shell of scars? "I need some air."

****

Noah waited until Emmit's taillights were no longer visible. With a sigh, he headed toward the woods, sure that was where Fletcher had gone. He called her name, not that he expected her to answer, but he figured she'd call him an asshole or some such thing and give away her position.

He stopped when he was deep in the woods. It was getting too dark to see a damn thing, much less find someone who didn't want to be found. Goose bumps rose on his flesh right before Fletcher attacked him. She was able to knock him to the side, but he grabbed her arm before she could hit him. "What the hell is wrong with you?"

She broke loose, then got into a boxer's stance. "Come on, Reed. What? Scared?"

Noah crossed his arms over his chest. "You want to fight? Be serious."

She bounced around him with her hands balled into fists. "I *am* serious."

"I'm not interested in this game."

"Fine," she growled and lunged at him. Fletcher

was fast, but he was faster. He had her over his shoulder in a matter of seconds. She cussed him out the entire way back to the house, and he smacked her butt a couple of times.

"Put me down, you overgrown oaf!" she shouted when they entered the house.

He did as she asked, not surprised when her fists came back up. He eyed her. She was wearing jeans, a sweatshirt, and had her hair in a sloppy bun. His body stirred. "Strip."

Fletcher dropped her fists. "Huh?"

He swept his gaze over her. "I said strip."

Fletcher blinked. What in the world? A laugh bubbled from her throat, and she covered her mouth with her hand. He got into her space; his maleness crowded her. Goose bumps rose on her flesh, and she licked her bottom lip. "I—"

"Your emotions are overwhelming you, you can't get control of them, so you need to do something. You being you, fighting is the first thing that comes to mind. It makes sense. You're a fighter."

He stepped even closer and tucked a hair behind her ear. His warm breath swept against her cheek, and her lady parts quickened. Parts that only woke for him.

"But why fight when you can fuck?"

She took a step back. Fletcher had never been spoken to like this. A thrill shot through her at the idea of the two of them…well… She swallowed. "Um?"

He rubbed his thumb over her bottom lip. "What do you think? Fight? Or—"

She smacked his hand and attacked his mouth with hers. The kiss was hard, almost violent, and it wasn't enough. She pulled away and stripped to her underwear, then latched back onto him.

His hot hands were everywhere. Fletcher didn't know if she wanted to scream or cry, but she didn't want him to stop. The heat from his palms was delicious. Her scars crossed her mind for a moment, but she cast the thought aside. All that mattered was this, right here and now.

Noah pulled away, and he stripped off his clothes. He was muscled and massive, with dark hair matting his chest, arms, and legs. He stripped out of his boxers, letting his erection bob, and her mouth went dry.

Fletcher looked into the swirling mercury of his eyes and returned the favor. She took off her bra and underwear. She was naked and scarred. "Don't mind the scars."

Noah let out a breath. "You're beautiful."

She stepped back. "Don't be sweet!"

It was his turn to step back. "I—"

"You said fight or fuck. We choose the latter," she reminded him. She needed the fervor, the fury, the thrill. Nothing soft. Anger, lust, passion for life.

Noah narrowed his eyes. "Fine, but we do it my way." He yanked her against him, then moved until her back was against the closet door.

Fletcher glanced over her shoulder, and panic stirred. "Not in there."

"Yes, in there." He bent to her ear, his stubbled cheek grazing her jaw, and whispered, "Scared?"

Her eyes searched his. Was it a test? A different kind of fight?

"Fuck it!" He opened the closet and brought them inside.

Fletcher gulped when Noah shut the door.

"Shh," he murmured against her lips. The kiss was forceful and demanded her full attention.

He grabbed her under her arms and pushed her against the wall. Fear of the closet had her adrenaline pumping so fast her chemicals must have gotten mixed up because she was so turned on, she couldn't think straight. She stuttered his name, then climbed his body until he was where she needed him to be.

Reed bent and positioned his erection at her entrance. He brought his mouth to hers and entered her in one strong thrust. She gasped, her body clenching around him. "Relax," he murmured against her skin.

She blinked back tears, glad it was too dark for him to see. Had she ever felt this…this what? Connection? She trembled.

His soft hair brushed against her breast as he sucked a nipple into his mouth. She moaned low in her throat and pulled his lips back to hers. She kissed him with all the fight she had and began to move her hips accordingly. Noah took the hint, grabbed her ass, and hammered into her.

Fletcher couldn't help the sounds slipping from between her lips. He'd adjusted his position again, and whatever he'd done had put him exactly where she needed him. She told him so with a violent, "Yes!" Every thrust sent little zings throughout her body. And he was doing things to her breasts that made her, for the first time in her life, happy she came equipped.

Tension was building in her thighs, and she squeezed her vaginal muscles around him. He felt so good inside her, perfect. Her hips moved to chase the pleasure that was just out of reach. So, so close…

"Fuck," he said against her ear and moved harder

against her.

Her moan echoed in the confines of the closet as her orgasm spiraled through her. She dug her nails into his shoulders and rode the wave of sweet release. She trembled with it.

Noah was only a couple of seconds behind her. Her name on his lips as he came was something she wouldn't forget. He wrapped his arms around her and rested his head against her heaving chest.

Once their breathing had slowed, Noah let her slide off him, then opened the closet door.

Fletcher stared at him. His seed ran down her inner thighs, but she didn't care; it didn't matter. This had been a glorious dance of bodies becoming one. Like the storm and the tide. Natural. Powerful. She glanced over her shoulder at the closet, then looked back at Noah.

His eyes were smoky. "Should I apologize?"

She rubbed her nose. "Why?"

He jerked his thumb behind him. "For the closet?"

Did he think he'd taken it too far? "If I'd said stop, you would have stopped—"

"Of course, I—"

She covered his lips with her fingers. "It was exactly right." She wouldn't tell him how true those words were.

"You wanted a fight or a fuck. And then you didn't want me to—"

She dropped her hand. "I wasn't saying I didn't want it to mean anything. I just"—she leaned her head against his chest—"I wanted it to be different from before."

Noah stilled. "Like with Daemon?" He tilted her chin so she had to look at him.

She nodded.

He cupped her cheek. "I'm sorry, cupcake."

Fletcher snorted. "If that ain't the sissiest damn thing I've ever heard; I don't know what is. I's ain't a cupcake."

Noah smiled, then sobered. "It wasn't though, was it? Like—"

"Don't worry, it wasn't the way I expected it, but it was what I needed." And she wanted him to do it again. She never wanted them to stop.

He pulled her against him. "You don't hate me then."

"I'm pretty fucking happy with you right this second."

He caressed her cheek with one finger. "You mean something to me," he began, but she stood on tiptoe and covered his lips with hers. He kissed her back, then swung her in his arms.

Chapter Fifteen

She was running down the stairs, but her legs weren't fast enough. She slipped.

"Where are you, Jamie, you little bitch!" the mother was shouting at her again. "It's time for your haircut."

No! Not that; she hated the scissors.

"There you are!"

Jamie cried as the mother put the scissors to the corner of her eye.

"Maybe you'd be a good girl if you couldn't see. Huh?" She dragged her to the closet and threw her in. "Take some time to think about what a spoiled brat you are," the mother shouted and slammed the door. Darkness enveloped Fletcher.

She was in the closet, but she wasn't alone. She was with her sisters. Uncle Evan was being murdered on the other side of the door. She turned the knob, but she was no longer a child, and she was no longer with her sisters.

"My beautiful Jamie. Come out," Daemon said, but he didn't have his face; he had his brother's face. He pulled her out of the closet, his icy fingers lingering on her neck, then heated the hanger.

"No, don't!" Was she telling Daemon or the mother? She wasn't sure. The hanger was yellowed with heat, glowing like an ember, and he came closer.

129

He drew his arm above his head, then brought it down in an arch. The heated metal singed her back. It was cold and hot, but cold. Burning flesh.

She sat in front of the mirror while he tugged a brush through her hair.

"We should cut your hair, Jamie. You'd look so sophisticated with your hair short and sleek. That would please me," he whispered against her ear.

"Where are you, missy?"

"Jasper? I'm here!" She was running through the woods. But it was dark, and the branches were slicing into her. "Jasper? I can't find you."

"Why are ya locking me in a box?"

She ran around the bend trying to find him. A thousand cuts. "Jasper?" she screamed.

"Fletcher? Fletcher!"

"What?" She jumped out of the bed. "I'm okay." Taking a couple of deep breaths to get her bearings, she focused on her surroundings; they were in Noah's bedroom and she'd had a—It was just a dream. She got out of the rabbit hole. "Go back to sleep, Reed. I'm fine."

Noah got out of bed and went over to her. He didn't do anything but hold her in his arms.

"I's fine," she said again and shoved out of his embrace.

"Do you need anything?"

"For you to go back to sleep." She searched the floor for her stuff. They'd brought their clothes up sometime after they'd decided to eat dinner. There. She put them on and went to find a brush. She hated the nightmares. She'd stopped having the ones from her childhood a long time ago. But after Daemon had held her hostage, they'd come flooding back. With a vengeance. A brutal montage created by some sadistic sandman.

Noah stood in the doorway, naked except for his boxers. "I take it you're not coming back to bed?"

Fletcher looked over her shoulder while she trapped her hair. "No."

"You can't leave. Protective custody, remember?" He crossed his arms over his beautiful chest.

She stared at him for a moment, thinking lusty thoughts. They could go back to bed. Do other things. She looked away from him and bit her lip. "Get dressed then," she said so he would stop tempting her. They'd had several sexual encounters over the course of the evening, and she was sore. She shivered. Sore in a good way.

"Where are we going at three in the morning?"

"What's this? An interrogation? I want to drive around or something, that's all."

He rose a dark brow. "Drive?"

"Around, yeah." Fletcher chewed her lip while he went to put on some clothes. Deciding she needed some coffee, she headed downstairs to the kitchen. Once she hit the on button, she rooted around in his junk drawer for some lip balm. She hit the jackpot with an unopened tube. She snorted as she applied the stuff. Cherry.

She capped the balm and hopped up on the counter. Noah came in wearing pajama bottoms and a black V-neck pullover. Did he know how fucking hot he was? He made her feel things—want things—that scared her.

"You're staring at me," she said.

"And your point is?" Her gaze went wide when he stepped between her legs and gave her a quick kiss. He rubbed his lips together and rose a brow.

Fletcher held up the tube. "I found your lip lube."

His snort was garish. "Help yourself to my—"

She cut him off with another kiss.

Noah stepped away with a chuckle. "Do you wake up like this every night?"

She shrugged. "Most nights. Since I was a kid. This is how I started picking locks. There wasn't anything better to do this late, and my sisters would all be sleeping. I'd get on my bike and ride into town."

"How old were you?"

"Seven or eight the first time I went." She didn't mention that the very first time she went she was with Casey. That was big sister's business.

He leaned against the counter. "Where did you go on these outings?"

"Broke into the sheriff's station." She laughed at the disbelief on his face. "I got in without incident the first couple of times, but Jasper caught me one night. I got into so much trouble. Grounded for two months. No bike, no playtime, and no show."

"*Murder She Wrote*," he offered.

She rose a brow. "Who told you?"

"Emmit." He smiled and got out two mugs.

"Figures." Did it bother her that Noah and Pops were so chatty? They were friends, which was annoying, but Fletch didn't tell her father who he could and couldn't be chummy with. But to mention her show... "I guess he told you about my name too?"

"He did." Reed prepared the coffee, then handed her a mug.

"Thanks." She saluted him and drank. That first sip was the best.

"I think your name gives you character."

"As opposed to being one, you mean? I'm not trying to start shit, Reed. I promise. Are you going to ask me why?"

He shrugged. "I didn't want to start shit."

She grinned. "I used to wake in the middle of the night when I was little. I know it still holds true today. But I'm talking about when I was with the woman who birthed me. I'd sneak out of whatever closet she put me in and turn on the TV. That late they showed reruns, and I watched *Murder She Wrote*—"

"And decided to change your name?"

"Well, I hate the name Jamie—Fletcher is much better."

"Why did Daemon call you Jamie? I'm not trying to be an ass; I'm curious."

She shrugged. "I'm not sure. He found out my middle name and kind of latched onto it." He wanted her to be Jamie. Short hair, fancy dresses, and a lady. "The first step in turning me into who he wanted me to be was to change my name. Identify me as who he wanted me to be. Our names are tied to who we are. Take them away…perhaps it's easier to lose sight of ourselves and be manipulated into a new identity."

He pursed his lips. "That makes sense."

"He did me a favor, really. By calling me Jamie, he gave me a way to compartmentalize things." Jamie got beat and branded. Fletcher got shot and driven crazy.

"I'm sorry you had to—"

She rested her mug over her heart. "Why are you being so nice to me?"

"Am I?" Noah kissed her cheek, then stepped back.

"Yeah. I don't know if I can handle all this"—she

133

waved her hand around—"pleasantness."

He rose a brow. "Try."

She made a noise in her throat. Whether she would *try* remained to be seen. She pointed to the clock on his wall. "We can go bug Jake in a couple of hours. He'll make us breakfast."

Noah rubbed his jaw. "Keller doesn't particularly care for me."

"That's because he's trying to protect me. See, if I didn't know better, I'd think you were the one after me."

He stiffened. "But you *do* know better."

She shrugged. "If you wanted me dead, you could have killed me at any time."

"Thanks for the vote of confidence." He would have turned away, but she kissed him.

"Look at it like this," she began after she'd kissed him thoroughly. "I could have killed you at any time too." She smiled when he paled.

Chapter Sixteen

Noah found himself in an odd situation. He was sitting at Alexandra's kitchen table while Jake Keller flipped pancakes. Fletcher had wanted to come to the B and B, so after they'd both showered and changed, here they were. Noah didn't care for the dirty looks Keller kept sending his way. Sure, it was around six in the morning, but Jake had been awake as Fletcher said he would. What was the big damn deal? If Noah'd had his way, they would be at the diner.

"You get much sleep?" Jake asked Fletcher.

"A bit." She poured a cup of coffee for Noah.

He waved a hand. "Thanks. I've had plenty."

"Suit yourself." She sipped her own and took a seat next to him. "I was thinking—"

"A dangerous pastime," Alex said, breezing into the kitchen. She gave him a look. "Good morning, Noah."

He nodded. "Alexandra." The revelation that Alexandra was his cousin still gave Noah pause. He had known her for years, yet he never noticed how much she looked like his aunt. Granted, his aunt had passed when he was a boy, and he'd only seen Alex once or twice when she was a baby. But Craig had known, and after he'd revealed the truth, Noah now saw his aunt whenever he looked at Alex. It was strange, but he was getting used to it.

Alexandra sipped her coffee and winced. "Did you make this, Fletcher?"

Fletcher grinned. "Too strong?"

"A little." Alex glanced from Noah back to her sister. "To what do we owe the pleasure of this visit?"

"I was hungry, and Jake makes the best breakfast."

Jake saluted her with his spatula. "Thanks, kid!"

"You need a guard to have breakfast?"

"She's in protective custody," Noah said and thanked Alex when she got him a glass of water.

"You didn't arrest her then?" Alex asked.

"I went willingly," Fletcher said. "After Jasper…"

"Oh, honey." Alex sat next to her and squeezed her hand.

"I keep telling myself he's with Laura now." She sniffled.

Noah shifted in his seat. Fletcher's grief was a powerful thing, and he wasn't sure he was ready for it. He would help her the best way he knew how. Jake caught his eye, and Noah sighed. He should just—

"I didn't kill my birth mother," Fletcher mumbled.

"What?" Noah and Alex said at the same time.

"Laura did," Fletcher began and filled them in on what she had found.

Guilt crept over Noah. She had spent years thinking she killed her birth mother, and he had burdened her with the guilt of his parents' deaths. Not that he believed she was responsible; he didn't. He hadn't. But Noah had needed closure after what happened, needed it in order to take his next breath, and Fletcher had hesitated. He'd hated her for that. Maybe part of him still did. He despised her for the hesitation, but also for giving him no choice but to stoop so low to get her cooperation. He shook himself. There was always a choice. *He* had chosen poorly.

Noah sipped his water. It did no good going down that road. It was bitter and made his feelings for Fletcher that much more complicated. What they'd done the night before. He'd never experienced anything like it. Passion, desire, lust, hate, want, and blatant need acted out in a meeting of their bodies. He turned his shiver into a stretch.

"So that's what Jasper meant," Alexandra said, bringing Noah back to the present.

"What?" Fletcher asked.

"After he had his heart surgery, Jake and I went to see him in the hospital. He said you hadn't killed anyone and neither had I. This explains you."

Fletcher sat back in her chair. "But what did he mean about you?"

"I don't know. He reminded me that self-defense is not murder. The guy who broke in and attacked me died because I fought back."

"That's an open and shut case," Noah reminded them. The first thing he'd done as sheriff was to read every file concerning the McKays, including the one they were discussing. A man had broken into the apartment above the garage, and Alexandra had walked in on him. There was a struggle, and Alex was the one left standing. Which, knowing the McKays, wasn't a big surprise.

"You think he was talking about Ruthie?" Fletcher pursed her lips. "The autopsy was inconclusive. I can get my hands on the—"

"You've seen the report, and so have I." Alex shook her head, and Jake put a hand on her shoulder.

"None of that really matters anymore."

"I was thinking more about getting my hands on the medical examiner."

"His body went to the city, so we have no pull," Alex said.

"I've got an ace in the hole." Fletcher grinned and stood up. "Jake, make mine a surprise."

"You just got here," Jake said from where he had moved to prepare plates.

"I know, but Noah and I have to check something out."

Noah shook his head. "No, we have to go to the station because *I* have to keep law and order in this town." Fletcher came over to him and got on his lap. He caught the look that passed between Alexandra and Jake, and heat flooded his face.

"Please, Noah? I need your help." Fletcher put her arms around his neck and kissed him. "Please?"

He hardened. The heat in his face increased, but he would be damned before he gave Fletcher the satisfaction of flustering him. "What do I get?"

Fletcher narrowed her eyes. "What do you want?"

"The governor's having a dinner party this weekend, and I need a date."

Alexandra burst out laughing, and Noah smiled. It was the first time he could remember her responding so openly.

Fletcher hopped off his lap and stuck her thumbs in the loopholes of her jeans. "What exactly do I have to do on this date?"

"It's a formal function," Noah explained.

"That means you have to dress all spiffy, kid," Jake said.

"Like how?" Fletcher looked between Noah and Alex.

Noah kept his face impassive. "It's black tie."

Alex's eyes went wide; then she bit her lip. "You should wear a dress."

"What do you mean by 'dress'?" Fletcher asked.

"Well, black tie usually means formal, so a gown—"

"Oh, fuck that. No way in hell am I gonna wear a damn ball gown. Nope. I refuse!"

"Then you'll go with me to the station and only there," Noah said getting out of his seat.

"But—?" Fletcher looked at Alexandra. "I need your connections to get to the city's medical examiner."

Noah straightened his spine. The look on her lovely face made him want to give in. To concede whatever she wanted.

"I've got an idea," Alex said and left the room. She came back with a familiar board game.

"Clue?" Noah sat back down. What in the hell?

"If Fletcher wins, then she doesn't have to wear a dress. And if you win, she does."

"Great idea, Alex!" Fletcher cheered and refilled her mug.

Noah sighed. "I don't have time for this."

"Scared, Reed?"

Twenty minutes later, the look on Fletcher's face was priceless when Noah came out victorious.

"It's settled," Noah began with a grin. "You'll wear a dress. I'm sure Alexandra will help you. Now, let's go to the station." He rose from his seat and put his dishes in the sink. "Thank you for breakfast." Keller was a damn fine cook.

"No problem," Jake said. "Kid?"

Fletcher stared at the board. "I can't fucking believe this!"

Noah rose both brows. "You're not going to back out on our bet now, are you?"

"Hell, no. I'll hold up my end, even if it bites my ass. But you still have to go where I want first."

"I'll graciously go." Noah went as far as giving a small bow.

Fletcher grunted and slammed out of the door.

"How did you beat her? The kid always wins."

Noah nodded toward Alex, who grinned.

"Oh, I helped him," she said.

Jake stared at his wife. "You did what?"

"I was the one who put the cards in the 'top secret' file. So I let Noah know. He never would have beaten her, and a night out would do her a world of good."

"You are so on her shit list if she ever finds out," Jake warned.

Alex shrugged. "I'm quite certain I have a permanent position on said list."

"Right next to me," Noah said, then waved and headed out the door.

Chapter Seventeen

Twenty minutes into their drive, and Fletcher still couldn't believe Reed had won. Hell's bells, the only person Fletcher ever lost to was her ma.

Reed gripped the steering wheel. "I won, period. Now we're doing what you want; even though I have multiple reservations about this."

"What's the big deal? The man's retired. All we're doing is paying him a social call." She turned in the passenger seat. "I appreciate you going out of your way for me on this, Reed."

He glanced at her. "I'm dependable like that."

"I'll do my part." She would hate every damn minute, but she would keep her word.

They pulled into a short driveway and parked. The house was a ranch-style, white brick, with an Asian esthetic. Noah knocked on the door before she could ring the bell, but that was fine with her. A tall, attractive man, maybe mid-sixties, with salt-and-pepper hair answered the door.

"Are you Leo Patterson?" Noah asked.

"I hope so. I'm wearing his underwear and sleeping with his wife." Leo winked.

Fletcher laughed, ignoring Noah's glare. He was annoyed he had agreed to this, but she was glad they were checking this lead. She should have come directly to the medical examiner years ago, but if the thought had crossed her mind, she'd dismissed it.

"I'm Sheriff Noah Reed with the Blue Creek Sheriff's Department, and this is Fletcher McKay. Would you mind answering a few questions for us?"

Leo looked Fletcher up and down. "You're the one Sheriff Hart always talks about?"

Fletcher snorted. "Probably."

"I heard Jasper was attacked."

Fletcher's gaze shot to Reed's.

"Jasper's at the hospital in critical condition," Noah said.

Fletcher's chest tightened. They weren't telling the public about Jasper's death yet. If the attacker thought they could get to Fletcher through Jasper, then they might get lucky with keeping the guard outside the empty hospital room. It was a chance they needed to take, and she understood that, but she hated lying to people. Folks loved Jasper, and they deserved to know. To grieve. She blinked away the tears that threatened.

Leo ducked his head. "I'll keep him in my prayers. Of course, I'll answer your questions. Come on in. Don't mind the mess. The missus is in Florida visiting her sister, and I'm slacking off."

A sense of warmth engulfed Fletcher the moment she stepped inside Leo's house. The place was cheerful, with portraits of kids and more kids lining every wall. It was a home and a happy one. She smiled.

"Have a seat," Leo said and turned the TV off. "Would either of you care for something to drink?"

"You wouldn't have any coffee, would you?" Fletcher sat on the plush red couch.

Noah stared at her. "Haven't you had enough?"

"One can never have too much coffee before

142

noon," Leo told Noah. "I'll get you a cup, Ms. McKay, and for you, Sheriff?"

"I'm fine," Noah grumbled and sat next to her.

Once Leo brought Fletcher and himself a cup, he took a seat in the worn recliner. "So, ask your questions."

"About sixteen years ago, you performed an autopsy—"

"About twenty minutes ago, I did something that I can't remember." Leo tapped his forehead. "The memory isn't what it used to be."

"This was a peculiar case," Noah said.

Fletcher finished her sip of coffee and set the mug on the end table. "The man was both shot in the head and stabbed in the heart."

Leo shifted in his seat. "The Ruthie case."

Fletcher took Noah's hand, and he squeezed hers in return. "You declared the cause of death inconclusive."

Leo gestured to Noah. "Is this off the record, Sheriff? Not that I've broken the law, but I want my bases covered all the same."

Fletcher turned to him. "Reed?"

He stretched his neck. "Fine."

"Sit tight," Leo said and left the room. He was back in a jiff with a manila envelope. "I owed Sheriff Hart several favors, and he asked me to leave certain things out of the report. Honestly, all I could give was an educated guess, so inconclusive fit."

"What favor did Jasper do for you," Noah began, "off the record?"

Leo sat back down with the envelope in his lap. "I used to work for Blue Creek before the city took away funding for the medical examiner's office. Something you may want to look into now that times have changed. Medical examination is sexy, thanks to TV."

"You're from Blue Creek?" Fletcher didn't recognize him.

"Originally. I moved not long after my divorce, nearly thirty years now. Jasper was the one who discovered Beverly's—that's my first wife— indiscretions, shall we say? He had the evidence against her, and it was concrete. Made the divorce smooth, and considering who she was sleeping with, that was a bargaining chip I was in desperate need of."

"Who?" Fletcher asked before she thought better of it.

Leo's eyes shone. "I'm sure you've heard of him. Despicable man. For years, Jasper tried to obtain enough evidence to prosecute the arrogant bastard, but money and clout too often speaks the right language. As does a big fish in a small pond. I found it fitting that Beverly married him."

Noah scooted to the edge of the couch. "Beverly as in Beverly Thomas? As in Ian Thomas?"

"Ah, the knowledge one possesses in a small town. Yes, Ian Thomas. Heard he died a few years back. Left Beverly and that no-good daughter of hers in a tight spot."

Fletcher elbowed Noah. "See, Reed, Leo doesn't even live in Blue Creek, and he knows Marylou's bad news. Like mother, like daughter, wouldn't you say, Leo?"

He harrumphed. "I'd say more than that."

"Please do," Fletcher said, and Noah glared at her.

"Ian Thomas was a criminal. He was charming and persuasive. Beverly had come from money, then

144

married me. She was happy until she met that man. He twisted her, changed her, and I guess one could say she left herself open for corruption. And that girl." Leo shook his head. "I've seen her around the city a few times. Sneaky and underhanded liker her daddy. Wouldn't have put it past Ian to have taught his daughter all his dirty tricks. Keep the family tradition alive."

"See." Fletcher smacked Noah's arm.

Noah sighed. "I heard him fine the first time, McKay."

"Best you keep yourself clear of that one, Sheriff," Leo told him.

Feeling a tad guilty, Fletcher said, "Reed has been trying to bring charges against her for fraud."

"The DA said they couldn't prosecute with the evidence I had," Noah explained.

Leo shook his head. "Jasper could never get anything concrete on her daddy either. Slippery like a snake that man was, like that organization Jasper was investigating—"

"What organization?" Noah asked.

Leo looked between them, his cheeks flushing. "Jasper never mentioned it?"

Goose bumps rose on Fletcher's arms. Another secret? "No, he didn't."

"Well, I…" Leo ran his hand through his hair twice. "I could be mistaken. As I said, my memory isn't what it used to be."

Noah nudged Fletcher and pointed to her coffee. She rolled her eyes and nodded. He should have asked for his own.

Reed took a sip from her mug, then handed it to her

and asked, "Could you tell us what you think you remember?"

"I…" He cleared his throat. "It was a long time ago, maybe twenty years now. I'd already moved, so I wasn't there. I remember Jasper mentioning it in an off-hand way, but I can't recall details. And if he didn't tell you, then…maybe it came out to nothing in the end."

Fletcher met Reed's gaze. Was he buying this? She was about to say something when Leo held up the envelope. "This I *do* remember."

Her misgivings forgotten, Fletcher set down her mug and took the folder from Leo. She pulled out the documents, and Noah shifted closer so he could read along with her. His heat embraced her, and she may have leaned into him if only to calm the chaos inside her. "Wait! You found two bullet wounds?" Fletcher bit her lip. That couldn't be. Alexandra had only shot once.

Leo tented his fingers. "Yes."

"I don't understand." Fletcher reread the ballistics report. Different bullets indicate different weapons—two shooters. "He had an entry wound dead center of his forehead. There's no way we wouldn't have seen another wound. And Alexandra would have noticed someone else outside."

Leo cocked his head to the side. "Alexandra?"

"Alexandra's my sister, Mr. Patterson. She had the rifle that night." She gave him a small smile. "I had the knife."

Leo sucked in a breath. "You're her, then."

Noah sat forward, almost obstructing her view. She swatted him until he backed up, then asked Leo what he meant.

"You've got his eyes. Strange—like Jasper."

Fletcher hid her surprise. Jasper had told this man?

Noah took the ballistics report from Fletcher and held it up. "About the second bullet?"

"It was a first for me." Leo shook his head and pointed to the ceiling. "Came from above. The second bullet was shot down into the top of Ruthie's skull. Going through his brain, his heart. It nicked a rib and embedded itself in the pelvic bone."

Fletcher shook her head. That wasn't possible. "There were six people there that night, not including Ruthie, and none of us knew."

"The gun probably had a silencer," Leo suggested.

Fletcher sat back against the cushions. A second shooter? There was no fucking way. Was there?

"What was it you did for Jasper?"

Fletcher looked at Noah. How could he think of questions right now? Her mind was blown.

"Well, Sheriff, off the record, I kept mum about the second bullet for starters and stated inconclusive on the report."

Noah nodded and picked up her mug again.

Was it weird that she liked him drinking out of her cup? She shook herself and motioned toward Leo. "But you said you could only make an educated guess."

"Ms. McKay, I'll have you know I'm quite educated." Leo winked.

Fletcher smirked. "What was your 'guess' then?"

"The mortal wound was the mystery bullet."

Her entire body went limp; then she straightened and asked, "If there hadn't been that bullet?"

"That *is* inconclusive, my dear."

Fletcher let out a shaky breath. Emotions threatened, but she brushed them aside.

"It may interest you to know that Ruthie would have been dead in less than twenty-four hours anyway."

Tension gripped her. "What?"

Noah held up the autopsy report. "Something else Jasper had you leave out?"

Leo nodded. "The man was dead, and with the circumstances surrounding the situation, didn't much matter that I left it out."

"What was it?" Fletcher wanted to know.

"He was poisoned."

Noah's dark brows drew together. "How?"

"Found a lethal mixture of ethylene glycol, methanol, and propylene glycol in his system."

Fletcher widened her eyes. "Antifreeze?"

"It was a matter of when, not if."

Noah stood and shook hands with the former medical examiner. "Thanks for your time, Leo. I think we got what we came for."

"It was nice meeting you," Fletcher said and followed Noah toward the door, stopping when Leo asked her to wait.

"This is a picture of Jasper and I when we were starting out. Thought you might like it."

She glanced at the photo. Her eyes filled with tears, and she looked back to Leo. "When did Jasper tell you about me? About me being his daughter, I mean."

Leo's cheeks pinkened. "He didn't. Secrets run deep in Blue Creek, but rumors run rampant, and years ago they threatened to destroy Jasper. Word got out that he'd had a one-night stand when he was away for a conference. You'd be about the right age if a child had come from that affair. It was an election year, and Ian Thomas didn't want Jasper to win. But Laura stood by her husband, said who better to be sheriff than a man who can admit to his mistake and take responsibility for it."

"That sounds like Laura." Fletcher smiled.

"Indeed." Leo rocked back on his heels. He opened his mouth, but the blare of Noah's horn shut him up. "I think the sheriff's getting a tad impatient."

Fletch snorted. "That's Reed for you. Thanks for everything."

"Take care, Ms. McKay."

Fletcher hurried her steps to Noah's vehicle.

****

"I need to check out Alex's ceiling," Fletcher said for the seventh time since leaving the medical examiner's house.

"Call her, and she can look," Noah said and took the turn to town. "You're coming with me to the station." He had already missed a couple of calls from his deputies.

"Reed, I have to see for myself."

"Then wait till I'm done. We can go right after shift." Was that asking too much? No.

She growled.

"McKay, I have a job to do," he said and turned the radio on.

She turned it off. "I have one to do too. I have to find out the truth. I'm trying to cooperate, Reed. I really am, but this is fucked up."

"I'm sorry you feel that way."

She huffed out a breath and crossed her arms over her chest.

Noah snickered. "Are you pouting? I can't believe it, you are!"

Her cheeks turned bright red. "I've never pouted in my damn life. Pouting is for sissies."

"Then you may want to consider a name change because you *are* pouting." He chuckled. Her face was priceless.

Fletcher smacked him upside the head.

"Watch it," he said, then pulled over on the side of the road. This gave her a chance to make her escape. "Damn it, Fletcher, were you trying to get us both killed?" He got out of the truck.

"I's ain't a sissy!" She headed toward town.

"Will you stop?" He picked up his pace. "Now you're acting like a drama queen."

She threw her arm in the air and flicked him off.

"McKay, if you don't stop, I swear to God I'll arrest you," Noah warned.

Fletcher stopped in her tracks, turned around, and walked right up to him. "You wouldn't dare!"

"Fletcher McKay, you are under arrest for assaulting an officer..." Noah began, then stopped wasting his breath. If he arrested her, there was no telling what the town would do. Mutiny probably. Instead, he picked her up and slung her over his shoulder.

"You best be putting me down!" Fletcher shouted.

A flashy red car drove by, and the driver honked their horn. Noah waved.

Fletcher grumbled. "That was Trixy Mae! Now everyone's gonna be talking about us."

"It's your own fault," Noah said as he buckled her in.

She slapped his hand. "I can do that myself, thank you very much."

"Why does everything have to be a fight with you?" He leaned in and kissed her, surprised when she kissed him back. Noah stood and shut her in. He got to the driver's side and started them on their way again.

Fletcher turned in her seat so she was facing him. "For the record. I am not now, nor have I ever been a drama queen."

He smirked. "Okay, you're not a drama queen. There, I said it. Happy?"

"No. I need to go to Alex's to check the damn ceiling. Can't you drop me off? I'm sure Jake will watch me for you."

"Please don't insult my intelligence. You have Jake Keller and all the other men in your family wrapped around your finger, so the answer is no."

"Pops ain't wrapped around anything. He's barely even speaking to me. You could let me stay with him."

"The answer is no." Emmit had other things going on.

"Fine!"

Noah pursed his lips. She had given in too quickly for his liking.

Chapter Eighteen

Fletcher got a ride with Jebb to the B and B later that afternoon. It had taken her two phone calls. One to Jebb to tell him where to meet her and the other to Mildred Lawrence. The woman got Noah out of the office and out of Fletcher's face at the agreed-upon time.

"Should I wait for you?" Jebb asked when he pulled into the parking lot of Granny Vaughn's.

"You're coming in with me. I might need your brain." Fletcher got out of his vehicle and went inside.

"Hey, Jebb." Jake gave a small salute, then motioned to Fletch. "Where's your bodyguard?"

Fletcher snorted. "Up a tree by now, I reckon. Where's Alexandra?"

"Right here." Alex came fully into the kitchen and pointed to Jebb. "Why aren't you in school?"

Jebb shuffled his feet. "I have work release this year."

Alex rose a brow. "Shouldn't you be working then?"

"I usually work at the garage with Casey, but—"

"He's working with me today," Fletcher said, rocking back on her heels.

Jake laughed, and Alex glared at him. She turned back to Jebb. "How are things at Charlie's house?"

Fletcher swiveled toward her brother. "Why are

you staying at Charlie's?" He hadn't mentioned that.

Jebb squirmed. "Ma and Pops said they needed some alone time."

The blood drained from Fletcher's face. "They're not having problems, are they?"

"Oh, please. They're like teenagers. Having problems?" Alex scoffed. "That's ridiculous. Now, what brings you here?"

"Did you ever have to fix a hole in the ceiling?" Fletcher closed her eyes and moved around the room, trying to remember where everyone had been positioned all those years ago. "About here?"

"I didn't, but Granny had the ceiling redone after…everything." Alex shrugged. "Blood spatter, she said."

Fletcher stared at the ceiling a moment, then turned to her sister. "You might want to sit down, 'cause you ain't gonna believe this shit."

They sat around the kitchen table while Fletcher explained what she'd found out from Leo. At one point, Jake took Alex's hand, and Fletcher held in a smile.

"I didn't kill him," Alex whispered, then rose to her feet. "Excuse me."

Fletcher grabbed her arm. "Don't go running off to be upset by yourself, Alexandra. We can be upset together."

"Who said I was going to be upset? I was going to go…oh, never mind." She sat back down and fiddled with her charm bracelet.

"Good," Fletcher said and looked at Jebb. "You go away."

"Why?" Jebb asked but stood.

"Fine, stay, whatever. What we need to do is find

out who the mystery shooter was."

"Why do you think Jasper kept that from us?" Alex asked.

From over his shoulder where he was rooting in the fridge, Jebb said, "Knowing Jasper, he was probably protecting someone."

Fletcher nodded. "He always told us the results were inconclusive. Maybe that was his way of letting us know as much as he could without breaking a confidence." Fletcher gripped her locket.

"But doesn't it mean that that person had to have known the truth about Ruthie? Who could have suspected him?" Jake asked.

Fletcher shook her head. Who was around then? She glanced at the clock on the wall. Her time was running short if she wanted to make it back before Noah. If she wanted to make it back. Which she didn't, did she?

"What about Granny Vaughn or Granddad?" Jebb asked, pouring a glass of tea.

Alex pursed her lips. "It had to be someone close to Granny. Close enough to know about the secret passageways. Know where they are and how to get in and out of the house with no one the wiser."

Jake leaned back in his chair. "Someone poisoned the man before that, though. Did the medical examiner say what kind of poison?"

"Antifreeze," Fletcher mumbled. She smirked when Jebb slurped his tea, making Alex bitch about manners. Fletch should let him go on to the garage. Casey would throw a fit if she found out Fletcher had absconded with her help. Wait... She jumped to her feet. "Holy shit!"

Alex sighed. "Really, Fletcher."

"No, I figured it out!" she shouted. It had taken her long enough. Of all the stupid—

"Don't keep us in suspense, kid," Jake said.

"Ward fucking Jessup." Fletcher waited for it to sink in. Ward Jessup, their uncle Evan's father, had died a couple of years ago, but he had run the only garage in town at the time.

"No shit!" Jake said.

Alexandra rubbed her fingers. "It makes perfect sense... He was good friends with Granny Vaughn, so he more than likely knew about the secret passageways."

"Evan told Ward his secrets. Who's to say he didn't tell his father his suspicions too. Ward would have wanted revenge." Fletcher would have.

Jebb hunched in his chair. "Poor Ward."

"He was never the same after Evan died," Alex murmured, looking out the window.

Fletcher swallowed. Blood, pouring out of their uncle's throat, tears streaming down his cheeks, his beautiful dark eyes closing for good. An envelope. Fletcher shook herself. That was a different rabbit hole, but it led to worse ones.

"Jasper keeping this to himself doesn't make sense," Jake said, standing. He gripped the back of his chair. "Why not tell you after Ward—"

"Jasper and Granny always said to let the dead lie," Fletcher reminded them. But it was another secret he had kept from her. She didn't want to think too closely on that either.

"Probably their way of telling everyone to mind their own business," Jebb said. "But we don't have to like it."

"No, we don't," Fletcher agreed, then pointed to her sister. "Did you ever hear about an organization in Blue Creek—"

"There are multiple organizations in Blue Creek," Alex began, "as you well know."

"I'm guessing she's not talking about the future whoever's of America," Jebb said.

Fletcher snorted. "Not unless there's a future criminals branch."

"One never knows," Alex said with a smirk. "Why?"

"Leo said something about Jasper investigating some organization—"

"In Blue Creek?"

Fletcher's gaze flicked to Jake. "Yeah, but Jasper never mentioned it to me. Ever."

"Could Leo have been mistaken?" Alex asked.

Fletcher shrugged. "He did say his memory wasn't the best."

"But you didn't believe him?" Jake asked.

She shook her head. "I think he was backpedaling."

"What about Jasper's files?" Jebb asked before he excused himself to use the restroom.

Fletcher stood. "I didn't bring all the files with me when I left the apartment."

"It's as good a place to start as any," Alex suggested.

She nodded, then headed out the back door.

"Kid?" Jake came beside Fletcher and stuck his hands in his pockets. "How are you holding up?"

"Let's see…my life has gone down the fucking drain, and I'm no closer to finding Jasper's murderer."

She choked on the last word. Someone couldn't be a murderer unless they killed someone. Killed as in made dead. Jasper was dead. She shook it off. No time for that rabbit hole either.

"Sorry." Jake put his arm around her shoulders. "Do we trust Noah now?"

"No." Did she want to? Yes. She wanted it so much it made her sick.

Jake pulled away. "Oh?"

Fletcher rolled her eyes. "I don't trust anybody but family." Thinking again of Jasper, and the files, she nodded toward the apartment. "The cops are done, aren't they?"

"Yeah, you want to get some of your stuff to take to 'protective custody'?" He smirked.

"May as well make the most of this visit," she said and headed up the steps.

Fletcher went about gathering her things. Noah was surely back at the station by now. He'd be pissed. But he'd pissed her off plenty of times. Fair was fair.

Jake snorted and shook a jewelry box. "What's this?"

"That ain't mine." She huffed. It was girly and gross.

Jake shrugged a shoulder. "Must be Alexandra's then." He started to lift the lid.

"Wait," Fletcher shouted making Jake jump. "Sorry, I just need to get this stuff downstairs pronto." She held up the box of Jasper's files. "Do you mind?"

"No." Jake set the jewelry box on the table. "I'll take it."

"Thanks," she said and handed the files over. She smiled, then waited until he was down the steps before she shut and locked the door. She stared at the box for a moment, then put her ear against it. No ticking. Slowly she unlatched the small lock. "In a minute," she hollered when Jake banged on the door.

She took a breath, squeezed her eyes shut, and opened the lid. She peeked out of one eye and released her breath when she didn't blow up. Looking in the box, she said, "Ah, fuck," then nearly jumped out of her damn skin and dropped the box when the door slammed open. She grinned. "Hey, Reed."

Jake pushed past Noah. "What in the hell are you doing?"

"That's what I'd like to know," Noah snapped.

"Alexandra's gonna kick your ass for breaking her door." Fletcher sniffed. "Someone left me a present. I thought it might be a bomb, but it wasn't. No lurker lyrics either." Her sister needed to get some cameras installed now. This was twice—

"Wait a minute." Jake took hold of her shoulders and gave her a shake. "You mean to tell me you thought that thing was a bomb and you opened it? Are you out of your fucking mind?"

She patted the hand on her shoulder. "Don't worry, Jake."

"What? He calls you crazy, and you don't curse him out," Noah said.

Fletcher sighed. "I like him, or I would have let him open the box."

"Kid, you're killing me here," Jake said stepping back. "You got any beer?"

"You know Alex keeps this place stocked," she said. That was all the invitation Jake needed to raid the fridge.

Noah crowded next to her. "What's in the box, McKay?" When she didn't answer, he took it from her. She swallowed when he pulled out a silver ring. "I don't understand."

Fletcher fiddled with her locket. She didn't say anything when Jake looked inside the box and pulled out a pair of scissors and a bent piece of burnt wire. Bile rose in her throat, and breathing was difficult.

"Kid?"

She opened her mouth, then closed it when Alex walked in.

"Jacob Keller, if you're responsible for this mess, you're in so much trouble." Alex looked at the three of them. "You didn't do it, did you, Fletcher? What *is* going on?"

"I'll have you know I could easily have broken down the door, princess, but Noah's like a bull—all charging and shit."

Fletcher laughed, and Noah shook his head.

Alex blinked. "Okay."

"Do you know anything about this box, or the things inside?" Jake asked.

"What things?" Alex stepped closer, then her eyes shot to Fletcher's. "Oh, honey."

"It doesn't mean nothing," Fletcher hissed. She shifted from foot to foot, not even believing herself.

"It means a great deal," Alex murmured.

Fletcher didn't want her sister to see the glaze of tears in her eyes.

"Look at me."

Fletcher blinked a couple of times, then met her sister's blue gaze.

Alex wiped a tear from Fletcher's cheek. "This is a

159

W. L. Brooks

direct threat."

Fletcher nodded. Still, she had to confirm her suspicion of something else. Grabbing Alex's hand and the ring out of Noah's, she pulled her sister into the bedroom, then shut the door, and lifted her shirt. "See if it fits." She was shaking like a ninny, but she couldn't help it. She needed to know. Under the scars on her back was a brand; one of the many mementos left by the mother. The ring was an exact match.

"Fletcher, no. I won't do it."

"Alexandra, I need to know. Do you think I'm enjoying this?" Fletcher waited another minute, but her sister wouldn't move. Fine! Snatching the ring out of Alex's hand, she held her shirt and went back into the den. She handed the ring to Jake and asked him to see.

"Kid?" Jake's voice shook.

"Don't do it, Jacob," Alexandra said. "Fletcher doesn't need to torment herself like this."

"See if it fucking fits. Damn it, I'd do it myself if I's could reach." Jake put the ring to her back, and Fletcher swallowed bile.

"It fits," Jake whispered.

"Now the wire." Fletcher looked over her shoulder and pointed Jake toward the box. "The wire."

"Kid, I don't... I'm sorry, princess," he said to Alex, who looked away. He took the wire and compared it with the scars on Fletcher's back.

"Are you happy now?" Alexandra demanded.

Fletcher put her shirt down and took the scissors out of the box. She didn't say a word as she headed through her bedroom door and into the adjoining bathroom. Stopping when Alex caught her arm.

"What are the scissors for?" Alexandra whispered,

then shouted, "Fletcher, what are the scissors for?"

"Ain't nobody's business but mine." Fletcher snatched her arm back and went into the bathroom. Locking the door, she unbraided her hair and ignored everything else. She used the tips of her fingers to find the right place, but she couldn't feel it anymore. Fletcher covered her mouth as a laugh slipped out. The scar was gone. She gripped the sink and sucked in air.

After exhaling a shaky breath, Fletcher opened the scissors knowing what she would find, but afraid of it anyway. Initials G. W. Greta Wayne. They were the same scissors she'd feared. The ones from her nightmares. They seemed so small now. Funny how something so insignificant could terrorize a body. She opened the door to find Alex staring at her.

"I'm going to call Casey to come home right this instant if you don't tell me what's going on!"

"You's won't do a damn thing." Fletcher tried to get around her sister, but Alex held her ground.

"Your speech regressed, which is a dead giveaway," Alex pointed out.

"It ain't my fault my subconscious makes me talk funny when I's emotional. When I'm emotional," she amended. "Now, let me out."

Her sister rose a brow. "No."

"I want out! This isn't for you; don't you get that?" Her voice cracked, and she squeezed her eyes shut.

Alex took Fletcher by the arm and pulled her down to sit on the bed. "You said I didn't have to be upset by myself. Neither do you."

Fletcher rubbed her nose. "The ring was hers. It fit perfectly on my back. Even felt the same. That's weird, right? The wire fits because it's from a wire hanger, which you can get anywhere. But how would someone know what Daemon used?"

"The court transcripts from his trial?" Alexandra suggested, her voice catching.

Fletcher nodded. That made sense. She'd had to tell the court what Daemon had done, everything. She had asked her family not to come that day. Of course, they came but sat outside the courtroom waiting for her.

Alex pointed to the small metal object clutched in Fletcher's hand. "And the scissors?"

Fletcher snorted. "Scar's gone. After all these years, it faded away."

"I don't think I want to know," Alex began, "but what scar?"

"Only good girls had pretty hair, so she kept mine close to my scalp. She cut me with them once, enough so that she had to take me to the hospital for stitches. Head wounds bleed something awful. She told the doctors some story. I don't remember. She engraved her initials in them." Fletcher held up the scissors. "See."

"The ring, the wire, and those are all the things that hurt you. How the hell did someone get the ring and the scissors?"

Good question. "Maybe Mommy Demented's estate had a sale, and our lurker lyricist friend attended."

"However they came into possession of these things, this is a direct threat, like I said before." Alex's brow pulled together. "Someone's bent on coming after you, but they want you to suffer first. The question is who—"

"The only 'who' that matters is *who* killed Jasper."

"What about *you*, Fletcher?" Alex narrowed her

eyes. "Are you willing to risk your life to find his killer?"

Fletcher glared at her sister. "What kind of question is that? Of course I am! I went after the person trying to hurt Casey. And I tried to help Charlie with the son of a bitch who was after her. I did my part with helping Pops way back when, and I'll do the same with Jasper. Family is family."

Alex ran a hand down the skirt of her dress. "They were all haunted by ghosts of their pasts—"

"Yeah." Fletcher stood and looked at the toes of her boots. "Our ghosts are beyond hauntings."

"So it would seem," Alex said with a sigh, then stood when the bedroom door opened.

"I hate to break up this party, ladies, but Fletcher and I need to be going," Noah told them.

Fletcher pointed to her sister. "You can leave me with Alex; she won't let me get away."

"We've been over this, McKay. There's no way in hell I'm leaving you here. Considering what you pulled today, you're lucky I don't lock you behind bars. Which I'm thinking might not be such a bad idea."

Fletcher threw her hands up. "All right already. I'll talk to you later, Alex. And don't you dare call Casey."

Chapter Nineteen

Noah sat behind the desk in his den. He'd taken Fletcher back to the station and hadn't let her out of his sight again. Now she sat on his couch with her legs curled under her. She was going through the files she had picked up from the apartment. He hadn't had the heart to ask her exactly what the ring and scissors meant. Considering he'd been over every inch of her naked body, he had a pretty good idea.

Jake and Jebb had also filled him in while the sisters were having their conclave. Jebb did most of the talking, if truth be told, but Noah had gotten more from Jake's agitation than from the young McKay's words. Keller had cursed a blue streak; Noah knew Fletcher was important to Jake, but today he'd seen to what extent.

Noah being on the McKay sisters' side wasn't a first. The simple fact that he'd put himself there instead of being forced was what made the difference. Mildred was right; life was more comfortable on the McKay side. Hell, half the town had gone out of their way to say hello to him today. Like he'd won the damn lottery or something. Trixy had obviously told everyone what she had witnessed on the road.

A couple of the deputies had mentioned they'd noticed a change in him. Which had surprised Noah. Was he different? He was happier. Content. How did he feel about people being able to perceive that? Not as bothered as he thought he'd be.

There *was* something troubling him, but he couldn't put his finger on it. A memory, an old case? It was right in the back of his mind, but he wasn't able to access it. It was something to do with that box—

"Whatcha thinking about?" Fletcher asked without looking up from Jasper's files.

"I'll let you know when the answer comes to me," he told her. "Have you found anything of interest yet?"

"No." She sighed and dropped what she'd been reading. "If there's a ghost from my past trying to torment me, I can't figure it out."

He motioned toward the files. "Anything about suspicious lurkers?"

"No," she grumbled. "I should have put cameras up the minute I started staying at the apartment, but I got waylaid with other stuff."

"It happens to the best of us."

"You don't honestly think we'll get prints off of the jewelry box, do you?"

They had taken the box to the station and sent it directly to the lab. Did he think they'd find anything? No, he didn't. "We'd be remiss not to check it out."

She pursed her lips. "True."

Noah stood and stretched, then asked, "Are you ready to go to bed?"

Fletcher eyed him. "I'll stay in one of the guest rooms."

"Fine. But I'm ready to go to sleep, and I don't trust you to be down here alone." Noah wouldn't tell her he wanted her in his bed, wanted her next to him, even if only to sleep.

She rolled her eyes and stood. "If you insist," she said and headed up the stairs. When she got to the landing, she pointed to the back guest room. "I'll take that one."

"Good night, then." He waited for a second, then went to his own room. He turned on the shower and put the water on cold. Stepping in, he waited until he had his lower body under control before changing the temperature.

He dried himself off, slipped on some pajama bottoms, and went to make sure Fletcher was still in her room. She was sitting on the bed, a crease at her brow as she looked over the files.

"What?" Fletcher asked when he came in through the door.

"Just making sure." He gave her a small smile. Was it his imagination or were there more files than before?

"Noah?"

He rose a brow. She didn't often call him by his first name. He liked it. "Yeah?"

"I'm not going to sleep tonight, but if you want, you can lie in here until you feel like going to your room."

"You want me to lie here but not go to sleep?"

"I said if you want to. You don't have to do anything." She shrugged and returned to her files.

"I'll stay. Do you want me to take a look at those?" She handed him a stack. Fixing the pillows so he could have something to lean back on, Noah sat next to her and started reading.

Fletcher may have scooted a teeny weenie bit closer to Reed. She had suggested the guest room in order to sneak to the attic and grab some of the files she'd left up there without giving herself away. She peeked at him from under her lashes. These were Jasper's personal files on the residents of Blue Creek. His suspicions, his theories, and his anecdotes. The old man had an opinion on everything and everyone, but he was fair, and he was honest. "What did you find?" she asked when Noah got off the bed with a piece of paper in his hand.

"We've had a run of vandalism lately, and this gives me a name. I need to double check my reports and see if there's any congruency."

"Oh," Fletcher said, hoping her disappointment wasn't obvious.

****

Fletcher stood on Alex's stupid stool in her bra and underwear. She tightened the towel on her head and rolled her eyes. Alex had a full-length mirror that Fletcher was sure she'd stolen from an evil queen in some fucking fairy tale.

Alex huffed. "You need to change your underwear, Fletcher."

Charlie made a face. "Those aren't sexy."

"Silk would be sexy," Casey said from her position on the bed. Casey McKay Keller was the oldest of the four McKay sisters. Her hair touched her waist when it was loose; it was jet black and had a slight curl. Her skin was a dusky gold, and her eyes were a strange violet color. She was also several months pregnant and getting bigger by the day. She and Ryan had returned home from their babymoon the night before. Just in time to torture Fletcher about this "date" with Noah.

Fletcher made faces at the suggestions: silk, lace,

satin, blah, blah, blah. She had to get all fancied up to go with Noah to the governor's dinner part tonight, and her sisters were purposely tormenting her. "What's wrong with what I've got on? They're clean."

Alex motioned toward her. "Your panty lines will show."

"I ain't wearing those damn wedgie things!" Sheesh. It was bad enough Alexandra had taken her to Trixy's salon to get waxed. Alex was an evil woman. Fletcher had had her eyebrows waxed, her legs waxed, even her damn private part had gotten special treatment. She hadn't known Trixy offered services like that. Hell, Fletcher wasn't sure those kinds of things were even legal.

Fletcher kept her lady parts neat and tidy, but Alex had told the waxing chick—who had a degree in cruel and unusual punishment—to shape it up. Fletcher said she wanted it shaped like an inverted heart. An ace at the hole or so she'd told Alex. Course Alexandra hadn't found it funny. And after the waxing chick had torn away the first strip, the tears in Fletcher's eyes hadn't been from laughter.

"They're called thongs, Fletcher. I wear them. Well, not right now," Casey told her.

"If you like having something jammed up your crack, that's your business." Fletcher crossed her arms over her belly. At least the worst of her scars would all be covered. Alex had made sure of that.

"Fletcher, trust us, okay?" Charlie smiled and pulled things out of a pink satin bag. "Here, put these things on."

Fletcher snatched the stuff from Charlie, stomped to the bathroom, and slammed the door.

Several minutes later, she came out and said, "What in the hell is this thing?"

Casey sucked in a breath. "Holy shit, Fletch!"

Fletcher froze. They were all staring at her, and she didn't like the smile on Alex's face. "What?"

Charlie giggled. "You look like a pinup."

Fletcher rolled her eyes. "Whatever."

"You're fucking hot, that's what," Casey said, then smiled a lecherous grin. "Noah's gonna die."

"Good," Fletcher said.

Charlie rolled her eyes. "You don't mean that."

"Maybe I do," Fletcher countered.

"They do say there's a fine line between love and hate," Casey reminded the room. Big sis had blown a gasket when she found out about Fletcher and Reed, but Ryan had soothed things over, so Fletcher didn't have to worry about it.

Alex gave a ladylike snort. "Typical of Fletcher to go crossing lines."

Fletcher gave Alex the one-fingered salute, jumping when her other sister patted her ass. "What the fuck, Charlie?"

"You're gonna get some tonight, Fletch." They all looked at Charlie, whose face turned bright red. "I said that out loud, didn't I?"

Casey laughed, hard. "You sure as hell did!"

"Oops," Charlie said and rubbed her baby bump. "Pregnancy brain strikes again."

Fletcher waved it off. "Don't worry about it."

Casey threw a wad of tissue paper at her, and Fletcher batted it away. "You have done the deed with Reed, haven't you?"

Charlie broke into a fit of giggles. "Done the deed

169

with Reed."

Then Alex started laughing. Fletcher's face, neck, and even her chest went pink. If she didn't tell them, they would never shut the hell up. "Yes."

Casey sat up straighter. "How was it?"

"Casey," Alexandra hissed. "A little tact for goodness' sake."

Charlie looked between Fletcher and the others. "I mean, I want to know too. If you want to share."

"No, I's don't wanna share. It's none of you's business."

Casey hooted. "That good, huh, Fletch?"

"She died of embarrassment" would be a stupid-ass epitaph, wouldn't it? Fletcher cleared her throat. "I'm only going to say this once, then we will never speak of it again. Agreed?" She pointed to her sisters.

"Agreed," the three of them said in unison.

She opened her mouth, then closed it. Shit. "I—it was better than, you know…before." It was like someone sucked the air out of the room. They stared at her, their fear palpable. The sex she'd had with Daemon had been consensual, and *before* he'd gone mad, but no one seemed to believe her on that point. "It's fine. I'm fine. I don't know how to say what you want to hear."

"We'll help you," Charlie said stepping closer to her. "How many times have you and Noah—"

"Several," she said, and the room relaxed.

Casey scooted toward the edge of the mattress. "Several what? Orgasms?"

Fletcher blinked. "No, several times that night. I don't know how many orgasms I had. Every time. Sometimes twice. Is that what you want to know? Can we be done now?" They were ogling her again.

"What?"

"You said 'that night,' " Alex said.

Fletcher stared at her toes. "We only had sex that one night." They'd spent most of their time together talking about fun stuff like unsolved crimes and—

"Several times," Charlie asked. "As in more than five? In one night?"

Fletcher shrugged. "Yep."

"And each time had a happy ending?" Casey asked.

Fletcher couldn't help but grin. "Fucking delightful."

"And you want to do it again?" Alex prompted.

She squirmed. "Yeah, but he hasn't initiated it again." He hadn't even kissed her again, since that last time in his truck. She wanted to kiss him but kept second-guessing herself. What if he was pissed about her ditching him? What if—

"You can initiate it," Casey said.

Fletcher rubbed her nose. She had planned to order some sexy e-books and get some ideas. But she hadn't done it yet. She couldn't go to the library, because the librarian, old Millie Mitchell, would tell the world. "How do I—"

"Jump him," Charlie said, and her other sisters agreed.

A thrill shot through her at the idea. "Okay, I will." She smiled. "As per our agreement, we never talk about this again."

Her sisters mumbled but acquiesced.

"Good," she said, then waved some sort of contraption at them. "Now, what the hell is this thing?"

"It's a garter belt," Alex said. She helped Fletcher put it on.

171

"But what's it for?"

"You connect your stocking to these little straps," Casey said and tossed Fletcher a pair of flesh-colored silk stockings.

"Oh." Fletcher chewed her lip and sat on the bed. She tried to pay attention as Alex explained how she was supposed to do this without putting a hole in the damn things. Her fingers and toenails had already been manicured and pedicured because her sisters said she had to do it. She hated nail polish, but she had enjoyed soaking her feet and the massage. "There." No holes or runs or whatever the hell Alexandra called them.

"Now sit here." Alex pulled out the vanity chair. She took Fletcher's hair down from the towel.

"What are you going to do?" Fletcher's eyes widened when Charlie brought out the blow drier and the curl gadgets. "Ah, man." Fletcher sat as still as she could while Charlie dried her hair, then rolled it in hot curlers.

Casey grinned. "You look like Medusa."

Fletcher made hissing noises, then shut up when Alexandra pulled out some high heels. What in the actual—

"Try these."

Fletcher stared at the shoes. "You can't be serious." Daemon had made her...she squashed the thought. She could do this.

"Balance yourself," Alex said for the tenth time. "Stand up straight and stick your butt out a little."

Charlie giggled.

Alex glared at her. "You're not helping matters. Noah is well over six foot; you're maybe five two, Fletch. You need a good four inches so you don't look ridiculous dancing."

"What do you mean, dancing?" Fletcher paled. "I didn't sign up for dancing." Dread turned her stomach; Daemon had danced with her every night. Icy fingers brushed her neck, goose bumps lifted on her skin, and bile filled her throat. Stop! No rabbit holes.

Alex pulled her into a hug. "It won't be like with Daemon, I promise. You'll be dancing with Noah." She kissed Fletcher's cheek, then let her go.

"Yeah," Casey agreed with a sniff.

Alex snapped her fingers. "That'll do."

Fletcher grumbled when Alex guided her toward the vanity seat.

"Make up," Charlie said clapping her hands. "I'll do it."

"No. I'll do it," Alexandra said. "You chose her hair, remember?"

"What's Casey gonna do?" Fletch sat her ass down.

"I'm gonna sit here and observe the operation," Casey said from her position on the bed.

"Good choice," Alex said and opened a bag. She got out a pink bottle and applied the contents to Fletcher's face.

"Smells nice," Fletcher said.

"It nourishes your skin."

Fletcher pointed to the little box Alexandra pulled out. "What's that?"

"An eyeshadow palette. Now, close your eyes."

The brush was soft against her skin, but Fletcher would never say anything good about this experience. She prayed Alex didn't make her look like a doll or a clown or a clown doll.

"Stop fidgeting," Alex complained as she applied

eyeshadow to the other eye.

"I'm not doing it on purpose." Fletcher blinked open her eyes and would have looked in the mirror, but Alex smacked her. Damn it, she wanted to see. She'd only worn makeup three times in her life, and that had only been because her sisters had gotten married. But her ma had only made her wear mascara. 'Course, mascara was the tool of Satan. Fletcher was sure of that.

Alex uncapped the eyeliner. "Look up. Good. Now close them." She put a bit on the upper lid and recapped the pencil.

"Done?" Fletcher sighed when Alex pulled out the mascara wand. An instrument of evil.

"Look up and don't blink."

Fletcher held her knees in a death grip and barely breathed.

"Okay, you can open, but I'm not done." She grabbed the compact and powdered Fletcher's nose. Then she put on a little blush. "Go ahead and get the dress," Alex told Charlie.

"What about my hair?"

"We'll fix it once we have the dress on," Alex told her.

Fletcher stood up, slipped off the spikes, and stepped into the pink dress. Alexandra said it was mauve, but it looked pink to Fletcher. She held the front while Charlie zipped it up. The dress was pretty, not that Fletcher would give Alexandra the satisfaction of saying so. The top, or bodice as Miss Priss called it, hugged her breasts and with the strapless bra, well... Was she gonna pop out of the damn thing? Her sisters swore up and down she wouldn't.

The skirt was long and poofy, the material was

smooth and shimmery, and there was a belt of small peony buds at the waist. Alex and Charlie had added that themselves to coordinate with her tattoos. It was the one part she liked.

"Wow." Charlie smiled. "You look fabulous."

"I feel like an ass." She sat back down so Charlie could mess with her hair. "Where are you going?" she asked Casey when she got off the bed. If big sister was busting out of this joint, then so was Fletcher.

"Mind your business," Casey said, then, "I'll be right back."

Fletcher pursed her lips and looked at her arms. "You don't think anyone's gonna notice the scars, do you?"

"No, honey, they'll be too enamored to see anything but you," Alex reassured her.

"Besides," Charlie began, "the ones on your arms are fading."

Fletcher inspected. They had faded some. "I guess you're right."

"Don't worry about it, Fletcher," Alex said and pulled out a lacy little top.

"Where the hell's that supposed to go?" There wasn't any room inside this thing.

"It's a shrug," Alex explained. She helped Fletcher slip it on. "The lace will disguise your scars, but you can still make out your tattoos."

"I don't want people to be staring at me all night, s'all." She hated that. "All right, let's do my do."

Charlie took off the first hot roller, then chewed her lip. "Should we put it up or leave it down?"

"Down," Fletcher said.

Alex tsked her. "No comment from the peanut

gallery."

"Reed likes it down," Fletcher mumbled.

"Does he?" Alex said in the inquisitive tone of voice Fletcher loathed.

"Did he tell you that?" Charlie asked.

"Yeah, so what?" She shrugged. He was the only man to say she had beautiful hair. He was always touching it. She fanned herself, hoping her sisters didn't notice her blush.

"Keep it off her face, so put it up in the front and let it loose in the back," Alex instructed.

They all turned when Casey came back in the room with a scrap of material. "Here," she said and handed it to Fletcher.

"What's this?"

"It's a bridal garter, but I had Ma fix it so you could have your knife with you." Casey smiled when Alex shouted at Fletcher for jumping out of her seat.

"Where does it go?" Fletcher asked holding the garter in one hand and her pearl-handled knife in the other.

"On your thigh." Casey held up Fletcher's skirt so she could put it on. "Figured there may as well be a little of you in that dress, or under it, as it were."

Fletcher did a little jig and kissed Casey on the cheek. "You're the best big sister ever!"

Casey smirked. "Tell me something I don't know."

Chapter Twenty

Noah waited downstairs with the rest of the McKay family. It was like prom all over again. He'd even bought a damn corsage. Apparently, this date was a big deal to everyone. And if he were being honest with himself, it was important to him as well. He only partly listened as Ryan and Emmit talked about the hardware store. Noah hadn't realized Ryan was taking over and buying Emmit out.

Savannah moved next to him. "Are you all right?"

"I'm fine. But we're going to be late if she doesn't hurry," Noah said and straightened his tie. He was wearing a tux, and until tonight that had never bothered him. He'd grown up in money and was used to the society crap.

Savannah smiled. "I'm sure it's not Fletcher that's taking so long. It's what her sisters are doing to her. If they hadn't kicked me out of the room, she'd be done by now."

Noah grinned. "You're not mad about that, are you?"

"Not in the least," she said with a wink.

"Is everyone ready?" Alex said coming into the kitchen. She wrapped her arm around her husband's waist as Charlie and Casey came into the room.

Casey shook her head and stood next to Ryan, while Charlie stood by Craig and called Mack inside.

"She's gotta see this."

"Okay, Fletcher, showtime," Alex called.

Fletcher's grumble echoed down the stairs.

Noah's breath caught. She was magnificent. Her long, tawny hair flowed down her back in a stream of curls, while the front was held back by two braids crowning her head. Her eyes were green, and her lips a soft pink. He was speechless.

"Auntie Fletch, you're a princess," Mack said clapping her hands.

"Thanks, Mack," Fletcher said and bent to kiss the little girl's cheek.

"Holy hell," Jebb whispered.

"Shut up, bullfrog," Fletcher and Casey said in unison.

Fletcher made a production of rolling her eyes. "Can we go and get this over with?"

"Let me get a picture," Savannah said and started snapping away.

"You've got to be kidding me!" Fletcher looked at Emmit. "Pops, do something."

"You look beautiful." Emmit kissed Fletcher on the forehead.

Fletcher sniffed. "Thanks, Pops."

"Y'all are going to be late if you don't leave now," Craig said.

"All right, let's get this over with," Fletcher said. She grabbed Noah's arm and headed for the door.

They were on the porch when Jake ran out. "Kid, you forgot your purse thingy. Oh, hey, you got a limo?"

Noah tried to lead Fletcher down the steps. "I thought it'd be nice."

"Bitchin'." Jake handed Fletcher her purse and

gave her a quick hug. "Have fun."

"Yeah, right." Fletcher slipped into the black stretch limo.

"Don't keep her out too late," Jake called.

Noah shook his head and slid in beside Fletcher. He told the driver to go and turned off the speaker. Sitting back, he glanced at Fletcher. "You take my breath away."

Fletcher shrugged. "Alexandra did everything."

"It doesn't matter. Here." He pulled out the small corsage. "It's more of a bracelet of petals than anything else."

"Thank you," she said and slipped it on her wrist, then brought it to her nose.

"Thank you for holding up your end of the bargain."

"I keep my word, Reed." She smiled and kissed his cheek.

"What was that for?"

"Because you look hot as fuck, and people will be too busy staring at you to notice me, thank God!"

"Believe what you will. I won't argue." Noah lifted her hand to his lips and kissed her fingers, not letting go as they drove in silence.

Noah guided Fletcher into the governor's house. The property was substantial and beautifully maintained. There were a number of people milling about in the entry hall.

"Are you all right?" Noah whispered in her ear.

She glanced up. "As long as I don't trip and bust my ass, I'll be fine."

He smiled and kissed her temple.

The governor walked over to them and held out his

hand. "Noah, or should I say Sheriff Reed now?" The other man was in his late fifties with brown hair and brown eyes. His smile was genuine as he shook Noah's hand. "And who is this lovely creature?"

"Fletcher McKay, meet Tyler Carter. Governor Carter, Fletcher McKay."

"Thank you for having us," Fletcher said and returned the man's handshake.

"Oh, posh. Thank you for coming."

"I didn't really want to." Fletcher smiled. "I'd rather be getting the bad guys."

"Fletcher was a deputy until recently. She's a private investigator now," Noah explained.

"You don't say." Governor Carter smiled.

"You may be acquainted with my sister Alexandra McKay Keller."

"Ah, yes, Alexandra. Another extraordinary woman," the governor said and led Fletcher farther into the room.

Fletcher mingled with the who's who in politics, and Noah couldn't take his eyes off her. There was a circle around her as there had been at dinner. The governor had asked for Fletcher to be seated next to him. She was intelligent, and Noah had enjoyed listening to her debate with the politicians. He smiled. Everyone wanted a piece of her.

"Noah," said a cool voice.

Noah glanced over. "Mrs. Thomas, I didn't expect to see you here this evening."

"Nor did I expect to see you here with a McKay. That one in particular." Beverly sipped from her champagne flute.

Noah eyed the woman. Her hair was white-blonde,

and her eyes were icy blue. She stared across the way at Fletcher and didn't try to disguise the loathing on her face.

"I'm enjoying the company I keep. Unlike other women, Fletcher can be trusted."

Beverly let out a haughty laugh. "Think with your other brain, Noah. That girl is the last person you should give your loyalty to."

"I think I'll trust my own experience, considering." Noah hadn't had feelings for Marylou, but it had annoyed him to discover she'd been sleeping with a handful of different men while they were supposed to be dating.

"My daughter is a confused woman, Noah. She wasn't getting the attention she deserved from you, so she sought it somewhere else. I can't blame her, now that I see where your tastes truly lie."

"Yes, they've greatly improved," Noah said and took a glass of champagne from the waiter's tray. "I met an old friend of yours the other day. Leo Patterson." Something like regret flashed across her face, but it was so fleeting Noah may have imagined it.

"How is Leo? Still cutting open dead people?"

"He's retired now. He and his second wife are doing quite well. They have a large family, if all the pictures are accurate, and a happy one."

"Good for him," she said with a mock toast. "I see your date is heading this way." She touched Noah's arm. "I do like you, Noah, and I'd hate to see what she turns you into."

"Was that Mrs. Thomas?" Fletcher asked.

"Yes," Noah said and put his drink down to take Fletcher's hand. He led her to the dance floor where the band was playing something slow and romantic.

"I'm not good at this," she whispered.

Noah took one of her hands in his, placed her other on his chest, then took hold of her waist. "It's like boxing but slower."

Fletcher nodded and closed her eyes to find the beat of the music. Her feet throbbed, like she'd been hiking in the woods for two days barefoot. She had a new respect for her sisters. She rested her head on Noah's chest. He smelled nice. Soft but masculine. She looked up after he kissed her temple. "This isn't too bad. Did you know the governor has tattoos? He got them when he was in the army. He liked my flowers."

"You never cease to amaze me." He smiled.

"I was thinking the same about you. I'm going to trust you, Noah," she said with a sigh. "Please, don't let me regret that."

The minute they returned to the limo, Fletcher took off her shoes and threw them out the window. "Alexandra will get over it," she said to Noah, who was laughing at her. She glanced at the chauffeur on the other side of the tinted glass. "Can he see us?"

Noah shook his head.

"Good!" Fletcher lifted her skirt and straddled his lap. She was going to do it, jump him. Her sisters would be proud.

Fletcher placed a featherlight kiss at the corner of his lips, then stared into his silver eyes. She shimmied out of the lace shrug, wrapped her arms around his neck, and kissed him deeply. The champagne they'd had, mingled with a spiciness that was all Reed, was an intoxicating temptation.

Noah pulled down the zipper of her dress. Fletcher

shifted off him to dispose of the garment.

"Christ," he whispered.

Her grin was wicked. "Alex said you'd like it." Fletcher would have to get Alexandra a present to say thanks. The fancy underwear was a win.

He pulled her back on top of his lap. "I more than like it."

"It's pink," she complained, then not so much when he caressed her through the soft material.

"It suits you."

She shook her head, then leaned it back when he started kissing her breasts. He was hard beneath her. She moved against the bulge in his pants, and they both moaned. Waiting to get home to have him wasn't an option. She ran her hands down his chest until she got to his belt.

He slipped his hand up her leg, stopping when he got to her knife. "What the hell?" He turned on the light.

"What?" Fletcher reached to turn the light back off. "It's just my knife."

"You wore a weapon to the governor's home?" he asked incredulous.

Fletcher blinked. "This is who I am, Reed!" She pulled her dress back on. He was so not getting any.

"Who exactly?" Noah rubbed his temple.

"I have an assortment of weapons, and I'm not afraid to use 'em either," she said and fumbled with the stupid zipper. "I've got it." She slapped his hand away. She didn't need his help or his disappointment. She didn't need anyone bringing her down.

He stared at her. "What? We're fighting now?"

"No, I'm going to sit here and pretend you don't exist."

"Fantastic."

Chapter Twenty-One

Fletcher was barely speaking to Reed two days later. Was she being juvenile? Probably. But he needed to understand she was who she was; she would not be anyone else *for* anyone else. No one would mold her into someone she wasn't. Not. Ever. She'd die first.

Did she ache for him—like actually fucking ache? Yes, she did. Fletcher wanted him next to her, she wanted to touch him, to talk to him. To let him calm the chaos inside her, the way only he could. And she didn't want to inspect any of those feelings. Because they scared the crap out of her.

At least she was going to get away from Reed for a few hours. Fletcher shook her head and waited for her brother at the end of the driveway. Noah was letting her—Fletcher snorted—go to Alexandra's. "Like he owns my ass or something."

"What's wrong with you?" Jebb asked when she slammed into the truck.

"Reed's done pissed me off!" She looked at Jebb. "How are you?"

"Good, I'm still staying at Charlie's because Ma and Pops are redoing the kitchen and want it to be a big surprise. I don't know what was wrong with the way we had it." Jebb shook his head.

"People change what they can when they can't fix what they need," Fletcher told him.

"I get that. So, I'm taking you to Alex's, right?"

"Yeah, I'm going to bug Jake for a bit." More like bounce ideas off Jake, but that wasn't for little brother to worry about.

Jebb snorted. "You mean to cook you something, don't you?"

Fletcher laughed. "That would be *your* stomach talking."

"Probably. So, are you going to rebuild your cabin?" he asked, his hands sliding over the steering wheel.

"I haven't decided yet. Hey, isn't that Beverly Thomas on the side of the road?" Fletcher sat up. The woman's white-blonde hair would stand out anywhere.

Jebb nodded. "Looks like she's got a flat."

"Pull over." She unbuckled her seatbelt.

His dark brows bunched. "You aren't planning on helping her, are you?"

"No, you're gonna change her tire for her," Fletcher said and got out of the truck. "Mrs. Thomas, my brother's gonna help you with that flat."

Beverly looked her up and down. "Why?"

"Because it's the right thing to do. Jebbediah, hop to it." Fletcher slipped on her sunglasses and helped Jebb get the spare and jack out of the trunk.

She stood back with Beverly while Jebb worked on the tire.

"What is it you want in return?" Beverly asked.

"I don't want a damn thing from you. But you need to give Noah a break." Fletcher couldn't help defending Reed. *She* may not be cutting him any slack, but that didn't mean others shouldn't.

"You two are an item then?" she asked.

Fletcher rocked back on her heels. "We're working together to find out who shot Jasper Hart."

"Oh," she said with a softness Fletcher didn't know the woman possessed.

"You wouldn't know anything about that, would you?"

Beverly's fists clenched. "How dare you insinuate—"

"I was asking if you knew anything about Jasper's shooting. I wasn't assuming you were involved." Fletcher sniffed.

"I never had a problem with Jasper. You may not know it, but he and I dated in school before I started seeing Leo. It's true." Beverly's smile was almost vicious. "Jasper was a handsome man; still is, not to mention smart and funny. But he fell in love with Laura, and I fell for Leo. Then life took us in different directions. Mr. Thomas was the one who didn't care for Jasper. But as my husband has been dead for quite some time, I'm sure he was in no way involved."

"Done," Jebb said and wiped his dirty hands on a rag.

Beverly went to grab her purse.

Jebb held up a hand. "I can't take your money, Mrs. Thomas."

"Suit yourself." She headed to her vehicle, then stopped and said thank you.

They waited until the other woman was gone, then got in the truck and heading for Alex's. "I don't know why you made me do that," Jebb said, putting the vehicle in drive.

Fletcher turned in her seat. "Firstly, it's the right thing to do."

Jebb grumbled. "And secondly?"

"Because I wanted to chat with the woman." Fletcher had also wanted to see how Beverly would react to her questions.

"Whatever," Jebb said, then remained silent until they pulled into the B and B. "Should I pick you up when I get done at the shop?"

"Nah, I'll get Jake to bring me back."

Jebb stared out the windshield and nodded. "I'm headed to the garage, then."

Fletcher snorted. "Tell big sister I said hi."

"I'm not going anywhere near her. She's bossy and mean one minute, then telling me things about her sore feet, back, and"—Jebb shuddered—"her lack of bladder control."

Fletcher laughed. "Yeah, she said she had to pee every five minutes. Stop by the diner and pick her up a PB and J sandwich. You'll be good as gold for the rest of the day."

He perked up. "Good idea! Thanks, Fletch."

She stood back and waved him off, then went inside the B and B. Alexandra was in the kitchen arranging a vase of flowers. "That looks pretty," Fletcher said.

Alex rose a brow. "Since when do you say things are 'pretty'?"

Fletcher rocked back on her heels. "I think plenty of things are pretty." She usually kept the thoughts to herself, though. "Where's Jake?"

"He's looking into expanding the diner to add a full bakery instead of only offering his baked goods in the pastry case."

Fletcher helped herself to a cup of coffee. "I

wonder if he'll wear the funny baker's hat."

Alex smirked. "I've already persuaded him against that." She took the flower arrangement to the other room.

"Y'all got any guests coming?" she asked when Alex came back in.

"Yes, we have a couple coming tonight, then a full house over the weekend."

"Leaf lookers?" Fletcher said and took a seat at the table. People came to the mountains to take in the array of fall foliage. She couldn't blame them; it was beautiful here.

"It's that time of year again. Though peak color has been coming later and later over the last couple of years. So booking isn't as sure a thing as it used to be."

Fletcher pursed her lips. "Yeah—"

"How did you get here, anyway?" Alex looked out the window. "Did Noah drop you off?"

"No!" Fletcher didn't want to talk about Noah. "Jebb dropped me off on his way to the garage and—"

"For goodness' sake, what is it?" Alex crossed her arms over her chest.

Fletcher blinked. Sheesh. "Talk about not having any tact, Alexandra."

Alex rose a brow. "You thought Jacob would be here, but he isn't, and your ride left, so you're small-talking me to death."

"You own a B and B." Fletcher snorted. "You're a master of chitchat."

She smirked. "That's for paying guests."

Fletcher toasted her with her mug. "So it is. You want to take me to get my truck? It's at my cabin. I could walk if you don't have time."

"Why didn't you just say so in the first place, hmm?" Alex grabbed her keys.

****

Fletcher started the engine and sighed. It was nice to have her vehicle back. If she were anyone else, she would keep driving until she was far away from her troubles. But she was Fletcher J. McKay, and there was a madman on the loose.

She pulled into Noah's driveway, surprised to see his vehicle. But it was the bright-red sports car parked next to his truck that set the blood in her veins to boil. Marylou Thomas was back in town. What in the hell was she doing here? Fletcher didn't knock. She was a guest after all. Inside, she narrowed her eyes; Marylou was slobbering over Reed. Some emotion rose in Fletch, one she wasn't familiar with, but she squashed it and ran upstairs to grab her duffel.

She took another glance into the den when she got back downstairs. Marylou was unbuttoning Reed's shirt. Fletcher would give him credit; he was trying to get the witch to stop. That was something at least. She coughed, cocking her head to the side when Marylou let go of her prey and turned around.

"Oh, Fletcher. How awful for you?" Marylou smirked, her blue eyes alight with malice.

"I was done with him anyway, Marylou. He's all yours." She grabbed her bag and walked out the door. Reed was hot on her heels.

"McKay? Fletcher!" he shouted and grabbed her arm. "I was trying to get her off me."

"I's saw that. But if you really wanted her off you, you would have tried harder, right?"

Marylou followed them out. "Is there a problem?"

190

"You're the problem. I'd like you to leave my home and never"—Noah looked straight at Marylou—"never come back. If you do, I'll arrest you for trespassing."

"You can't be serious, Noah!" Marylou stomped her foot. "You're choosing her over me?"

"Yes!" Reed tightened his grasp when Fletcher tried to pull away.

"Fine. Have it your way. It'll be a shame too. Everyone knows Fletcher McKay destroys everyone she comes into contact with. Like a cancer or something." Marylou sneered, got into her car, and sped off.

Noah opened his mouth, but Alexandra pulled up. "Great! More fucking drama!"

"Was that Marylou I saw?" Alex scowled and pointed to where Noah was holding Fletcher's arm. "I'll ask you nicely to let go of my sister. Now."

"Not until I'm done talking to her."

"There ain't shit to say. I's caught you sucking face with that slut." Fletcher tugged at her arm, but his grip was intense.

"You were kissing Marylou?" Alex looked Noah up and down. "I'm utterly disappointed."

"This is none of your business, Alexandra." He turned to Fletcher. "I was trying to get her off me, and, yes, I could have tried harder, but I didn't want to hurt her," he explained. "I was angry, and I didn't want to do something I'd regret."

"I's don't care!" Fletcher spat.

"The change in your speech says otherwise."

Fletcher glared at him. "Just 'cause a body has sex with someone doesn't mean they care. It's the body

191

reacting to stimulation, that's all."

"I did not need to hear this," Alex said, but she didn't move.

"Shut up, Alex," Fletcher hissed. "Reed, if you don't let go of me, I's gonna hurt you."

"Damn it, Fletcher, I'm in love with you," he shouted and dropped her arm. "How in the hell could you not know that?"

"You's what?" Fletcher swallowed.

"I love you. Christ, for someone so fucking smart, you can be incomprehensibly dense." Noah ran a hand through his hair, then stared at her. "I love you."

Fletcher blinked back the mist in her eyes and glanced to where Alexandra stood with her mouth hanging open. She looked at Noah, then drew back her fist and slugged him. "I don't believe you," she said and jumped in her truck, missing Alex by inches as she sped away.

Noah worked his jaw and headed inside. He left the door open; Alexandra would be right behind him. He got a beer and went to sit behind his desk.

Alexandra raised a brow and pointed at the beer, then went to pour two tumblers of scotch. Handing one to Noah, she said, "Welcome to hell!"

"I've been in hell." Noah downed the scotch and then sipped his beer. This was gonna hurt later. "What brought you here anyway?"

"I forgot to ask Fletcher if y'all wanted to come to the B and B for dinner sometime next week."

Noah snorted.

Alex took a seat resting one arm across the back of the leather sofa. "How long, Noah? How long have you loved her?"

Noah got up and would have poured himself another tumbler full but decided he'd take the entire bottle. If he was going to drown his fucking sorrows, he'd do it right.

"You may as well tell me."

"Since the moment I laid eyes on her."

All the color drained from Alex's face. "Excuse me?"

"When I hired her to find out about my mother, I opened my door, and there she was." He could still see her when he closed his eyes. She'd been wearing a white tank top and green cargo pants. Her hair had been in a braided bun at the top of her head.

Alex motioned with her hand. "And?"

"I saw her and I knew. But it was more than that," he said when Alex scoffed. Did it sound foolhearted? Was it out of character for him? Yes, and yes. That's what had made their connection so tempting. "While Fletcher was investigating my mother's case, we got to know each other. We would talk on the phone for hours every single day for three weeks. We spoke about nothing and everything. Brainstorming together."

"The locket." Alex shifted. "When we're trying to find Fletcher and unravel her clues, you knew her locket was the key. Or as you said then, you 'guessed.' "

"Like I said, we talked about everything and nothing." The best conversations of his life, and he remembered nearly every word. Had replayed them in his mind countless times.

"You didn't tell her your feelings?"

"Fletcher was nineteen. A kid. I couldn't—"

"You've been her sworn enemy."

Noah licked his lips. "She made me take my mother out of the cult. It wasn't like I wanted her to stay there, but she was happy and obviously didn't need or want me in her life. Fletcher wouldn't give in, and I—I couldn't say no to her." He would have given Fletcher anything. Everything. And then...

Alex closed her eyes. "Oh, Noah."

"We got Mom to the hotel. I talked to her for a while, and she seemed fine—more herself. We'd called Dad, and he was on his way. We were going to work out the particulars when he got there. Mom wanted to soak in the tub, decompress, and I didn't think anything of it. Then we found her. I can't explain to you the feeling of knowing your parent would rather be dead than live a life with you."

"She was troubled, Noah. Surely you know that."

He nodded. "But knowing and living with it are two different things. My father couldn't live with that knowledge. And then both my parents were gone. I needed closure. I needed it to be done, wrapped up in its box, and buried forever. But Fletcher wouldn't take the money. It left things open. Unfinished. I needed her to take the fucking money." Anguish bubbled inside him. He would have given her the world, but she had denied him his peace.

"And you what? Blamed her for your parents' deaths." Alex poured herself another finger of scotch.

"I said what I had to say. I paid her for her services, and I paid her well. She held it against me. Never let me forget." As if he would.

Alex put the tumbler to her temple. "And you stopped loving her then?"

"No." He swirled the scotch in the bottle. "But if

she'd known how I felt, she would have had all the power. I pushed down my feelings until they turned to resentment; then the resentment turned to hate. It's a vicious cycle."

She rose a brow. "But you love her again now?"

"You don't understand. Even when I hated her, I loved her—wanted her. You're not the only one who can make people believe what they want to, Alexandra."

"It must be a family trait," Alex said with a small smile, then straightened. "You dated Marylou to get back at Fletcher, didn't you?"

"I knew Fletcher would fly off the handle. Part of me, I'm ashamed to admit, wanted to hurt her if possible, like she hurt me."

"How on earth did she hurt you?"

"Have you ever loved someone, and not only did they not share your feelings, but they despised you? Then all this shit with Daemon. She came to me with her suspicions, asked for my help, sought me out, and I let myself hope. Then when I found out she'd slept with him—I said some vicious things." Noah shook his head. He'd wanted to beat something.

"She was a virgin," Alex whispered.

"Don't remind me." Noah set the scotch aside and switched to water. He needed his wits about him.

"You never acted like you cared. Even when she went missing, you wouldn't help at first. You thought the worst of her."

"As did you, cousin, and you claim to love her."

She toasted him with her glass. "Touché."

"By then I was numb to every feeling for her but animosity. I could barely look at her. When we found her with Daemon, I wanted to kill him. The marks he put on her." Noah squeezed his eyes shut. "When we were at the hospital after finding Jasper…there was this moment, when—I couldn't pass it up. You see, she's it for me."

Alex ran a hand down the skirt of her dress. "You never slept with Marylou, did you? I always thought there was something odd about the two—"

"The only person I've been with since I met Fletcher is Fletcher. I don't want anyone else." And neither did his body. He hadn't slept with Marylou; he hadn't been able to go through with it. Noah was loath to admit it, but he'd kept the woman on the line by buying her expensive gifts and jewelry.

Alex sat hard on the arm of the couch. "I don't even know what to say."

"Someone wants Fletcher dead, and I'll do whatever's necessary to make sure that doesn't happen." No matter what.

"Even sacrifice your relationship? Because when she—"

"I'd rather have her alive and hating me than… I've lived with her hate." He could keep doing it.

"You're willing to be alone for the rest of your life because my sister holds a grudge like the Statue of Liberty holds a torch?"

"Now that you have Jake, could you be with anyone else? If he left or died, would you be able to share your life with someone other than him? Honestly?"

Alexandra blinked a few times. "No."

Noah sighed. "This time I've spent with her has been worth it. To sleep next to her, be with her, and her

196

want me. Want to be with me and only me. I'll take what I can get and be happy with that." He didn't have much choice. "I'll go looking for her in a couple hours, give her time to cool off."

Alex shook her head. "Oh, Noah…"

Chapter Twenty-Two

Fletcher rested her head on her folded arms and looked at the sky. It was a deep, rich blue that demanded you take notice. The grass was dampening the sleeves of her sweatshirt, but she didn't care. Her life was so fucked up.

Noah said he loved her. Could she believe it? Let herself grasp on to this hope? This temptation of being able to be with Reed, really be with him? He'd hated her and had for years. Sex was not love. The only other man to claim to love her romantically had been a psychopath who had kept her chained to a wall, so her field of reference was fucked.

Things with Noah were different. When they'd made out in her truck…neither of them had even been naked below the waist, and they'd found completion. Being intimate with Noah had been carnal. She'd never been so turned on in her entire life. She would have remembered. But that was good sex, right? Okay, mind-blowing sex. Closets weren't even as scary. Instead of being freaked out when she was near one, she was aroused, of all things.

Fletcher rubbed her nose. When she'd walked in to find Marylou all over him, Fletcher thought she might have a heart attack. But then she'd let anger take over. It was a defense mechanism a lot of people used to protect themselves. Not a smart one, but it was all she had on hand. Wrath was one of the deadlies, and she was on friendly terms with it.

Then he'd gone and told Marylou off. He chose her, Fletcher J. McKay, over the simpering sexpot. Could he love her? The truth was plain in his eyes. He'd meant the words, but drama had brought them together, and that easily confused connections. She couldn't put faith in a love based on circumstance. One based on life-or-death situations. Could she? Deciding she needed to talk to someone, she got to her feet and put a stone on Laura's tombstone.

****

Sweat stung her eyes, but she ignored it and hit the bag again. Diaz had let her in before he locked up to go on patrol, and she was making use of the gym. When Jasper was sheriff, they'd come in here and hit the bag. Tiny would come sometimes, and they'd make a night of it. It was great.

The Nu metal was on in the background, and she let her body be the weapon of the singer's words. Fletcher kicked the bag, then spun around and kicked with her other leg. Her muscles strained and pulled under her skin. Right jab, left hook, side kick, again and again.

She took off the boxing gloves and patted her face dry. Casey had been too busy to talk, and when Fletch had gone by her parents', she hadn't even made it to the door before her ma came out and stopped her. Jebb was either right about their parents not wanting anyone to see the kitchen renovations, or Pops didn't want her there. Fletch hadn't wanted to dwell on the latter, and her ma had been fidgety and weird, so she'd left.

Needing another distraction, she went to the hand

weights and started lifting. After she'd done fifteen reps, she went over to the weight bench. She did several reps, then sat up.

"That's dangerous without a spotter," Noah said from the doorway.

Fletcher sipped her water without taking her eyes off him. "I can take care of myself."

"Fine," he said and walked away.

Fletcher shrugged. If he wanted to be an ass, so could she. Deciding she'd had enough, she shut off the speakers and went to the locker room. At least he hadn't accused her of breaking in.

Going to the showers, she turned on the middle faucet and went about getting rid of the sweat. She took her time washing her hair and body. No one was here, except Noah, so she wasn't worried about anyone seeing her. She turned off the water, patted herself down, then wrapped the towel around her, securing it across her chest.

She went to her duffel to get some clothes, pausing at the music that echoed from the hall. She found Noah taking a swing at the bag himself. He only had on a pair of shorts, and sweat glistened on his toned body. She couldn't help but stare. He was beautifully built.

Fletcher wasn't the only one with old wounds. About two inches from Noah's spine was a jagged scar; someone had literally stabbed him in the back. Her fingers ached to touch it, touch him. Take away the space between them, the hurt.

Noah looked up from the bag. "Could you get dressed?"

She shifted from foot to foot. "Do you really love me?"

Noah closed his eyes and unwrapped the tape on his hands. He looked over at Fletcher. Her hair was wet and hanging down to her butt. And her only clothing was a sorry excuse for a towel. "Yes," he said and walked over to her. "I love you." He kissed her forehead and went to his office. He'd go back and lift weights later.

He sat at his desk and pretended to go through his paperwork. Fake it till you make it, or so someone said. The door creaked, and he glanced up. "I thought I asked you to get dressed?" He wasn't a saint, damn it.

Fletcher cocked her head to the side and closed his office door.

Goose bumps rose on his flesh, and he scooted his chair back. Maybe he should have put his shirt on. She walked forward until she was right in front of him.

"How much do you love me?" she asked. Her voice was husky, sexy, and made him hard.

Noah sighed. Could he give her this power over him? "I'm not playing games with you, Fletcher. I love you." He stared into her bright-green eyes. "Can you comprehend that?"

"I think so," she said and dropped her towel. She brought her hands to his shoulders and straddled his lap. The chair moved, but Noah braced his feet. She brought her lips to his, her tongue seeking entrance.

Noah wanted to devour her. His hands tangled in her wet hair, and he pressed her body to his. Her hard nipples pebbled against his chest, and he deepened the kiss. He couldn't get enough.

Fletcher wrapped her arms around his head and nibbled on his lower lip. He groaned, then kissed her neck and down to her shoulders. She moved against the bulge in his shorts, and they both moaned. He kissed his way to her breast, used his teeth to tug at a nipple, then cupped her ass.

Her heat burned through the thin fabric onto his erection, making each slight movement intense. He pulled her to him so he could kiss her pouty lips. Her hands drifted toward his shorts, and Noah stood. He lifted her and put her on his desk. A fantasy come true.

He dropped his shorts, and Fletcher reached out to run a finger along his erection. He gritted his teeth and moved between her thighs. Noah cupped her, and wet heat met his hand. She was ready for him.

"I love you," he said and entered her with one sure thrust.

Fletcher gasped and wrapped her legs around his hips. She leaned back and rested her forearms on the papers on his desk. She bent her head back, and her wet hair spilled behind her.

"Look at me," Noah demanded and pushed into her again.

Fletcher opened her eyes and took one of his hands from where it gripped her hip to the juncture of her thighs. She intertwined her fingers with his and brought his hand between their bodies. He knew what she wanted. "Like this," he whispered.

She licked her lips. "It's not enough."

Noah paused. His heart was thudding in his chest, but he was frozen. What did she mean? It wasn't enough?

Fletcher leaned up to nip his lip. "I wanna be on top."

A heady flood of relief and lust flowed through him. He looked around. The chair. He sat.

Fletcher smiled and hopped down from the desk. "Move it so the back's against the wall."

Noah did as instructed and braced his legs when she straddled him again. He held her waist while she positioned herself over him. Her eyes met his as she lowered onto him with a sexy moan. Her heat was intense. He leaned in and sucked on her nipple.

Fletcher hummed low in her throat, then moved faster. Noah gripped her hips. His fingertips played over the scars marking her flesh. He opened his eyes to find her nose to nose with him. Her hair cascaded around his head, and she leaned in to kiss him. His mouth made love to hers while his hips tried to keep pace.

Fletcher tore her mouth away, moved her hair over her shoulder, then grabbed the back of the chair and rode him harder. Christ, she was beautiful. Her muscles tightened around him, squeezing him, embracing him. She cried out, throwing back her head as she reached orgasm. Noah rose, almost standing, and gripped her hard. He moved faster, harder, then found his own release.

Noah put his arms around her back and hugged her to him. "I love you," he whispered in her ear.

Fletcher's gaze searched his. "I—"

"You don't have to say anything." He kissed her again for a long time, then said, "Let's go get washed up and head home."

****

Fletcher's gaze was held captive by the flames dancing across the logs. By the time they'd returned to Noah's, the temperature had dropped enough that she was able to cajole him into using the fireplace. He'd built a roaring fire in the hearth and put down several blankets and throws to make a comfy pallet.

They'd played a couple rounds of Clue, which she won, and argued about the use of the candlestick as a weapon. Reed said it was elegant in a way, a steadfast beacon shedding light on darkness or some shit. You could have knocked her over with a feather when he said she was like that. A delicate but deadly weapon hiding in plain sight, alight with a fire that burned fierce and bright. Fletcher had kissed him then, so enamored by his words and how they left his lips. Reed had deepened their connection and taken her again. Right here on the floor.

She stretched across the blankets, enjoying the heat caressing her bare skin. There was something sensuous about being naked in front of a fire. Their combined musky scent lingered in the air. She wanted to revel in it. These were new experiences for her. They were thrilling and terrifying, and she wanted more.

Fletcher sat up when Reed returned to the room. His muscled body was in full view other than the parts hidden by the throw blanket he'd slung across his hips. She shivered. How was it possible to want someone so much? Gluttony was one of the deadlies, but she wasn't sure if this counted. It was a decadent indulgence, but it was backed by—Nope, she wasn't going there.

Noah handed her a mug, then sat behind her. Fletcher leaned against his chest, loving the feel of him, the heat of him. She sipped her drink and sucked in a breath. "Oh."

"I added a little Irish to the coffee."

"It needs whipped cream, and you didn't put it in the right kind of mug," she said, then snorted. "I've been spending way too much time at Alex's."

He chuckled. "I'll ask your sister or Craig where I can procure the correct drinkware."

"Alex lives for that shit. This is nice."

"It is," he murmured and place a featherlight kiss on her shoulder.

Fletcher's phone chimed, and she hopped up to get it. "It's Jebb. Checking on me."

"He's a good kid," Noah said and helped her back down to the blankets.

"He's the best. He's staying with Charlie and Craig right now because my parents are remodeling the kitchen and want it to be a surprise or some shit like that." She shook her head and sipped her Irish coffee. "It must be a big fucking deal too because my ma freaked when I showed up this afternoon. Are you okay?" she asked Noah when he choked.

He nodded, his eyes watering. "Went down the wrong tube." He coughed again, then took another sip. "Were you able to see any of the remodel?"

Fletcher rolled her eyes. "No! If it wasn't for Jebb being displaced, I'd be of the mind that Pops was making excuses not to have me there."

"I'm sure that's not the case."

She pulled a blanket under her arms. "I'm not."

"Your dad loves you—"

"Jasper's my dad," she said before she could stop herself. Noah's expression went slack. Was he hurt? "I'm sorry. I should have been more considerate." Reed didn't have a father anymore, and here she was complaining about hers. She scooted away from him. His father—his parents—were dead because of—

"Don't," Reed said, pulling her back to him.

A bead of panic unfurled in her chest. This was a dangerous subject for them to discuss. Would they have to be enemies again? Would he hate her? "I'm not trying to start shit."

Noah set his drink down, then brought her hand to his chest and looked her in the eye. "I don't blame you for what happened to my parents, Fletcher; I never did. I said the only thing I could think of that would make you take the money. It was like leaving that bill unpaid kept the tab open, and I couldn't live with it out there. Do you understand? I needed that tab closed so bad I couldn't think straight, and I did whatever I had to in order to make it so. Do I wish I'd never done it? Yes, but I did it, and I'm so fucking sorry."

Fletcher's chest heaved, and tears filled her eyes. "You don't blame me?"

Reed kissed her fingers. "Never."

Her lips parted. "That's some fucking truth bomb."

He threw his head back and laughed.

Fletcher grinned. She loved his laugh. He'd never blamed her; he was just hurting. She frowned. "Damn it."

"What?"

She sighed. "People do things they don't mean when they're hurt and/or angry. One of Pops' favorite things to remind us of."

"And that upsets you?"

Fletcher fidgeted. She wanted to tell him; talk to him about it. Get his perspective.

"Cupcake?"

Fletcher quirked up her lips. "Yes, it upsets me. *Pops* upsets me. He stopped fighting for me a long time ago. He sure as hell fights against me on things, but he doesn't fight *for* me anymore. Once Jasper was in our lives, after everything with Evan and Kyle, even before he knew I was his daughter, he never stopped fighting for me or my sisters. A lot of times it was behind the scenes, but Jasper did it. Pops..." She shrugged.

Reed ran a hand through her hair. "Emmit loves you."

"It's not his love I doubt. It's his character."

He flinched. "You don't mean that?"

Didn't she? Fletcher gripped the ends of the blanket. "I do."

"That's what you'd call a truth bomb, right?"

"Yep."

Noah stretched his neck.

Was he worried? Upset? He was friends with Pops; maybe she shouldn't have put this on him. Fletcher glanced at the fire, then back to the blankets, and Reed. She needed to touch him, needed him to touch her. Calm the chaos of her admission. "Are you ready for another?"

He drew back. "I—"

She covered his mouth with her hand, kissed her way to his ear, and whispered her sexy desires. Reed growled, snatched her to him, and proceeded to fulfill her wishes.

Chapter Twenty-Three

Fletcher moved a loose strand of hair behind her ear and peeked at Noah from the corner of her lashes. They were in his truck headed out on another call. They had gone to the diner for breakfast, which would have been fine if Noah hadn't insisted they didn't sit at the counter. A booth was private, intimate, and people had been gawking at them. She didn't like people staring at her, and she expressed her displeasure vocally, which cost her ten extra bucks for the stupid profanity jar.

If that wasn't enough, Tiny had made a comment that kept circling her brain. The big man had smiled, gold tooth flashing, and said, "It's about time, shug." Then he'd kissed her forehead.

Anytime Tiny showed her tenderness, Fletcher would get emotional. It's not like he wasn't an affectionate person—he was a big freaking teddy bear—but he was her coach. He had taken over her and her sisters' training from Pops not long after Jebb was born. Tiny had taught her more about boxing, how to protect herself against bigger opponents, and how to be lethal in a fight if her life was on the line. He had been extra tough on her, so whenever he was sweet, Fletch turned into a silly puddle.

The sappiness had distracted her from contemplating his comment. Fletcher wasn't oblivious; he was talking about her and Reed. Tiny saw things others didn't, things most people missed, so if he had seen—

"What are you plotting?"

Fletcher glanced at Noah. "Huh?"

He smirked. "You're awfully quiet over there, which makes me think you're plotting something."

It was her turn to smirk. "Not currently."

He reached across the console, took her hand, and brought it to his lips. Heat spread across her cheeks. A strange, happy, fluttery she's-lost-her-f'ing-mind sensation swept through her. He did that to her.

"I love you," he said, kissing her hand again, then letting her go.

Fletcher blinked. He had repeated those words many times in the last twenty-four hours, and it filled her with both joy and dread. Her feelings for him were substantial, and unlike anything she'd dealt with before.

"Has it ever been like this for you?" she asked, unable to stop herself. She didn't have to explain what she meant. They had shared an intimacy last night…it was potent…it was more. They had made love—that's what Noah called it: making love—many times over the course of the evening and even this morning after her nightmares had woken them up.

Noah glanced at her, then back to the road. "No."

Fletcher let out a shaky breath. "Okay."

He gripped the steering wheel. "I don't expect anything in return."

Was there an underlying of hurt in his tone? The truth he'd shared last night had been even more shattering than the lovemaking. And having been able to share hers too, to talk to him about—She adjusted the seatbelt and turned in the seat. Fletcher studied his strong profile. She couldn't give him all he was asking from her, not yet, but she could give him something, right? "It's not that I don't feel the same—"

He pulled the truck to the side of the road and parked.

"I hate when you do that," she said, throwing her arms in the air. "People will pass by, and more rumors will spread."

Noah shrugged. "I don't care."

She tried not to smile at his staunchness. Well, fuck. "I'm only going to say this once, and I don't want to dissect it afterward, agreed?"

His gaze flicked over her face. "Agreed."

Fletcher took a breath. "Time for another truth bomb. I just got my power back."

Noah's dark brows drew together. "I—"

She reached over and cupped his cheek. "Let me explain."

He leaned his face into her palm, then nodded.

Fletcher brought her hands to her lap and squeezed them. "I'm not saying Daemon took my power, he didn't. He fucked with my head and…he hurt me, but he couldn't ever completely break me. I could've killed him at any time, I knew that, and it was my saving grace." She had spent many hours alone, chained to a wall, dreaming up different scenarios of ending Daemon Randle.

Reed's chest rose and fell. "Why didn't you?"

Good question. One she'd asked herself many times. After the beatings. Especially then. "Sometimes I wish I had," she murmured.

"We don't have to talk about it."

Fletcher met his gaze. "You read the court

transcripts, didn't you?" They recounted her testimony of everything Daemon had done to her. It wasn't a read for the weak at heart.

He stared at her, then nodded.

Her shoulders sagged. "I would have too."

"I'm—"

"Don't apologize, Noah. I'm glad you read them."

His eyebrows shot up. "You are?"

She gave him a small smile. "Relieved. I want you to know, not to burden you with—"

"It's not a burden. I had to know what you went through."

Fletch blinked. His knuckles were white on the steering wheel. "Why?"

"Because you shouldn't have to be the only one who remembers what you suffered."

Her nose burned with unshed tears. "Let me see if I understand. You're taking on my trauma, so I won't be the only one haunted by it?"

His eyes were stormy. "I can't explain it. I—I love you." He leaned across the console and kissed her long and hard.

Did she look like a strawberry? Her cheeks were on fire. She ducked her head. "Thank you for doing that for me. I wanted you to know what happened, but it's hard for me to talk about. I'm still working things out in my head. That doesn't mean what we've shared hasn't affected me or doesn't matter. It has and it does. I can't—"

"No defense against matters of the heart," he murmured.

She sat back. "Huh?"

Noah shook his head. "Something Jasper said."

"What'd he say?" They'd talked about her? First Pops, then Jasper? Who else had he—

"Jasper said you have no defense against matters of the heart."

She crossed her arms over her chest. Fletcher had a defense; it wasn't the healthiest type was all. "And when did you two have this little tête-à-tête?"

Noah blanched. "The night he was shot, I went over there to talk to him. He was tinkering at the workbench in his garage when I pulled up—"

"He liked to fiddle with things, but he didn't have Pops' skill," she said, her throat closing at having to use the past tense. "Silly old man."

Noah stared at her. His Adam's apple quivered. "I—"

The radio on the dash crackled. "Sheriff? Everything all right out there? Over."

He grabbed the receiver. "Had to make a quick stop…" Noah began, his tone official.

Fletcher turned in her seat while he discussed things with Deputy Hewitt. Mildred had called, again, wondering why Noah hadn't arrived yet.

"Headed that way now. Over," he said and put the truck in drive.

"We need to think of what we're gonna say about Jasper," Fletcher said.

Noah tensed. "What about him?"

Fletcher rolled her eyes. "Mildred is no doubt calling you out here because she wants the latest. You need to put her mind at ease first thing because if she homes in on me…" Fletch squirmed. She'd break like a sissy crybaby, but she didn't want to tell him that. "Mildred's been a family friend for years; she was Ma's

212

secretary way back when, and she can see through the McKay girls quicker than a perve at a wet T-shirt contest."

Noah's snort was garish. "Understood. I know she's—"

"The queen of the rumor mill?" Fletcher shook her head. "She doesn't start the shit...people 'round here just blab to her. And when I say 'people,' I mean everyone! It's one of the reasons Charlie offered her a job at the diner."

"All the gossip?"

Fletcher chuckled. "No one can say Charlie doesn't know what she's doing. Mildred draws all kinds of crowds."

They pulled up to a pretty cottage-style house. The yard was beautifully maintained, and in the spring, it would look like a florist shop. When people weren't stealing the flowers, that is. Fletcher waved when the older woman stepped outside the front door. Mildred was in her late sixties and fit as a fiddle. She had short, styled gray hair and was wearing a light pink McKays Diner sweatshirt.

Fletcher waited for Noah to go first, then whispered, "Remember, you need to handle the Jasper situation right off the bat."

"Got it," Noah said. He put up a hand. "Afternoon, Mildred. What can we do for you today?"

Mildred's sharp gaze went from Noah to Fletcher. "Ain't seen your hair down like that before, Fletch."

Her face turned eight shades of red. She never wore it down, and she wanted to trap it so bad it was making her batshit, but...Reed liked it down. And it was just a small thing. Before she could answer,

Mildred asked if she was back on the job.

"Protective custody or some shit." Fletcher made a production of rolling her eyes.

Mildred snorted. "Y'all come on in."

The mistress of the rumor mill's home was cluttered and cozy. Fletcher had spent more than one morning here when she and Jasper were on the job. She fidgeted and hoped Noah hurried the hell up.

"Jasper's in protective custody too, before you ask," Noah began as Mildred ushered them into her kitchen. "Only his doctors have access to him."

Mildred pursed her lips. "That answers that, doesn't?"

Fletcher sagged. "May I use your bathroom?"

"You know where it is," Mildred said pointing behind her. "I'll put the coffee on."

"We don't have time—"

"Sounds great, Mildred," Fletcher said. "I'll be back in a sec."

"Go on and have a seat, Sheriff."

Noah grumbled but did as he was told. Fletcher must have a reason for wanting to stay. Other than for the coffee and danish, that is. "Like she needs more coffee."

Mildred snorted from where she was pulling out a stainless-steel canister. "They haven't taught you yet, have they?"

His brows bunched. "Sorry?"

The older woman looked toward the hall, then back at him and grinned. "This past summer Alex devised a plan—any time after twelve p.m., we give Fletch decaf. We can't stop her when she prepares her own. 'Course Alexandra makes her a canister of half café when she can, but we all know—"

Incredulous, Noah sputtered, "You mean to tell me—"

Mildred swatted him with a towel. "Shh, ask Alexandra or Charlie to fix you a canister of their grounds, keep it on the counter, and Fletch will never know. She can't tell the difference."

"Keep it on *my* counter? That's presumptuous, isn't it?" Not that he didn't like the idea, he did. Too much. That's why he'd chosen the booth at the diner this morning, wasn't it? A signal.

Mildred gave him a droll look, then turned back to the coffee pot. "Trixy told everyone what she saw, Sheriff. And there's no way on God's green earth Fletcher McKay'd let you manhandle her like that if y'all weren't courting."

Who the hell still said "courting"? Noah shook his head.

"Don't even try to deny it. We know. We *all* know!" Mildred got mugs down while the machine began gurgling.

Fletcher came back into the kitchen. "Smells good, Mildred."

Noah blinked. Not only was the entire town in his business, but there was some sort of conspiracy to keep Fletcher's caffeine consumption down. He wasn't sure how to feel about either of those things. He wanted to claim Fletcher as his, but his business was his own. Their relationship was theirs.

Fletcher snapped her fingers in front of his face. "You okay, Reed?"

"Fine," he said.

She nodded and gave him a small smile before

launching into a conversation about upcoming events with Mildred. He tried to keep up, but he was still caught on the decaf thing.

"Here you go, Sheriff." Mildred handed Noah a hot-pink mug that read Sassy, Classy, and Smartassy.

He smirked. "Thanks."

Fletcher toasted him with a cat-shaped mug before she took a sip. "That's good."

The older woman put a plate of danish on the table and took a seat. "Got it from the boss." Mildred winked at Noah.

Flabbergasted, he sipped his coffee. It was good. His eyebrows rose when Fletcher put a danish on a plate and set it in front of him. "Thank you."

She smiled and fixed herself a plate. "Reed prefers custardy delights, Mildred."

The other woman paused, then motioned to Fletcher with her fork. "Gotcha!"

Noah had the pastry halfway to his mouth, then lowered it. "How did you—"

"I know things." Fletcher winked at him, then turned in her chair.

His heart turned over in his chest. If he wasn't already head over heels in love with Fletcher, this would be the moment he fell. She moved her long, tawny hair behind her ear. She'd worn it down for him and blushed every time someone had mentioned not having seen it down before.

They had both dropped "truth bombs" last night, as she called them. He was relieved by dropping his and unnerved by hers. Emmit was his friend, and someone Noah respected, but Fletcher's admission was… distressing. A heaviness weighed—

"Mildred, we have to ask you something uncomfortable, and you have every right to plead the Fifth."

The older woman straightened her spine. "Okay."

Noah blinked. He hadn't realized this had been Fletcher's intention. They had discussed broaching this subject with Mildred, but—

"Go on, Reed," Fletcher said, motioning with her mug.

He turned his jerk into a cough and looked between the two women. "Certain things have come to light recently that put a new spin on an old case, and we need to ask you about it."

"What case?" the older woman asked.

Noah stretched his neck. "The Ruthie case."

Coffee sloshed over the rim of Mildred's mug. She glanced between Fletcher and Noah and whispered, "Oh."

Fletcher dabbed at the spill with a napkin.

"Yes, 'oh.' " Noah sat back and waited. He and Fletcher had hashed out the aspects of the information they'd received from Leo Patterson. Fletcher was certain the mystery bullet and the antifreeze were both supplied by Ward Jessup.

Ward had died a few years back, and though Noah had only met the man a couple of times, he had liked him. Fletcher said one of the biggest secrets in Blue Creek was the relationship between Mildred and Ward. If anyone knew what happened that night, and how Ward fit into it, it would be her.

Mildred fiddled with the handle of her mug. "Jasper tell you something?" It wasn't a secret Jasper had been with Ward when the other man died, but if there had been a deathbed confession, Jasper never mentioned it.

Fletcher bowed her head and shook it.

"No," Noah said. "We spoke with Leo Patterson."

Mildred harrumphed. "That old fool. Doesn't have the good sense God gave him."

Fletcher patted the other woman's hand. "We have it figured out, Mildred, but confirmation would be helpful."

"Off the record, of course," Noah said, thinking of Leo.

Fletcher shot him a dazzling smile. "Yeah, this isn't for everyone. We'll keep it to ourselves."

Mildred's bottom lip wobbled. "Ward figured out who'd killed his boy, and he took action."

"The antifreeze," Noah prompted.

She nodded. "He slipped it in the iced tea. It was winter, and cold outside, but Ward couldn't think of what else to put it in." Mildred's wet eyes went to Noah's. "Those words came out simple enough, but the doing wasn't so easy for Ward. Hell, wouldn't have been easy for any of us. Even living with the truth all these years, a part of me still doesn't want to believe it of him."

Noah's brows bunched. "Of Ward?"

Fletcher gripped her mug and murmured, "Kyle."

His gaze shot to her. Noah had read the files on the case, and he'd heard the story from many of the residents of Blue Creek, but he hadn't known these men. Hadn't loved them. These women had. This town had.

"Those boys were thick as thieves since kindergarten…" Mildred stood and grabbed a tissue.

"Pops, Uncle Evan, and Kyle," Fletcher explained. "They spent a lot of time at the garage with Ward when they were growing up. Pops and Kyle were like second sons."

Mildred blew her nose and nodded. "Like I said, the telling is easier than the action was. Ward gave Kyle enough of the stuff to kill him, but not enough to do it fast. He left, and Ward followed. He was worried Kyle might be on the road and pass out; Ward didn't want to be responsible for hurting innocents."

Fletcher ran her hand over the tablecloth. "But Kyle didn't go far."

"No, he didn't." Mildred sat again. "Ward and Sadie were close friends. He knew about the secret passageways Sadie's first husband had built in the house, so Ward figured he would go in just to be sure."

Craig had told Noah the ins and outs of the B and B, so he was familiar with the layout. "But the ceiling?"

Mildred sighed. "Old Johnny Madison liked to keep tabs on guests when Sadie was entertaining. There were two holes. Ward grabbed one of the guns Sadie had stashed, used one hole for his sight, and the other for a pillow and a barrel. Messed his hearing up a bit."

Fletcher lifted her mug in mock toast. "And the rest is history."

Not only history, but it was also another trauma in Fletcher's life, another scar. Her truth bomb in the truck on the way over would stay with him forever. Yes, he'd read the transcripts. Every sick detail was implanted in his brain. Noah wished he could take it for her, carry it, but he couldn't. Nor could he protect her from what was to come. Hell, he couldn't protect either of them. At least he—

"Leo mentioned something else I wanted to ask you about," Fletcher said.

Mildred pursed her lips. "Awful chatty, wasn't he?"

Noah snorted. "Sorry," he said when both women glared at him.

"Did you ever hear about a group Jasper was investigating? An organization of some sort?"

Mildred looked at the ceiling. "Well, now...I can't think of any you wouldn't have heard of. Nothing stands out."

Fletcher sighed. "I was afraid you'd say that."

Mildred patted Fletcher's arm. "Leo's no spring chick. Heck, who is! He may be remembering something wrong."

Noah sat back as the ladies launched back into town gossip. Fletcher told him she thought Leo had been backpedaling, but Noah wasn't so sure. He stretched his neck; he could always ask—

Mildred cackled. "Serves her right, Sheriff!"

"He wasn't paying attention," Fletcher said with a smirk. "I was telling Mildred how you told Marylou you'd charge her with trespassing if she came on your property again."

Heat filled his cheeks, and he cleared his throat.

Mildred patted his arm. "It's best to make your stance and keep your distance. Ian Thomas had an ungodly amount of pull in this town when he was alive, and the last thing any of us want is for his offspring to acquire those skills."

"Here, here!" Fletcher cheered.

Noah sighed, then raised his mug. "Agreed." The ladies clinked their mugs with his.

Chapter Twenty-Four

Noah's cell vibrated on the nightstand. He snatched it up. "Reed," he said, rubbing his face and sitting up in bed. Fletcher made a noise and rolled over beside him. He checked the time. It was six thirty. She hadn't woken with one of her nightmares.

"Hold on a sec," he told Diaz and made his way out of the room. If there was a chance Fletcher could sleep longer, he was damn sure going to give it to her. He pulled the door closed. "Go ahead."

"Sorry to call so early, boss, but I just got in, and the results are back. The lab didn't find anything on the jewelry box or its contents other than y'all's prints," Diaz said in his quiet gruff tone.

He pinched the bridge of his nose. "We figured that would be the case." But they'd had to do their due diligence. "Any news on the prison logs?" They had put in a request to subpoena the list of people who visited Daemon in prison but had so far been blocked.

Diaz grunted. "No."

He cursed, then asked for a general update. "Fine. I've got a few things to do here, then I'll be in."

"Got it, boss."

Noah ended the call. Would the logs hold the answers they were looking for? He doubted it, but he wanted all the puzzle pieces. He rolled his neck and searched the contacts on his phone. He was loath to do it, but he didn't have much choice. The man would be up already. He hit the name and waited.

"Keller," Jake answered on the third ring.

"It's Noah."

"Is the kid okay?"

The corner of Noah's mouth lifted. "She's still sleeping."

"Really?"

"Yes. Look, I need a favor—"

"You need another fucking fa—" Jake was cut off, but there was no mistaking the bitterness in his tone.

"Noah?"

He sighed. "Good morning, Alexandra."

"Is Fletcher all right?"

"Yes, I was calling for a favor." Noah curled his toes into the carpet.

"Calling Jacob? This time of morning?"

He almost growled. "Yes, I haven't been able to get the logs from—"

"The prison? Daemon's visitor logs?"

Noah looked at his phone. "Yeah?"

"There're no names we recognized."

"You have the logs?" Noah gritted his teeth. "And you didn't think that was pertinent information?"

"Didn't you warn Craig you didn't want us getting in your way?"

Did she have to sound so damn smug? Noah paced the hallway. "Things have changed."

"So it would seem." Alex's sigh echoed across the line. "She doesn't know."

Was Alex a mind reader? "Fletcher, you mean?"

"Obviously."

The knot in Noah's gut untangled. "Why didn't

you—"

"She gets this look at the mere mention of his name, so we decided we wouldn't bring it up unless she did."

He would have done the same. He rubbed a hand over his stubbled jaw. "Did you read the transcript from the trial?"

The pause was long. "Did you?"

Noah bowed his head. "We really are too much alike, cousin."

"Gluttons for punishment, you mean?"

He snorted. "Something like that."

They were both quiet for a moment, then Alex asked, "Do you want the logs?"

"Yeah."

"Do you want the video and intake forms too?"

Noah froze. "Visitations aren't recorded."

"No, but there are cameras in the prison, and we were able to obtain that footage."

Noah tamped down his temper. This was why he had called Keller in the first place, wasn't it? The twins had an uncle with unimaginable connections and an unprecedented proclivity to cut through red tape. It was obvious they had used his services. "Yes, I'd like to see that as well and the intake forms."

"I'll get Jacob to email it to you. Was there anything else?"

You tell me? "No, thank you."

"Bye then," she said, and the home screen appeared on his phone.

Noah should have called Ryan. He got along better with him, but he'd been trying to…what? Make friends with Jake? Extend an olive branch? Noah shook his head. It didn't matter. He needed to shower and get moving.

****

Fletcher blinked awake and stretched across the mattress. She ran her hand along the empty side of the bed, where was Reed? She glanced at the clock. Holy shit! She'd slept through the night. No nightmares. It had been so long since she'd done that. It had to be the sex.

She covered the lecherous grin spreading on her face. Noah had been insatiable last night; doing things to her body…a delicious tingle began in her lower regions. First, he'd prepared a bath for them in his big-ass soaking tub, with bubbles, candles, and champagne. It had been provocative, luscious, and one of the most sensual experiences of her life. The lovemaking in the hot, steamy water…goose bumps lifted on her skin. "Reed?" No answer.

Fletcher flung the sheet off her naked body and ran to the bathroom. After washing her hands, she brushed her teeth. She rolled her eyes at her silly reflection, slipped on a sports bra and pajama bottoms, then trapped her hair in a sloppy bun.

Noah was in the kitchen, decked out in his uniform and about to make coffee. She pursed her lips. "It's not noon yet," she said, impressed he didn't flinch.

He glanced over his shoulder. "Sorry?"

Fletch smirked and pointed at the stainless-steel container. Mildred hadn't sent them away empty-handed yesterday. Nope, the older woman had given them a bag of pastries and a canister of coffee. "I said it's not noon yet. Make the high octane, Reed."

His lips twitched. "You know?"

She snorted. "Damn straight! Fuck with my coffee once…"

"And?" he prompted.

"That's it. Once was enough." She shooed him out of the way and prepared the coffee herself.

"Everyone thinks they have you fooled."

She shrugged. "It makes them feel better."

Noah shook his head. "You never cease to amaze me."

Fletcher reached for a mug as Noah came up behind her. She shivered when he pressed his lips to her neck, then her shoulder. His fingers traced the brand Mommy Demented had left, and he paused. She wouldn't squirm. He'd seen every mark on her body, kissed most of them too. She shivered. "Anything wrong?"

Noah's hand lingered for another moment. "No, cupcake." He kissed her temple, then stepped around her. "Do you want to go with me?" He poured coffee into his thermos.

Fletcher ignored the sissy-ass endearment. "I get a choice?" She enjoyed going in to the station with him; she missed being a deputy. Being in the thick of things. And working with Reed was…more than she could've hoped for. Not to mention fun. Though she'd cut out her tongue before she admitted that.

"Can I trust you to be good?"

She snorted, then sighed when he kissed her.

The kiss turned into an embrace. He held her tight and said, "I don't want to go."

He wanted to stay here—stay with her. That strange, happy, fluttery she's-lost-her-f'ing-mind sensation swept through her again. Fletch frowned, then her eyes widened. Was she…giddy? Well, fuck! He let her go.

He tweaked her nose. "What?"

Fletcher poured her coffee and eyed him over the rim. "Nothing."

He rose both dark brows. "Nothing?"

Fletcher set her mug down, moved his arms out of the way, then slid her hands up his chest. She stood on tiptoe, smiling when he bent to her level. She said, "One for the road," and attacked his mouth.

Chapter Twenty-Five

Fletcher pulled into Jasper's driveway and shut off the engine. She'd promised herself she wouldn't cry, and she was keeping that promise. So far, at least. Should she have stayed at Noah's? Maybe. He hadn't specifically said she couldn't leave.

The grass was getting high; it could use one more mow before fall set in for the long haul. Maybe she should get out the mower. Or, better yet, pay Jebb to do it. Teenagers were all about making their own money, right? She would talk to him about it later. That decided, she unlocked the door and went inside.

She was sure she'd missed something. Jasper was anal about keeping notes, and there had been nothing about Ward in his files, not even an address. And no mention of any organization, which was nagging her. Could Leo have gotten things mixed up? Yep, but Fletch's gut wasn't listening.

Her cell rang, and Reed's face popped up on the screen. Fletcher smirked. "Well, hello." Were they going to have phone sex? She'd never done that before either, but—

"How's everything at Jasper's?"

She grinned. "Tracking my phone, are we?"

"I figured it would be a good idea."

Fletch would have done the same thing. In fact... "I'm tracking yours too."

"Why am I not surprised?"

She laughed. "You're a smart man. I don't think I could have phone sex at Jasper's house."

After nearly a minute of silence, Reed cleared his throat. "I—that wasn't why I—"

"I don't think I would like it anyway." She went around checking the house.

Another pause. "Why?"

"I like touching you too much." She blushed, then rolled her eyes. There wasn't even anyone here to hear her. What a ninny!

"I feel the same," he murmured.

Fletch shivered. "You're so fucking sexy on the phone. Maybe we could try another time."

"Tonight?"

"It's a date," she said in a tone she hadn't even known she was capable of. She could leave here and go to the station. Make use of his desk again. Fletcher suggested it.

Reed groaned. "You're killing me, McKay."

"Noah?" she said after a couple of minutes of dead air.

"One reason I called was to see why you were at Jasper's."

"I have the feeling we missed something. You were the last person to talk to him." When he was alive. Tears prickled her eyes, but she continued. "You're sure he didn't hint anything?"

"No, I pulled up, he was at his workbench, then we went in and had a chat."

"About me?" Fletcher made her way to the garage. What had the old man been working on?

"Yes…I asked him why he didn't offer you this

job."

Fletch stilled with her hand on the garage door. She turned and leaned against the wall. She wished she could see Reed. "Can we video chat?" she asked at the same time she pressed the video option.

It only took a second for Noah's handsome face to fill her screen. He was in his office at the station. At his desk. She grinned. "Hi."

He smirked. "Hi, cupcake."

Fletch made a production of rolling her eyes. "You know what I'm thinking, right?"

Noah leaned back. "I'm never getting rid of this chair."

She laughed. "You better not." Her gaze flicked down Jasper's empty hall, and she sighed. "About the sheriff's—"

"Jasper said you wouldn't have taken it."

Fletch shook her head. "No, I—"

He glowered. "Why? I mean, I had figured you wouldn't; you like being bossy, but prefer not to be the boss."

She burst out laughing. "That's true enough. Casey was always the one in charge. I'm the snarky sidekick."

It was his turn to laugh. "First Casey's, then Jasper's."

She loved the sound. "Yep. A motley crew."

His brow furrowed. "But there's more? That's why you wanted to video chat."

"Smart and sexy!" She winked at him.

"Truth bomb time?"

"Yeah." She straightened. "I couldn't have taken the position, even if I wanted to—which I didn't." The other deputies—well, Hewitt—drove her batshit, and she did not want them in her face and up her ass twenty-four seven.

"Why? I've seen your scores from basic. You were top of your class, not to mention you have a degree in criminal justice."

She could make a joke about her psych eval, but it was best not to give any question to her sanity. "There may have been a bit of fibbing on my physical."

Reed rose a brow. "How so?"

She rubbed her nose. "Technically, I don't have full mobility in either of my shoulders."

His gaze flicked there. "The bullet wounds."

Fletch shrugged. "I was a kid, I hadn't fully grown, and there was scar tissue. Don't get me wrong, I'm not that far from the passing mark. It was close enough that the doc checked the box. But—"

Noah pinched the bridge of his nose. "The doc's local."

"How and why my shoulders got this way isn't a secret in Blue Creek, and I don't know for sure if that's what swayed the doc in the end or—"

"If it was Jasper pulling strings."

"Like he was fucking Lachesis or something."

Reed groaned. "It's a little early for Greek mythology, cupcake."

She grinned. Tickled he got the reference. "String puller of epic proportions is what I meant." Jasper had gone out of his way for her entire family. He had used up chits and banked favors to ensure the McKay girls were taken care of. "All Jasper said was to take my good fortune and roll with it, so I did. It's been fine. Like you said, I got great marks in basic, but the sheriff's position would take on more scrutiny from outsiders. Especially since I don't have a dick."

His lips twitched. "Would you want the position if it wasn't an issue?"

"I thought you'd be more upset."

"Maybe I would be if you hadn't been damn good at your job."

Fletcher blushed. "Thank you, Noah." They stared at each other on the screen. She needed to touch him again, but that wasn't on tap until later. "What was the other reason you called?"

Reed hesitated. "The brand on your—"

"What about it?" He had paused over it this morning, hadn't he? Fletcher cocked her head to the side. "Reed?"

He shifted. "Do you know what Daemon's tattoo was of?"

Fletcher's grip tightened on the cell. "What does that have to do with—"

"Did you ever see it?"

She shook her head. "He told me he got a tattoo, but it was before he changed his face, and I didn't see it, you know…later."

Noah nodded. "Nick Flowers, the man Daemon killed so he could fake his suicide, had a tattoo on his back. That was how Daemon's sister identified the body."

Fletcher swallowed. Daemon had put a big hole in Nick's face, making identification nearly impossible. But with Daemon's sister's positive ID, they hadn't needed to investigate further. "Meaning Daemon would have had the same tattoo, right?"

"That's my guess."

"What was it? Just tell me, Reed," she said when

he hesitated again.

"Two snakes forming a circle. With ruby-red eyes."

Her knees buckled. Oh, for fuck's sake. She took a couple of deep breaths.

"Are you okay? Damn it, I should have waited to tell you in person."

"It's fine, I'm fine. That's one hell of a coincidence." Jasper didn't believe in coincidences, and neither did Fletch.

"My thoughts precisely. I prefer when people knock," Reed said with an undertone of venom when someone entered his office.

The screen filled with a view of the ceiling. Fletcher rolled her eyes as Hewitt's voice echoed over her phone. He wasn't a bad guy, or a shitty deputy, but Lord, was the man an annoying ass-kisser. And he had more gab muscles than the ladies at Trixy's.

Reed's face filled the screen when they were alone again. "Duty calls. I'll make further inquiries into this, and we can discuss it tonight, okay?"

Wanting to lighten the mood, she said, "Before or after we try the phone sex thing?"

His gaze turned smoky. "Whatever you prefer."

A thrill shot straight to her lady parts at the tone of his voice. He should be illegal. God, she lo— "See you later." Fletcher ended the call. She was terrified of the words lingering on her tongue. Or, more accurately, she was afraid of the power Noah already had over her. Her heart.

She slipped her phone into her pocket and opened the door to the garage. Fletch's nose burned with unshed tears at the sight of the uproarious rust bucket.

Jasper had loved his ridiculous old truck. She'd take care of it for him.

Fletch shook herself and went to the workbench. She quirked up her lips at the mess. Jasper didn't have Pops' skill, but the man had loved to fiddle with shit. She pulled up a drop cloth and found his latest project. "Silly old man," she murmured.

He'd made a shadow box for his badge. Jasper had shined the damn thing twice a day. He'd had a habit of fiddling with it... Shaking her head, Fletcher opened the box and tried to pull out the badge. Something pinched her. What the hell?

She leaned against the workbench and wiggled out the box's backing. A single cassette tape lay inside. Fletcher squinted at the date written on the label; it was a day before he'd gotten shot. Without hesitating, she went inside to his office and put the tape into the old player he kept on his file cabinet. Jasper's voice came over the speakers, and her eyes filled.

"Well, missy, if you're hearing this, then the threats were real. No doubt you found them in the safe already. Ain't gonna do me no good being I'm six feet under the dagnab ground." He took a sip of something, then cleared his throat.

Fletcher took the player to the kitchen and made some coffee while Jasper told her what Laura had done and the lengths he'd gone to in order to keep it secret. She put her hand to her heart, they had done so much more to protect her than she could have ever imagined. Fletch closed her eyes and bowed her head. "I don't know if y'all can hear me, but thank you. Thank you for all that you did for me. For my sisters. I's love you both so damn much."

Fletch grabbed a tissue from the box on top of the microwave and blew her nose. She poured herself a mug of coffee, then hopped on the counter when Jasper began talking about Kyle's death. After Leo Patterson had performed the autopsy, Jasper had gone to Sadie's to investigate. They'd found gunpowder residue, and together realized, taking into account the antifreeze, it had to have been Ward. Jasper had then asked Leo to keep things quiet.

"I know that's not the most ethical thing to be doing, but I figured it was for the best. So make sure you tell Alexandra. She's suffered so much, and I wanted to tell her, ease her pain, but I didn't want her to feel like Sadie had let her suffer for nothing. You know your granny wouldn't have done anything to hurt y'all. Truth be told, I don't think the old girl could handle the weight of it. We all lost so much, with Evan and, and…well—" He cleared his throat. "—speaking of Alexandra, it's about damn time you forgave that girl."

Fletcher rolled her eyes. She had forgiven Alex, but she got a kick out of busting her sister's dainty balls.

"I forgave her a long time ago. If you look at things from her point of view, you might understand how she came to the conclusions she did. We're all human. And it ain't like they knew our genuine relationship, so you can't hold a grudge that long, missy. She's your sister and nearly died for you—for all of you. Who does that sound like? That's right…you. Sometimes your head is brick hard, girl. That said, I'm gonna hope you don't hold what I say next against me."

Fletcher stopped the tape. Was she ready to hear this? She took a breath and hit play.

"Here goes. I was investigating this organization 'bout twenty-five, thirty years ago; it was a group of powerful people in Blue Creek and the surrounding areas. I uncovered some of their dealings and tried my damnedest to break it up. There are a few names you might recognize though. Kyle Ruthie, Ian and Beverly Thomas..." Fletch grabbed a notepad and pencil from the junk drawer. There were names she knew quite well and several she didn't. "And finally, Greta Wayne. That one I didn't know until much, much later. They had a crest of sorts. Two snakes joined to form a circle."

Her coffee sloshed on the paper after the mug wobbled in her hands. She grabbed a towel to clean up the spill. Thoughts revolved around her brain like a game of Russian roulette. It was only a matter of time before one hit home.

"If I've learned anything over the years, it's that no matter what face it takes, the serpent can't hide the truth behind the mask. I doubt it will surprise you that the leader of this group was—"

And there it was. Fletcher stopped the tape. She didn't need to hear the rest. Like a veil being lifted. The ring was a symbol of this group, proof of membership...a tattoo representing belonging. And the leader of the group—she grabbed her keys and rushed to her truck. She was reaching for her seatbelt when the barrel of a gun pressed an icy kiss to her temple.

Chapter Twenty-Six

"Good to see you again, Ms. McKay. You wouldn't mind if I called you Jamie, would you, poppet?"

"Why not?" she mumbled. All the psychos did. Fletcher glanced in her rearview mirror at the man and woman in her back seat. Alex was right. No one in this damn town stayed dead. "Mr. Thomas, I presume, always a pleasure. Sorry, I can't say the same about you, Marylou."

"I knew it was only a matter of time before you figured it out. How like your father. Drive."

"Daddy, kill her," Marylou whined.

Ian climbed into the front seat with Fletcher. "Good things come to those who wait, Marylou."

"Dr. Dan did an excellent job on you, Mr. Thomas, but you should seriously consider contacts. The blue eyes are a dead giveaway." He looked like he was fifty instead of pushing seventy. He'd been the leader of the group. The serpent. Fletcher's ma had told her once that Mr. Thomas was like a pair of snake-skinned boots, when you took away the shiny veneer you were left with the truth. The snake.

"Yes, Daniel was quite the talent. Pity Daemon burned that bridge."

"Did you kill Daemon?" Fletcher gripped the steering wheel while he screwed a silencer onto his gun.

She could crash the truck, but she hadn't finished putting her seatbelt on, and doing so now would be a dead giveaway. Bad choice of words. Sheesh!

"A liability, you understand."

"Daddy," Marylou hissed, "you said she did it."

"I've said a lot of things." Ian turned toward Marylou. "Like you. Sniveling, whiny girl. Time to say good-bye."

Marylou's head splattered against the back window. Fletcher swallowed. That was not going to come out.

Ian straightened and put his seatbelt on. "Messy business."

"You killed your daughter."

He laughed. "Haven't you learned anything, Jamie?"

"Um?"

"She wasn't mine." Ian shook his perfectly coiffed head. "My wife philandered. Should have known, huh? A zebra doesn't change its stripes."

Fletcher snorted. "You cheated on her with Gracie McKay." She and Alex had seen them. Gag.

Ian hummed low in his throat. "God, she was a knockout; the best fuck I ever had. If she hadn't toyed with Kyle, things would have been different. She underestimated him and paid the price. It's a shame too—her skills were important to the group. Gracie could manipulate paint off a building."

Fletcher had no misgivings where the first Mrs. McKay was concerned. "So, who's Marylou's father?"

"I do not know, nor do I care. She did try to please me; I'll give her that. Unfortunately, her meddling exacerbated things."

Fletcher nodded. He wasn't wrong. "Where am I taking us?"

"To the beginning, of course. To your parents' home." He sighed. "None of this would have been necessary if Kyle had succeeded in acting out his revenge. But as I've learned, the old adage is true; if you want something done right, you need to do it yourself."

Fletcher pulled into her parents' driveway, utterly grateful no one was home.

"You first," Ian said and kept his gun trained on her. "And leave your phone."

She rolled her eyes but complied.

"After you, poppet."

Fletcher opened the back porch door and walked into the kitchen. "Mind if I had one last cup of coffee?"

Ian laughed. "One would think you would have given up coffee after yours was drugged. But, yes, go ahead."

"It's in my veins."

"I understand. Considering what's in those precious veins of yours."

"You knew her, didn't you? Greta Wayne?" She filled the reservoir with water and measured out the coffee.

"She was my sister." Ian laughed when Fletcher spilled loose grounds on the floor. "I see that bit of information slipped by you."

Fletcher bent to clean up the mess. She peeked at Ian out of the corner of her eye. He was looking out the window. Using his carelessness against him, she took her knife out of her boot and slipped it in her pocket. She straightened and threw away the paper towel. She circled around the room. "My parents said they were redoing the kitchen, but nothing looks different. Pops just didn't want me here!"

"Poor poppet," Ian said and used the gun to motion her to sit. "Did you find my gift?"

"The box of goodies? Yep, definitely registered on my oh-shit-o-meter." It made sense. Mommy Demented's belongings would go to her next of kin.

He snorted. "I thought you'd appreciate a few familial trinkets. Greta was never a well woman, you understand. I'm not a monster, Jamie. Had I known she was abusing you, I would have helped. But she never told me about you. I found out later. Jamie was our father's name, by the way."

Fan-fucking-tastic. "How nice."

"It's fitting; he was a lot like you."

"How so?" Was he sane?

"He was an expert tracker in his time, like you, and he was intelligent again like you. He would have enjoyed knowing you despite your sex. Pity he died when he did."

"You?" Great, she was from a line of murderers.

He frowned. "Heavens, no. It was Greta. She was rather disturbed, not that we allowed that bit of dirty laundry to air. Father wanted another boy, and he never let Greta forget it. She killed him, and Mother sent her away."

"Hurt people hurt people," Fletcher said. She would never feel pity for that woman.

"Going away was the best choice for Greta. She grew up and got married. After her husband died, she moved closer to home, and, thankfully, the people of Blue Creek had forgotten all about her."

W. L. Brooks

"Jasper sure as hell didn't know she was a Thomas." He would have seen the trap coming. Of course, then she wouldn't have been born...

He chuckled. "No, he was clueless."

She studied his smile. Ian Thomas hadn't been what she considered a handsome man, but with his new face that had changed. He was fucked in the head, but his face was pleasant. "Dr. Dan did an excellent job. I can't get over it. Daemon didn't turn out as well. Or Nick," she said thinking of the man whose body had once lain in Daemon's burial plot. He'd been paid handsomely to become Ian Thomas in order to empty the real Mr. Thomas's secret bank accounts.

"Nick made a dashing replica of myself, don't you think? Daemon shouldn't have killed that boy either."

"You didn't approve." That was interesting.

"No, the order needed a new start, and with some guidance, Nick would have fit right in."

She pursed her lips. "Jasper didn't do as much damage to your organization as he thought."

"Oh, he did his fair level best," he said, his face twisting. "Jasper kept asking questions, stirring up trouble. Despite my efforts to keep him in line. He put doubts in the wrong people's heads, and I had to disappear."

She sat back in her chair. "You were the mastermind of this entire thing?"

"I've been enjoying my new life overseas, or I was until Daemon's arrest. Marylou kept me abreast of all the goings-on. She tried so hard to please me; I'm sure you understand."

"No shit. Marylou was the one in charge?"

He smirked. "Her initiative surprised me too."

"If that don't just beat all," Fletcher said with a shake of her head. "Marylou found the one person in the world who wanted Casey dead and brought them to Blue Creek to do her bidding. She must have found out about Charlie having been with Rick after the divorce, and she set that ball in motion. But...Daemon would have been in on that."

"Think, Jamie. You started putting your nose where it didn't belong. Looking into Rick's murder. I paid Daemon quite well to kill his brother. I couldn't have Rick destroying my empire, could I?"

Fletcher fiddled with her locket. "You had high hopes for Rick, so you encouraged Marylou to marry him. But he was nothing but a petty thief. Luckily, the marriage brought Daemon into your life, and he was everything you were hoping for. Daemon was to be your heir apparent. You took him under your wing, and he helped you fake your death. He connected you with his old school chum, Dr. Dan, a renowned plastic surgeon. A new face was the least Daemon could give you as repayment for what Rick did. You could live comfortably, and Daemon would get your empire." Greed was one of the deadlies, and perhaps the most dangerous.

He sighed. "You do please me so."

Fletch steeled herself. Icy fingers ran up her spine. Daemon had said those exact words to her. With the same creepy connotation. She did her secret breathing.

Ian motioned toward the coffee pot. "I'll take a cup too, poppet."

"Marylou was after my sisters." Fletcher poured the coffee. Did she feel bad for Marylou, of all people? Maybe. But she wouldn't give that away. "I can understand why you got rid of her. How do you take it?" she asked, pointing to the mug.

"Black with sugar."

"Daemon would have enjoyed helping Marylou act out her petty revenge. Then again, he would have been the one tying up loose ends. Marylou's loose ends." He would have enjoyed doing that too. She handed Ian his coffee, prepared her own, and reclaimed her seat.

"And I do believe one of your brothers-in-law took care of the other Randle."

She pursed her lips. "You'd chosen Daemon to be your heir. He divorced his wife, but he didn't want Marylou."

"His first wife lacked vision, and Marylou wasn't mine. You, on the other hand, are made from the same stock. You were the better choice." He sipped his coffee.

"Daemon was molding me for the part." The sleek, sophisticated lady, Jamie Thomas. Queen to his mad king.

"Indeed, he was quite taken with you."

"No shit," she murmured.

Ian shook his head. "The extensive surgery and the drugs did something to him, made him reckless, and I couldn't have him telling anyone I was alive. All those things added together spelled liability to me."

Fletcher nodded. Extreme plastic surgery can wreak havoc on a person's psyche. And to take the identity of the brother you'd murdered? Yeah, that could do some damage. She had known the minute she'd opened the door to find Daemon standing there with his brother's face that psychosis had set in. She shook herself. She couldn't afford to go down any rabbit holes right now.

"You must have been disappointed in Marylou's performance. I mean, she's been coming after us for years and never beat us. That's a pretty shitty track record."

"That's why I said 'initiative.' Her follow-through was utterly disappointing. You beat her at every turn. You helped both your sisters succeed against her, stole Daemon away, and I even heard Noah Reed chose you. See, Jamie, blood will tell."

"Marylou was my mystery lurker." Marylou—lurker and lackluster poet. Fletch shook her head. "And she has to be the one responsible for blowing up my cabin. Without Daemon to do her pyrotechnics, she had to do it herself. I'll give her credit; the bomb was amateur but effective."

Ian sighed. "Daemon was skilled at destroying things with fire."

He had been skilled at destroying things period, but she didn't say that. Instead, she said, "I can't see Marylou shooting Jasper though."

"Oh no." He saluted her with his mug. "That was me. Jasper's wife killed my sister, and I finally avenged her death. An eye for an eye. But your cabin? Yes, that was Marylou. She so loved to torment you."

Fletcher sipped her coffee. "No one came after Alexandra."

"Alexandra is a legacy, not to mention a well-respected woman amongst highly influential people, and Marylou adored her."

Yeah, right. "And hated me."

"As the last in the Thomas line, you were a threat."

"More like 'the threat.' She must have been the one

hanging around my cabin when I was out of my mind on that cocktail of your meds and herbal supplements."

"That was quite devious of Marylou. She made it look like someone was framing us. A bit of reverse psychology."

"Agreed. She used our families' mutual distaste to her benefit. It was smart. She tied up loose ends too, which is good form. Then you killed Daemon so he wouldn't talk. I guess I should thank you for that." Fletcher scratched her bun. She was glad Daemon was dead.

He patted her hand. "You're welcome. Though if not for him wanting you, Marylou would have no doubt finished you off. It may have been her only success."

Daemon's obsession with her saved her life? Nope, not going there. "What about Beverly?"

Ian's face clouded. "A mistake is all she's been. So much potential wasted. Had I known, I would have gone after Gracie right from the start."

She slid her mug over the table, then back again. "Beverly doesn't even know you're alive, does she?"

"No, but she will. One last hoorah before I go back overseas."

No loyalty. Fletcher huffed. "I finished my coffee."

He cocked his head to the side. "Eager to die?"

"I've had a shitty time of it, Ian. I've been drugged, shot at, closed inside a burning building, kidnapped, and beaten." She stood and stuck her hands in her pockets. "I've got more scars than Frankenstein, you murdered Jasper, my home was blown to bits, and Marylou's brains are ruining the interior of my truck. There was the whole losing-my-grip-on-reality thing; that sucked. And does this place look like it's being fucking remodeled?" She stomped her foot. "No! Add my mother lying to me to that list. So, you see I've had the fucking worst—"

"Dagnabbit, girl, don't you ever shut your yap?"

Fletcher glanced between where Ian stood and the kitchen door. "And now I'm seeing dead people." She turned to Ian. "This is pretty fucked, don't you think?" Ian raised his gun, but her knife was out of her pocket, then it was in his chest. He sputtered and looked at the handle of her blade sticking out of his heart. "Your day sucks more."

"Watch out!"

Fletcher dove. Ian got off a shot before he hit the ground. She sat up and kicked Ian's body with her foot. He was dead. Thank the Lord. But she turned her arm to see where the bullet had grazed her. The arm of her sweatshirt was bloody. "Why am I the one who always gets shot?"

"Ya ain't the only one, missy."

"You're still here?" Fletcher shook her head, blinked, and jumped up. "Jasper! You're alive! You ain't a ghost," she said, hugging him. He was real! She wasn't losing her mind again. Fletcher took a breath and held on.

"Did you think I was staying here because I love McKay's cooking?" He squeezed her back.

"You were gone. The alarms were going off and— and—" She swallowed and studied his face. Tears fell freely. "I's love you so much."

His cheeks pinkened. "I love you too, missy."

She wiped her tears on her shirt. "I's thought you were dead."

Jasper sniffed. "Was wondering why you didn't

come see me."

"You look good for a corpse." She laughed, floating on this high. "I thought I lost you."

"You could never lose me. Now let's sit for a minute, okay?"

Fletcher rushed to get Jasper a chair. She guided him into it. "Did you hear him? That's Ian Thomas?"

"Heard every word. I hope you didn't pay no attention to his bologna. You're all Hart!" Jasper winked. "I called Noah, so he should be here soon."

Reed! She couldn't wait to see him. "Everyone will lose their shit when they see you. Even Reed, and wait till until I tell you about that. What?" she asked when he held up a hand.

"I've done seen everyone. Either in person or on that app thingy." Jasper scratched his whiskers. "Your folks brought me here I don't know how many days ago; today was the first day they left me by myself."

Fletcher's stomach cramped. The reality of what was happening was sinking in. If he was staying here, then her parents knew he was alive. They—"Did Jebb know?"

"I ain't seen him. But everyone else's been checking in, like I said." He reached a hand up to his breast pocket, then dropped it. "But, ah, you didn't know."

Sirens blared, and car doors slammed. She glanced out the window. Noah and her parents heading their way. She pointed to Jasper. "Go get your things. Now!" she shouted when he hesitated.

"Don't do anything rash, missy."

Fletcher crossed her arms over her chest. Noah and her parents came running inside. She didn't uncross her arms when Noah grabbed her and held her tight. She steeled herself against leaning into him.

"Are you okay?" Noah asked. He let her go to walk around the table to where the body was. "Who is that?"

"Ian Thomas or I should say the new and improved Ian Thomas." She tossed her keys at Reed. "Marylou's in the back of my truck. Her brains are all over the place, so have the techs go in first. The gun over there on the floor is what he used to kill her."

"Ian was alive all this time?" Emmit pointed to her arm. "You got hit?"

"It's a graze."

Her mother stepped forward. "Fletcher? What is it?"

Jasper came into the room with a plastic shopping bag. "I got my stuff. Ain't much, but I sure would like to go home. Hey, folks," Jasper said. He leaned against the counter and pointed to the body. "It was self-defense, Noah, and I'll testify to that."

"Come on, old man." Wait, her truck was a crime scene. She bit her lip, then thanked the good Lord when Jebb's truck slid to a stop next to their parents' vehicle. Great timing, little brother.

Jebb skirted the deputies and ran into the house. "Jasper! Look, Fletcher, Jasper's alive?" Jebb took in the room. "What's going on?"

Fletcher met her brother's worried eyes. "Could you give us a ride, please?"

"Um." Jebb's gaze shot to his parents, then gulped. "Sure."

"Go on with Jebb, Jasper." She guided him into her brother's capable hands and ignored the older man's muttering.

W. L. Brooks

"Fletcher, let us explain," Savannah began.

"Explain?" Fletcher's laugh bordered on hysteria. "You've known all this time Jasper was alive!"

"It was my idea," Noah said. He radioed to his deputies to give them a minute.

Her body didn't reflect the violence his words inflicted. "Why doesn't that surprise me?" Fletcher sneered, then went to the door.

"Fletcher," her mother said, taking hold of Fletcher's hand.

She flinched away. "Don't touch me."

"Don't you dare," Emmit hissed. "Don't you dare—"

She stalked toward him, her hands clenched into tight fists at her sides. The desire to slap him surged inside her. "Me? This goes beyond a lie—beyond keeping a secret. I was dying inside, and y'all made the conscious decision to let me suffer. So don't stand there strung out on self-righteousness and tout your bullshit. How dare *you*!" Her voice had gone from icy cold to utter disdain. She was numb.

"Fletcher, please. It was my idea, I—"

"This is your idea of love, Reed? Well, fuck it and you. I'll give my statement to one of the deputies. You stay the fuck away from me." All of you. The door rattled on its frame when she slammed it shut.

Chapter Twenty-Seven

Jasper stared toward the front of the house where someone was pounding the bejesus out of his door. Fletcher was finishing up in the bathroom, and he was hesitant to let in any visitors. The banging got louder. He was pretty sure it was Jake's voice on the other side. With a sigh, he went to let the boy in. He'd get a peephole installed. Soon.

"I need to talk to the kid!" Jake lifted Jasper out of his way.

"Boy, she don't wanna talk," Jasper said once he regained his dignity. The nerve of the man picking him up like that. He followed Jake as the younger man hollered and carried on through the house.

"Kid?" Jake yelled.

Jasper shook his head. "Check the kitchen."

Jake nodded and went in that direction. Jasper was making his way there. Maybe it wasn't his business, but it damn well was his kitchen, and he had every right to be in it.

"Kid?" Jake said.

Fletcher was sitting at the table in her jammies; her hair was wet from her bath. She wouldn't look at Jake. Jasper harrumphed and went to pour the coffee.

She rose from her seat. "Jasper, sit down, I can make—"

"I can do it. You want some, Jake?" Jasper asked

and returned Fletcher's glare. "This is my house, missy. I can offer a beverage to whomever I please."

"No, thanks," Jake said and moved a chair so he was sitting right in front of Fletcher. "You're gonna hear me out, kid."

She crossed her arms over her chest. "I don't have to do a damn thing."

Jasper handed Fletch her mug, then went back to the counter to lean. He didn't want her to know standing was a bit of a struggle. They had more important things to be concerned with. "Listen to the boy. Ain't like you got anything else to do."

"Fine," she said. "I'll start the conversation with a simple *how could you?*"

"I didn't want to. You've got to believe me," Jake said. "But everyone agreed it was the only way to keep you and Jasper safe."

She looked inside her mug. "I heard you, now go."

"Fletcher, you're my best friend," Jake croaked. "Don't shut me out."

Jasper blinked to clear the glaze in his eyes and poured himself a mug. The boy was upset. The girl was shaken. He should have known something was up whenever he would ask where Fletch was and they changed the subject. No one had said a word about knowing Fletcher was his either. That would have made a difference. If they'd told him—

"If I talk to you and not Alexandra, she won't like it. Then there will be issues, and I won't be responsible for discontent in your marriage."

"Then talk to Alex. Talk to the family. They're all at my house right now."

Fletcher stared at him. "I won't do that, Jake. I

can't look at them—"

"Girl," Jasper warned.

"Not this time, old man. I will not put on a brave face and pretend nothing's changed. This isn't about a simple lie or keeping something secret. You let me believe Jasper was dead. You let my heart break needlessly; you stood by silent and watched as I suffered. So no, I don't want to hear this. I'm trying not to act out in anger, because I would tell you all to go fuck yourselves, and I don't want to do that. Even if everything in me is raging to. So, forgiveness isn't in my wheelhouse at the moment." She stood up.

"Kid, please listen to reason."

"Jake, I love you." She smiled. "Next to Jasper, you're my best friend too. But don't you see that's why it hurts? I've sacrificed so much of myself for the people I love, for my family."

Jake sat up. "I—"

Fletcher held up a hand. "I've done so willingly, don't get me wrong. I've sacrificed my heart, my mind, and my fucking body," she said, holding her scarred arms out. "I've been shot, driven insane, and tortured by a madman. I did it protecting my family, and I'm almost ashamed to say, because how fucking masochistic does it make me sound, that I would do it again."

"Kid." Jake shook his head.

Jasper grabbed the box of tissues on top of the microwave. He was going to hand it to Fletcher, but his own eyes were leaking. She was laying herself bare, and not just for Jake's sake, but for his too.

"You want to know why I was with Judge Mason?"

Jasper blew his nose. "Whatcha talkin' about,

missy?" He'd asked her a million times what she'd been doing with the judge, but she wouldn't go into it. His chest tightened, which scared him for a second, but he breathed through it.

"Judge Mason helps run a shelter for battered and abused women. She and Julia got me a place there and pulled strings so that I could come and go as I needed. Come and go so none of you would know. I didn't want to burden *you* with *my* pain." She swatted tears from her cheeks.

"You coulda told me!" Jasper choked out. He wanted to hold her, but he didn't want to make a scene. His poor girl. He gripped the edge of the counter to quell the trembling.

"Haven't you lost enough hair on my account? You want to be bald, old man?"

Jake put his hands over his heart. "I'm so fucking sorry, Fletch."

She kissed Jake's cheek. Before leaving the room, she said, "Tell them I've paid my pound of flesh."

Jasper swallowed and dabbed at his eyes again. "I'm sorry, Jake. I really am."

"It's not your fault, Jasper." Jake stood. "Take care of her. She needs a keeper."

"Girl's head is brick hard like her father's. And I mean McKay; everyone knows I'm a reasonable man." At least that got a laugh out of the boy.

"Thanks, Jasper. I'll see you around."

Jasper stood until the front door shut, then he sat and fiddled with his coffee mug. "Oh, Lord, Laura, what am I gonna do?" His wife would tell him to go to their girl. He patted the table and got up to get some ingredients.

He carried two glass mugs down the hall to the bedroom his girl had picked out as her own years ago. It had made Laura so happy to decorate it for Fletch. Hell, they'd even redone the bathroom with one of them garden tubs because their girl loved to soak in a nice bath. Those had been good days, turning his and Laura's house into a home for three.

Talk about turning a nightmare into a blessing. Jasper paused and closed his stinging eyes. He missed his wife something awful. Laura had stuck by him after the morning he woke up in his birthday suit next to a strange woman. She'd believed him when he told her that he didn't remember a thing about that night. In fact, it had been Laura's idea to have Leo take a blood sample.

The test had come back positive for GHB. It wasn't until he and Fletcher had their DNA tested that Jasper knew for certain what had happened to him that night. Laura and he had agreed never to tell Fletcher, and he'd sworn Leo to secrecy. Their girl had enough trauma; what good would it do to know she was the product of—Jasper shook himself. Fletch was their girl, and she was in pain; that's all that mattered right now.

The door was open a crack. "Fletch?" With his hands full, he used his back to enter after Fletcher said to come in. The room was already getting dark, but he could make out her curled-up form on the bed. "Brought something to warm you up, missy."

She sniffled but sat up on the bed. He took a seat next to her and handed over one of the mugs. She smirked. "A hot toddy?"

Jasper shrugged. "It'll warm you."

Fletch rose a brow. "Are you having one too?"

He harrumphed. "Even the doc would agree this one drink is for medicinal purposes. And considering the lemons in the fridge hadn't spoiled, I figure the good Lord gives his consent."

She laughed and kissed his cheek. "I missed you so much, old man." Her tears fell freely, and Fletch shook her head. "Sorry for being a sissy crybaby."

He patted her knee. "What a bunch of bologna! You ain't got nothing to be sorry for."

She snorted, then sipped her toddy. "You do make a damn fine beverage."

Jasper took a tiny sip. It was good. "You wanna talk about things? I saw the cassette player in the kitchen. Figure you might have some questions." He was thankful he hadn't told her the truth about what happened to him on the tape. Jasper had wrestled with it, but ultimately, he stuck with what he and Laura had agreed upon.

Fletcher held the mug to her chest. "I was pissed when I found out you were keeping important shit from me."

He reached up to his breast pocket, then dropped his hand. "I'll tell you whatever ya want to know." If she ever asked about that night, he would tell her the truth.

She maneuvered next to him and put her head on his shoulder. "I really don't give a shit at the moment. I'm too fucking happy you're here with me. Alive."

He sighed, put the past back where it dwelled, and kissed the top of her head. "You want to tell me what all happened while I was out of it?" He had ideas, but he wanted the full story.

"Did you read the transcripts?"

Japer stilled. He didn't have to ask what she was talking about.

Fletcher turned to face him. "No more secrets."

He took a gulp of his toddy. "I did." It had nearly killed him.

"Why?"

"It may be your burden to carry, but I wasn't gonna let you carry it alone." And he'd wanted to be prepared if and when she ever wanted to talk about it. He told her so.

She nodded.

He rubbed her back for a couple of minutes, then asked, "Whatcha thinking?"

"Nothing."

"Girl." He didn't want to pressure her, but he needed to have some idea of what was going on in that head of hers. "Go on and tell me."

Fletcher took a big swig of her drink.

If she needed some liquid courage, then he surely would too. Jasper took a bigger sip. "I got enough to make you another one."

She smiled. "This is plenty. Thank you."

They sat there long enough for Jasper to need a bathroom break. He came back to her room after doing his business and reclaimed his seat. Maybe she wasn't ready to talk. Jasper could respect that. He sighed, they had time. "Oh, I forgot to ask ya where you put my files?"

****

Noah slammed the front door and headed for the kitchen to grab a beer. The house was quiet, which had never bothered him before. Now it did.

The silence was deafening. There would be no late-night talks on unsolved crimes, no brainstorming, and no intense lectures on the badassness of Dame Angela Lansbury. His chuckle died in his throat. He hadn't laughed so much in—

He sipped his beer. It was over. They were over. "One for the road," she'd said this morning. Christ, had it only been this morning? They'd made love right here on the kitchen table. He ran a finger across its surface. It had been fast, frenzied, and so fucking fulfilling.

Then she'd turned their phone call into a video chat. Had she wanted to see him as much as he'd wanted to see her? To touch her. Fletcher had even talked about phone sex. Of all things. She had been letting him in, bit by bit, over the last couple of days. Dropping truth bombs.

He snorted. Truth. He brought his drink back to his lips, then threw it at the wall. She was gone. Rubbing his hands through his hair, he left the broken glass where it was. His life was in pieces, so the bottle may as well be too. He couldn't bring himself to care.

He had stopped by Granny Vaughn's before coming home. Emmit and Savannah were staying at the B and B, and he wanted to tell them that the crime scene techs had finished at the house. Noah had already called a cleaning crew, and they would be working through the night to get their place taken care of. He'd pulled into the parking lot at the B and B to find all the McKay vehicles there.

Inside, they'd sat around Alex's table, each of their phones laid out in front of them. He reminded them Fletcher's cell was in evidence, but no one had seemed to hear him. They all sat there staring blankly at each other. Except for Jake and Charlie, who'd been fighting for cooking space.

Then Jake had rushed out of the house, leaving Alexandra to pretend not to worry. She'd done a good job, Noah would give her that, but her gaze kept going to the window. Jake had been the last one told about the plan, and he'd been against it, adamantly. But after much discussion, they'd worn him down, and he had agreed.

Deputy Diaz and Deputy Hewitt had taken Fletcher and Jasper's statements. Noah had explained to the McKays what had happened. Years before, Ian Thomas had his sister set Jasper up so he could blackmail him out of office. His sister hadn't told him about the baby until later. It took some digging, but Ian eventually found out about Fletcher.

Marylou had found out too and had been systematically trying to destroy Fletcher ever since. Marylou had been behind most everything that had happened to the McKays over the past few years, not that they were surprised. She was dead; the end.

Noah went to the den and attempted to drown himself in paperwork, but Jebb's words kept playing in his mind. Right when Noah was about to leave, Jebb had shown up. He'd been agitated, having dropped Fletcher and Jasper off. He had filled them in about how Fletcher couldn't look at any of them right now. If she did, she might write them off. Noah was familiar with her fury and didn't doubt the sincerity of her words.

But when Jebb said Fletcher might have loved him, Noah had had to use all his strength not to react. He'd made his excuses and left with his head held high. Had he fooled them? No, he was pretty damn sure he hadn't.

He was raw, but he couldn't help thinking what Fletcher must be feeling. She'd said not to make her regret trusting him, and he had. Again.

The front door opened, and Noah's heart leapt. She had the key, and some of her things were still here. Footsteps echoed. He called her name.

"It's me," Fletcher said standing in the doorway of the den.

Noah could barely breathe. She was here. She came back. He got to his feet and moved toward her. He didn't want to get his hopes up.

"Jasper wants his files."

"Oh." Noah stood there like a jackass while she ran up the stairs, then back down. Her arms were loaded. He took ahold of her elbow, forcing her to drop the box of files. He cupped her face, her eyes fluttered shut, and he pressed his lips to hers. She kissed him back.

Noah lifted her in his arms, and Fletcher wrapped her legs around his waist. He walked to the den and sat on the couch with her on his lap. She untangled herself from him and stood. Her green gaze held his as she undressed before him. Noah slipped his shirt off, then unzipped his pants. Before he could divest himself of them completely, Fletcher reached down and freed his erection.

Their gazes held while she straddled his thighs. Their breaths quickened. She lowered herself onto him. They both moaned. Her heat was decadent. Noah reached up and undid her hair from its bun. He ran his fingers through the tawny strands. God, he loved her.

She brought his hands to her naked breast. He squeezed, then suckled her. Her fingers ran over his shoulders in slow circles. He inhaled her spicy scent and kissed his way up her neck.

Fletcher leaned closer, put her mouth to his, and began to move. It was slow at first, then frantic; neither spoke. Noah slid his hand into her hair and held her tight as she increased her pace. Skin slid against skin as their bodies slickened. More, more, more. He wanted her beneath him, he wanted to be pounding into her, imprinting himself on every cell, but this was hers to lead. The sexy little noises she made echoed in the room, and he gripped her harder. He was desperate. Her inner muscles were squeezing him, and he wouldn't last another second. They came together, their breathing a chorus of release.

Noah kissed her again, and Fletcher sank into him. Tears slid between their cheeks; whose they were he wasn't sure, but he let her go when she made to get up. She got dressed without a word, and he stood to put himself to rights. She headed to the entryway without looking at him.

She wiped her eyes on her sweatshirt and picked up the boxes.

Noah swallowed. "You just came back for the files."

"Jasper wanted them."

Anger and fear battled inside him. "Then why fuck me?"

She sucked in a breath; her icy gaze collided with his. "Fuck you!"

"Why? Damn it, I deserve an answer!" He slammed the front door shut so she couldn't leave.

"You deserve nothing! Now let me out," Fletcher hissed.

"Why make love with me?" he whispered.

Fletcher closed her eyes; more tears spilled from beneath her lashes. "I wanted…"

"What?"

"The memory. Please, move." She put the box on her hip and tried to open the door.

"Do you love me? Did you love me?" he asked to cover his bases.

She searched his eyes. "Don't."

"Answer me."

"Yes," she told him and pulled on the knob. "This is false imprisonment, Reed. Holding a body against her will is unlawful, as you damn well know."

"I don't give a fuck. Tell me when?" He slapped his hand on the door again when she'd gotten it partly open.

Fletcher shook her head. "I's fell in love with you the moment I laid eyes on you. Then you manipulated me into taking your fucking money when I never would have said anything to anyone, because it was *you*. And I would have died before I hurt you. But you had no reservations about hurting *me*. And I hated you for being able to do that so effortlessly." She spat and turned toward the back of the house.

"And now?" he asked hot on her heels. "This time we had together, did you love me then? Do you?"

Fletcher got the back door open but turned to him. "Yes." Her voice broke, but she cleared her throat. "And look what you were able to do to me again. Fool me once, shame on you. Fool me twice, shame on me."

He swallowed. There was another truth he could relinquish, an ace card, but…he couldn't do it. "I love you," he whispered.

Her chest heaved; then she ran out.

Noah went to the front of the house and stood on the porch until the taillights of Jasper's truck were out of sight.

He closed the door behind him and tried to breathe. His chest tightened. Noah went behind his desk; then he lifted it and flung it as far as he could. Anything within arm's reach was collateral damage; he went around the room smashing whatever got in his way. At some point, there was nothing left. He'd destroyed everything.

"So be it," he said and went to the kitchen to grab a beer. He shut the refrigerator, then leaned against it.

The pain slid around his throat to choke him. She'd loved him back. Then and now. She'd loved him, and he'd destroyed it not once, but twice. If he had thought for a second she returned his feelings, he wouldn't have taken the chance. But what was done was done, and he couldn't take it back now. He hung his head, and for the first time since his father's death, Noah let his grief off its leash.

Chapter Twenty-Eight

Jasper inspected the new flooring Fletcher had installed. She had pulled the old stuff up after the entire fiasco a couple of weeks ago. She had gone to Noah's to get Jasper's files and come back a mess. Jasper had sat with his girl for hours while she spilled her guts. The next day they'd started on the carpet.

"Looks good!" She beamed.

"I reckon it does," Jasper said and toasted her with his mug. "Better than the blood-stained stuff for sure." It was good to have a fresh start. They had done a lot of cleaning and such things around the place. Once people knew he was recovering at home, the good folks of Blue Creek had loaded them down with casseroles, cakes, and all kinds of things. He'd already finished the bear claws Mildred had brought him.

With meals covered, they only needed to leave the house to get supplies and go to his appointments. Jasper was getting cabin fever, but he didn't tell Fletch that.

"I did a damn fine job, if I say so myself."

He sipped his coffee. "You know what Laura would say?"

Fletch rolled her eyes, but she grinned. "Do tell."

"Pride's one of the deadlies, missy."

"It is indeed," she said with a snort. Then she got up from off the floor, brushed her hands on her jeans, and poured herself a cup of coffee. "What do you want to do today?"

"I think I'm gonna go to town. Doc gave me the all clear to drive, so I figure I'll stop at the diner," he said and pursed his lips. She was getting better at concealing her feelings, but she couldn't fool him, not yet. "You don't gotta go with me."

"I wasn't planning on it," she said with a shrug.

Jasper huffed and went to top off his coffee. The girl was irritating. She took out her tablet thingy and started typing on it. "Whatcha doing there?" he asked. She was always on that dagnab thing, her fingers flying over the screen. She'd gotten him one of his own when she'd replaced her phone, but he still had no idea how to use it.

Fletcher looked up. "I think we should take a vacation. Just you and me. What do you say?"

A vacation? He couldn't remember the last time he'd taken a vacation. He and Laura had wanted to travel, but they never got the chance. They'd kept putting it off, but time waited for no one. "We'd need to clear it with Doc."

"I already cleared it with Dr. Lowell."

He raised his brows. "Ya did?"

"At your last appointment."

"Well, then if she said it's okay, I think it'd be a fine idea. A change of scenery would be nice." Better than staring at the four walls, that's for sure. Not to mention it would do his girl a world of good to get away. Hell, it'd do them both good.

"Great! You go to the diner, and I'll look at some options."

"Deal," he said.

****

Jasper opened the door to the diner and snagged his stool. It was after lunch, so there wasn't a crowd. He strummed his fingers on the counter. "Is there anybody working today?"

"Sorry, Jasper," Mildred said as she came out of the kitchen. "How are you feeling?"

"Not too shabby," he said. Glad his ordeal wasn't at the top of Blue Creek's gossip mill. Nope, everyone was still losing their minds over the fact that Ian Thomas had been alive. He glanced around at the empty tables. "Sure is quiet in here today."

"The place was packed twenty minutes ago," she said with a wink. "Oh, put on your best behavior. Here comes the boss lady."

Jasper waved at Charlie and thanked Mildred for the cup of coffee she put in front of him.

"Jasper. How's Fletcher?" Charlie chewed her lip.

"Annoying." Jasper huffed.

Charlie smiled. "Other than that, though?"

"She doesn't want to see nobody yet, if that's what you're trying to get out of me. I'm sorry, Charlie girl, but that's the way the cards fell. I've been trying to get her to come to town with me, but she won't. And I'm sorry if I can't cold shoulder her into it." He wouldn't push his girl. She'd gone through so much. He'd finally got her to tell him all about the women's shelter and Judge Mason.

Jasper thought he had done a good job of keeping his emotions in check while she'd recounted everything. He had waited until he was alone in his room to weep. Reading the transcripts was nothing compared to hearing it from Fletch's mouth. His girl had suffered, and she'd done so in silence to spare them her pain. He shook himself and looked at Charlie. "Sorry?"

"I said it's not your fault." She patted his back and went behind the counter.

"She died inside." His cheeks heated.

Charlie stopped what she was doing. "What?"

"I ain't good at this stuff." Jasper harrumphed.

"I appreciate you trying, Jasper." The door opened, and Charlie murmured, "Speaking of someone who's dying inside."

"Charlie. Jasper." Noah sat next to Jasper and handed him a set of keys. "I had Fletcher's truck detailed after the investigation was closed. It's at the station."

"She ain't gonna want it," Jasper told Noah. The boy looked like shit warmed over. His hair was bushy, his jaw stubbled, and his eyes red. Sheriff shouldn't look like that.

Noah shrugged his shoulder. "It's done if she changes her mind."

"I'll tell her." Maybe he should start carrying a damn notepad again. Everyone was looking at him with puppy eyes. Like he could fix everything. Well, he couldn't; he couldn't do a damn thing to help anybody. He shrank down on his stool.

"Thank you. I'll have my usual, Charlie."

"I think I'll be getting along myself," Jasper said and put money on the counter. He couldn't get out of there fast enough. He didn't even get a dagnab bear claw.

****

Fletcher put her suitcase in her room and stretched out on the bed. They'd had a great vacation. They'd

265

seen all the sights Jasper had always said he'd wanted to see. She had a new haircut and a new tattoo. She grinned; she'd even gotten Jasper to get one. His covered the wound on his chest. It was an outline of a heart with both Laura's and her name inside.

Fletcher had made fun of him for doing it, but she'd been touched. She'd covered the brand Mommy Demented had put on her. Jasper hadn't understood her choice until she'd told him it was so there was always a candle lit, not only for those they'd lost but to offer light in the darkness. The old man had gotten weepy about it, and, truth be told, she had too. No one needed to know it was the candlestick that held the meaning for her. That light would burn on. Always.

Later that afternoon, there was a knock at the door. She looked in on Jasper, who was too busy snoring to hear it. Jasper had had her put in a peephole before they'd left for vacation, but she forgot to check it.

"Can I come in?" Pops asked.

Fletcher's heart hurt to look at her father. She glanced behind her. "Jasper's asleep."

He stared for a moment. "Can we speak out here then?"

She hesitated. "Okay." Fletcher shut the screen door, another new addition, and sat in one of the rocking chairs. She should have grabbed some slippers; it was chilly.

Emmit sat next to her. "I'm sorry I hurt you, Fletcher; sorrier than you can imagine, but I did it to protect you and Jasper. We shouldn't have kept it from you, but at the time it was the best option. You—you cut your hair."

"Only some of it." It was cut to the middle of her

back, but it was shorter than she'd ever worn it.

"It looks nice."

Her cheeks heated. "Do you want a beer?"

"I'll take one, sure."

Fletcher brought out two beers, handed one to Pops, then reclaimed her chair. She took a sip from the bottle and waited, bringing her legs up in the seat so she could fiddle with her toes. They'd been painted by a spiritualist in New Orleans. The woman said it would keep Fletch out of shit. Jasper said it couldn't hurt and even had his done too.

"I was jealous of Jasper."

No shit. "Why?"

"Because you love him more than me."

"That's the stupidest thing I's ever heard come out of your mouth. I never thought you loved Casey more than me, and we all know she's your favorite."

"Why is it that everyone thinks Casey's my favorite?"

Fletcher snorted. "Because she is."

"If that's what you want to think, that's fine." Emmit sipped his beer. "When did you find out about"—he shrugged—"you know?"

"I was ten," she said. "Jasper gave blood both times I was shot. He made the connection and was curious. Then when I was ten, we were talking, and he said he had my blood type. I asked him if we could get a DNA test."

"You asked him?"

"I'd read about DNA testing, and we looked into it. He didn't see a problem, so we got the test done. I've known ever since. Legally he could have taken me, but he told me it was my choice." She'd made her choice.

Emmit put a hand to his stomach. "You could have lived with your real father, but you stayed with me?"

Fletcher rubbed her nose. "Calling him my 'real father' says more about your feelings than mine."

He stared at her. "I—"

She shook her head. Was he so selfish? "I'm Jasper's only child, but I carry your name. I grew up in your house. Jasper let me choose, and he respected my decision. He never complained, even though Laura wanted me with them; they fought about it. It hurt her—I hurt her. She put her life on the line for me, but she didn't hold my choice against me. Neither has Jasper. I love him as I love you. The same but different. Jasper's my best friend. What y'all did hurt me." Well, more than hurt; it was devastating.

"I'm sorry. I never knew."

"You didn't ask. I understood, Pops. More often than not, people don't want to know the answers for fear of what they'll find. That's human." Pops had never wanted to know about their pasts. They were his, and that was it as far as he'd been concerned. But the world didn't work like that.

"Why didn't you ever come to me? Not just about Jasper but in the last couple of years. You haven't even talked with me about what happened with…when you were with Daemon. Didn't you trust me enough?"

Her grip tightened on the bottle. At least he got the name out this time. "It's not about trust, Pops."

"Then what's it about?"

"Honestly?" Usually she would spare his feelings, but she wasn't in a charitable mood. She would let him choose.

Pops eyed her for a moment. "I've never known

you not to tell the truth."

"I'm giving you an out."

He swallowed. "Tell me."

Fletcher looked him over. He was more disheveled than usual, and the dark circles under his eyes told their own story. "Did you read the court transcripts?"

He set his beer on the seat between his legs. "You asked us not to be there when you gave testimony, so I figured you would tell us what you wanted us to know when you were ready."

He had been a sharpshooter, not an investigator, so maybe that was the difference. Both Noah and Jasper had read the transcripts. And from the looks she'd caught her sister giving her, Fletch had a sneaking suspicion Alexandra had too. But Pops hadn't taken the extra step to find out what kind of hell she'd suffered. What did that say about him? "You can't handle what happened to me."

Pops shook his head. "You have so little faith in me?"

Harsh, bitter words leaped to her tongue, but she bit them back. She rubbed her arms. "That's kind of my point. It's not about *you*."

He sat back in the rocker. "Okay." They sipped their beers in silence for a while. "Jebb said you were going away again."

"In a few days."

"Where are you going?"

Fletcher smiled. "I'm gonna check out a small town in Maine."

He laughed. "I should've known." He started down the steps and got to his SUV before she called out to him. "Yeah?"

"You'll always be the first adult I ever loved."

Chapter Twenty-Nine

It was dark by the time Fletcher arrived at Granny Vaughn's. She had parked at the end of the drive and walked the rest of the way up. Jake, Ryan, Craig, and Noah were all squatting in the dirt and watching the house. She turned to Jasper when they got close to the group. "You go sit with them."

"Kid!" Jake pulled her toward him. "Thanks for coming."

"Of course we came!" Jake had called her, but she hadn't answered, so then he'd tried Jasper. Jasper had relayed the message to Fletcher; then they'd hopped in his rust bucket and hauled ass here.

Jake nodded. "I was out running errands when Emmit called and said Alexandra was taking care of dinner, so I didn't need to hurry home. Alex doesn't cook. Burns everything."

"We know." Pops had left a voicemail saying he was glad they'd reconciled, and he wanted to celebrate with her and her sisters at the B and B. Red flags all around.

"What are we going to do?" Ryan asked.

"I say we go into the secret passageways and ambush the bitch!" Craig punched his fist into his hand.

Fletcher eyed Craig. He and Ryan both had pregnant wives in that house, so their being on edge was expected. She appreciated Jake was trying to keep his cool, even though Alexandra was his entire world. Jebb was watching Mack at Charlie's place, so the kids were safe.

"Who is it anyway?" Jasper asked. He had refused to stay home, not that Fletcher really thought he would.

"Beverly Thomas." Noah put down the binoculars. He glanced at Fletcher. "You cut your hair."

Fletcher rolled her eyes.

"Can we get back to the situation at hand?" Craig growled.

"We need to wait for my deputies," Noah said.

"No need," Jasper told him. "You've got citizens on patrol right here."

"All right, boys, if I'm not back in…let's say ten minutes, come barging in." Fletcher stopped when Noah grabbed her arm.

"She wants you in there. No, I refuse to let you do this."

"Reed, for once in your life, trust me." It hurt to look at him. She wanted to close her eyes and bask in the heat of his hand. Fletch yearned to touch him, hug him, breathe him in, but she did none of those things.

Noah let go of her arm. "I love you."

Fletcher believed him, but she couldn't let it matter. "I have to go." She made her way toward the house, then turned. "Noah?"

"What?"

"If anything should happen, take care of Jasper." Fletcher walked to the porch and opened the screen door. Her family was all trussed up like Thanksgiving turkeys. "Why does this look familiar?"

Beverly pointed her gun at Fletcher. "Shut the door, Ms. McKay."

She sighed and did as she was asked. "You know this is fucked up, right?"

"Give me your weapon. I'm not stupid. I know you have one." Beverly waited while Fletcher emptied her pockets. She had a gun and two knives. "Is that all?"

"Yep. You wanna let my family go? This isn't to do with them, not really." Fletcher shrugged. "May as well keep this between us girls."

Beverly's face pinched. "You ruined my family; it's only fair I ruin yours."

Fletcher laughed. "If you hadn't cheated on Ian, he wouldn't have killed Marylou. He wouldn't have faked his own death to get away from you either. He was planning on paying you a visit though, did you know that?"

"You're just like Jasper. He never could mind his own business either."

Fletcher rocked back on her heels. "Jasper has an unnatural tendency to be inquisitive."

"What?" she screeched.

"Means he's nosy." Fletcher glanced at her sisters and mother restrained on the floor, leaning against the kitchen cabinets. Her father was tied to a chair, with duct tape over his mouth. How the world circled round. "Y'all okay?"

"Don't speak to them," Beverly hissed.

Fletcher tsked and took a step toward Beverly. As expected, the woman stepped back.

"Stop where you are, or I'll shoot them."

Fletcher grinned when the other woman swung the weapon toward Fletcher's family. Amateurs. Fletcher reached out and snatched the gun from the other woman's grasp. "Never take your eyes off the target,

Bevy baby." She kept the gun trained on Beverly while she untied Alexandra.

Alex stood, and Fletcher handed her the weapon. "The safety's on," Alex whispered.

"I know," Fletcher said and turned back to Mrs. Thomas.

Beverly, shoulders slumping, inched away. "What are you going to do?"

Fletcher cocked her head to the side. "You tied up my sisters, two of whom got my nieces and nephews brewing in their bellies. You bound my parents, intending to hurt them, maybe even kill them. Now, I'm gonna have to be all forgiving because they could've died and life is short. Too short to stay angry and blah, blah, blah." She walked closer to Beverly. "I wasn't planning on moving past my hurt anytime in the near future. I had plans, but you've taken away my choice. I hate that. But do you know what I hate more?"

Beverly's back hit the wall, and she swallowed. "No."

"I's hate getting shot. Been shot twice, and it isn't any fun. So, if you've got some issues, we can work them out the old-fashioned way."

Beverly's botoxed forehead didn't budge. "What?"

"We're gonna have us a fight." Fletcher rubbed her hands together.

"You're crazy!" Beverly said, then didn't say anything because Fletcher knocked her unconscious.

Fletcher rubbed her hand and glared at the woman. "That's the one thing I hate more than getting shot. I am not crazy." She turned around to see her family untied and staring at her. "What? I'm not."

"Did you mean what you said about forgiving us?"

Savannah asked.

"I reckon y'all are going to hold me to it." Fletcher sighed.

"Does that mean yes?" Charlie asked. "Because the animosity is driving me batty."

Fletcher weighed her feelings. She could have lost them all tonight, and then she wouldn't even have anyone to be mad at. "I'll forgive y'all. But you are so on my shit list!"

Chapter Thirty

Jasper harrumphed when there was a knock at the door. "Come in."

"You know, Jasper," Emmit began, "after recent events, one would think you'd lock your door."

"This is still Blue Creek, McKay. Take a seat." Jasper poured Emmit a cup of coffee and sat. "I reckon with the Thomases out of the picture I'm safe enough."

"Beverly's behind bars, and the skeletons are out of their proverbial closets."

Jasper fiddled with the handle of his mug. "Say what you need to be saying, Emmit. We're too damn old to beat around the bush." The girl was out doing whatever it was she did when she wasn't bugging the crap out of him. She wasn't here to keep him in line either. But Jasper would put a lid on his temper and do the right thing.

Emmit sighed. "I know she asked you not to tell me."

Jasper eyed the other man; he loathed this crap and wished like hell he didn't have to suffer through it. But such was life when one's secrets were out in the open. "I would have been proud to announce to the world that Fletch's my girl. But she's a McKay. If that damn hard head of hers isn't proof, I don't know what is."

Emmit laughed, then sobered. "I'm jealous of you."

"And I of you," Jasper admitted and stared at his wrinkled hands. "To Fletch, you'll always be her father. The man she loved first, and the one she picked to stay with. I'll admit her decision cut me to the core. Especially after Laura got sick." He looked into Emmit's blue-gray eyes. "Figure it's only right that at some point you'd feel the same. That may make me an old cuss, but there you go. Fletcher loves us both, and I reckon that's all that matters."

Emmit nodded. "You're right. I was jealous of your relationship before though. I didn't mind so much at first. You were the other man in my girl's life, and I figured I'd have to get used to that. But when she said she was your daughter, it broke my heart. I realized that's why Evan never wanted to tell me the truth face-to-face."

"When we got the DNA results, I wanted Fletcher for my own. She's my blood and my only child, but I let Fletcher make her own decision. Laura took longer to come to grips with Fletcher's choice, but my wife did it because staying with you and her sisters was what Fletch wanted."

"Yeah." Emmit finished his coffee and stood. "Thank you."

"For what?" Jasper asked as they made their way to the door.

Emmit pulled out his keys. "For my daughter. Thank you."

Jasper squashed the pinch of bitterness. Envy was one of the deadlies. "Sometimes mistakes aren't always the worst thing. Sometimes when you least expect it, the wrong you did in your life turns out to be the best thing that ever happened to other folks. Secrets can destroy people, and the truth more often than not hurts; but when it's out for the world to see, well, you ain't gotta hide no more."

"And you think Fletcher was hiding?"

Jasper shrugged. "She's mending, and that's gonna take time."

"You're right."

Emmit headed down the drive, and Jasper hesitated. He didn't like making waves, and they had resolved things. Lying to Emmit all these years hadn't been easy, but he'd done it. And he would do it again. He would do anything for his girl, but what he needed to do right now made him ill. It was risky with how dagnab angry it made him, but if he didn't do it, Jasper never would. He took a breath. "McKay?"

Emmit stopped, then came back. "Yeah?"

Jasper steeled himself. He would not let his temper flare. He would be reasonable. "You gotta tell her."

Emmit's brow pinched. "Who?"

"You gotta tell her," Jasper said again through clenched teeth. "You know what I'm talking about, McKay. The line between right and wrong can get muddy, but you're fixing to cross it. The boy gave you an out, and you took it, but hell and tarnation, it ain't fair to those kids, and you damn well know it!"

The other man's face went deathly pale, and he gagged.

"Go in the bushes," Jasper said, then hurried into the house and got an icy green can from the fridge. He got back outside as McKay was wiping his mouth. "Here, this always helps my stomach."

Emmit took the can, popped the top, and took a big gulp. Had a long belch after, but that was to be expected. "Excuse me," he said, then took another sip. "How did you know?"

Jasper rocked back on his heels. "I wasn't sheriff for thirty-odd years for nothing, McKay." He'd had a long talk with Noah and seen right through the boy.

"I—"

Jasper held up a hand. "Sometimes a body takes the easy way out, and that's fine. We all do it. I've done it, probably do it again. But your easy way comes with a high price tag, one *you* don't have to pay for. And you're hoping the girl's gonna see sense soon and it won't even matter. But it *does* matter because that girl's head is brick hard and you're better than this." He wouldn't beg. But damn it. This was his girl's heart on the line.

Emmit rubbed his hands over his face, then stared at Jasper. "I'm scared of losing her."

Jasper nodded. "I've been sitting at your table for years lying to your face about Fletcher being mine." He took too much pleasure in saying that. Pride was also one of the deadlies, and Jasper needed to be humbler. "I was scared as hell waiting for that shoe to drop. Thinking I'd lose my friend, my family—that's what y'all are to me. But here we are. Hell, I'm scared right now bringing it up. I don't want to lose our friendship, Emmit, but you gotta tell her. She's already forgiven you, and she may be perturbed, but it won't be as bad as you're thinking. Besides, I've known you all your life; you ain't ever done nothing easy!"

The other man chuckled.

"Savannah, on the other hand, might not be as gracious." Bless that woman.

Emmit squeezed his eyes shut and sipped from the

can.

****

Fletcher walked around the rubble that was once her cabin. The insurance company was being dickish about her claim, not that she could blame them, but it was annoying. She had the money to rebuild it on her own if she wanted to. Did she want to? The first cabin had been a testament of sorts to her relationship with Casey; this had been their spot when they were kids. Now Fletcher kicked a pile of ashes. What did she want?

She chose a cleared spot, lay on the ground, and took a deep breath. The air was thick with the scent of an upcoming fall storm. She rested her head on one folded arm and used her other to fiddle with her locket. Fletcher had had a long talk with her mother this morning. If there was one thing she couldn't stand, it was Savanah McKay's tears.

Her ma had cried buckets, which had made Fletcher cry too. She'd forgiven her family, but trust was harder to give back. Her mother understood that; hell, her family understood. Who knew better than the McKays what lies and betrayal cost?

She arched her back and glanced in the direction of footsteps. "What are you doing out here, Alexandra?"

Alex took a seat next to her. "Looking for you."

"Give the woman a prize."

"Funny," Alex said, then spread the skirt of her dress out on the ground. "Are you going to rebuild? Word around town is you're planning on leaving."

"Maybe." She peeked out of one eye. "Why do you care, Alexandra? What's in it for you?"

"Well, Jacob loves you, and for some reason that's

beyond my personal comprehension, he wants you to stay. Then there's Casey, who on normal days is bossy, but now she's even ruder than usual. Jebb is bugging me to death. And Charlie's trying to ignore reality again."

"Jake doesn't want to be left alone with all the females and his prissy brother." Fletcher smiled, thinking of Ryan. "Jebb will get over himself once he starts dating. Casey's hormonal. She doesn't need me; she just doesn't want to be left with only you to fight with. And let Charlie alone before you break her."

"What about Mama, Daddy, and Jasper?"

"They can all take care of themselves. Well, Jasper needs a keeper, but Jebb's gonna cover that for me." She had already discussed it with her little brother. Bless him, she loved that boy.

Alexandra narrowed her eyes. "And what about Noah?"

Fletcher shifted. "What about him?"

"Do you love him?"

She closed her eyes again. "I can't trust him."

Alex nudged Fletcher with her fancy boot. Hard.

Fletcher sat up. "Hey!"

"You avoided a direct question, Fletcher. You don't do that. Now, do you love Noah?"

Fletcher batted away the stupid tear that rolled down her cheek. She didn't think she could ever stop loving him. She yearned for him. "Yeah."

"Then go fight the good fight, as you used to say."

"This is the time to walk away." Before there was nothing to leave with.

"Who the hell are you?" Both Alex and Fletcher looked over when Casey came to join them. "Fletcher J.

281

McKay never backed away from anything in her fucking life!"

"I told you," Alex said and scooted over so Casey could sit.

Casey snorted. "I heard that, Miss Priss."

"Is Charlie coming too?" Fletcher asked as blonde curls came around the bend. "Hail fucking hail, the gang's all here." Hell's bells, it was an intervention.

"Hi!" Charlie looked at the ground, then pointed to Casey. "How did you get down there?"

"I've got skills." Casey winked.

"You didn't walk here, did you?" Fletcher asked. That was a long-ass walk for pregnant women.

"Hell, no," Casey said. "I drove us."

Alex raised her hand. "I drove too."

"Huh." Fletcher pursed her lips. Since when did she miss vehicles approaching?

"Now, let's get down to business," Casey began. "If you love Noah, go after him. Fight for him."

"Yes, do, the poor man looks awful," Charlie told them. "And Craig said he destroyed his house. Noah did, I mean."

"Did he ever," Alex said. "I have to find all new furniture to replace what he busted. I almost told him to redecorate himself, but I live for decorating."

Fletcher whistled. "That ain't got a damn thing to do with me."

"It's got everything to do with you." Casey shook her head. "I'm not a big Noah fan, Fletch, and you know that, but the man loves you. He doesn't want anyone else, and he's willing to live alone with his memories of you like some sort of saint or something. Do not make me feel sorry for Noah fucking Reed!"

"Bullshit," Fletcher called out. "Reed can have any woman he wants." He was beautiful, and that wasn't just his hot-ass body, either. He cared about people, cared about Blue Creek.

"He doesn't want anyone but you," Alex said, holding up her hands. "Don't ask me why. I think he's as crazy as you are."

"I's ain't crazy."

Casey snorted. "I don't know, Fletch. Not fighting for the person you love sounds bent to me."

Fletcher shot to her feet. "Look who's talking, Miss Emotionally Disinclined."

"She's right, though," Charlie said and patted Fletcher's foot. "Sorry, honey, but she is."

Fletcher glared at her other sister. "You're supposed to be on my fucking side, Charlie. And you can't talk either! Craig went through the wringer with you, and we all know it. And don't you say a fucking word, Alexandra, because you didn't go after Jake. You didn't fight for him." No, Fletcher had gone and brought Jake back for her. She'd gotten Ryan back here for Casey. Well, sort of. And she'd helped Craig put an end to their problems.

Alex narrowed her eyes. "I made a bad choice. Learn from that."

"Holy shit, Miss Priss admitted she made a mistake."

"Shut up, Casey," Alex and Charlie said in unison.

Casey flapped her hands in the air until Fletcher helped her up. "Fine. Y'all be bitchy together. I'm outta here." She turned to Fletcher. "Think about it." She gave her a tight hug, then walked away.

Charlie bit her lip, smiling when Fletcher helped

283

her up as well. "She's my ride," Charlie said. She leaned in and whispered, "She probably has to pee, and she can't go squat in the bushes so easy anymore."

Fletcher laughed at that. It was more than likely true.

"But really, Fletcher, think about things, okay?" Charlie kissed her cheek and headed back in the direction they came from.

Alex looked at her nails. "Goody, it's just the two of us."

"What fun!" Fletcher huffed and kicked at the rubble. "Maybe I'll hand the place over to Jebb along with the check and let him do what he feels is best."

Alex shook her head. "Running again?"

She shuffled her feet. "I need to."

"Why? Because we all know the truth and it's uncomfortable for you? We love you, and—and we love Jasper."

Fletcher's gaze shot to Alex's. "You do?"

"I can only speak for myself and Jacob, of course, but I'm fairly certain it's a unanimous thing. The fact that he's your birth father is moot. You forgave us for our poor judgment, and we are all ready to move on. With you."

Fletcher sat back down next to her sister. "I'm listening."

Alex sighed. "The only reason for you to leave is so you won't have to see Noah. And he's staying because your soul is here."

"What's this talk about my soul?" She picked at the grass while her sister told her what Noah had said. Fletcher couldn't help but laugh. They'd loved each other at the same time. Fate was a fucking bitch. "Ain't that some shit?"

"It's deplorably cliché, and don't tell her I said so, but Casey was right, there is a fine line between love and hate, honey."

She tossed away a blade of grass. "Yeah, well, it lies."

Alex stared at her. "Explain."

"The 'fine line' part, it's a lie. It's not a fine line at all, it's a fucking minefield." Fletcher shook her head. "A step in either direction and you're screwed."

"How?"

"Boom," Fletcher said, using her hands to demonstrate.

Her sister was quiet for a couple of minutes. "What if it's not a bad boom?"

She rubbed her nose. "Huh?" When wasn't a boom bad?

Alex made a noise. "Don't 'huh' me like I'm the one who's talking in riddles. You're saying the line between love and hate is a minefield. Okay, I'll give you that. But what if some of those mines don't kill you? What if they're fireworks? What if they turn into something beautiful?"

Alex being poetic was creeping Fletcher out, but she wasn't going to mention it. Instead she said, "That's a lot of what-ifs."

"That's life, isn't it? It's been ours. What if Dad hadn't adopted us together? What if Gracie hadn't died? What if we'd given Dad Uncle Evan's letter that night? There are a lot of what-ifs, Fletcher. You've always been willing to take the chance. Why not now?"

Fletcher shrugged. "I…" She didn't want to admit she was scared. "Why do you even care, Alexandra?"

285

Alex fiddled with her charm bracelet. "Out of everyone in our family, not including Jacob, I trust you the most. You kept our secret about Evan's letter. Even when Casey left, you tried to take some of the blame. You always insisted it was you who killed Kyle and not me. And even after you told me to go screw myself, I knew my secrets were still safe with you. I love you, Fletcher. You're my baby sister."

Fletcher blushed. "I's love you too."

Alex smiled. "I need you here. You know damn well Casey starts arguments with me when you're not around. And who else would antagonize big sister with me, hmm? You're always willing to fight for us." Alex tilted Fletcher's chin so she could look her in the eye. "Now you need to fight for yourself. A wise man told me once that people make mistakes, we're human. And despite popular belief, so are you. Noah's intent was never to hurt you, Fletcher. He'd rather live with your hate and live without you than let you come to harm. That's love. That's the gift."

Fletcher swallowed. "But what if he stops loving me? I's couldn't survive that."

Alex stood. "Love isn't for the weak of heart, Fletcher. It's hard and demanding, but trust me when I tell you it's worth it. If anything is worth fighting for, it's this."

Once she was alone again, Fletcher took her time studying the darkening sky. The rain should start soon; it would be the kind of storm that stole your breath. She looked at the remains of her cabin. Did she want to rebuild? No...not alone. "Noah," she whispered in the wind. She took a step, then looked over her shoulder when another vehicle pulled up.

Fletcher glanced toward the path that would lead her to Reed's house and promised herself she would go as soon as she heard whatever Pops had to say. She let out a shaky breath, then raised a hand to wave. "What brings you out here?"

Chapter Thirty-One

Pops' cheeks were pale. "I wanted to talk to you."

Fletcher pursed her lips. "Okay."

He exhaled a shaky breath. "It wasn't Noah's idea."

Her entire body went hot, then cold. "Huh?"

Her father rubbed a hand over his jaw. "Keeping Jasper's recovery a secret wasn't Noah's idea. It was mine."

"I…" Fletcher sat. There was a roaring in her ears.

Pops took a seat next to her. He was shaking. "When they were able to resuscitate Jasper after you left that day, I told Noah the best thing would be if we didn't tell you. If you knew Jasper was alive, you'd want to be with him. That would've been dangerous for both of you."

She stared at him. "I understood wanting to keep us both safe; that wasn't my issue. My issue was that y'all fucking let me think he was dead. Who does that?" She hit the ground with her clenched fists. "You's could have told me, asked me, talked to me about it, for fuck's sake. I wouldn't have liked it, but I would have stayed away. Hell's bells, I could have video-chatted with him, that would have been enough."

"I know that now."

Her mind raced. It was one thing for Noah to have devised this plan, but for it to have been Pops' idea…

The truth hit her. "You've been punishing us this whole time."

He sucked in a breath. "I—"

"I don't think you did it deliberately. You're not cruel. But you're hurt and angry. People do things they don't always mean when they're hurt and angry, right?" She flung his words back at him.

He looked at her, his cheeks ashen.

Fletcher fisted her hands in the grass. The time for pulling punches was drawing to a close. "You've been hurt and angry for a long, long time, haven't you? So much betrayal. More than you deserve." She shook her head. "I understand where your pain stems from, Pops; hell's bells, we were right there suffering with you. For fuck's sake, Alex and I've got blood on our hands protecting this family from *your* past. Which is funny considering you couldn't even be bothered to look into ours. But you punished us for finding it on our own, didn't you? For keeping Casey and Charlie's from you. You punish Jasper, when he's suffered enough, because he's the only one left to take the hits, for Evan, for Kyle. I chose to stay with you. But this...for the first time in my life, I'm questioning that decision."

Pops gagged but didn't move to get up.

Tears filled her eyes, but she refused to let them fall. "You let Noah take the blame for your dumbass idea. I'm sure he offered because the man is noble as fuck. He knew our relationship was strained, and he was willing to take the fall to protect it. Protect you. And me." He'd done it for her. Being a McKay meant the world to her, and Reed hadn't wanted her to lose that. Noah hadn't wanted her to lose her family, even though she'd had a hand in him losing his.

He had sacrificed his happiness for her family. Even after she'd told him her concerns about Pops. Concerns that turned out to be valid. Hadn't Noah been distressed when she'd confided in him? Had he doubted his decision then? Fuck. Perhaps the McKays were the minefield. She didn't think her brothers-in-law would disagree. That at least cheered her a bit.

"I'm ashamed to say I let him."

"You damn well should be!" Fletcher scoffed. "I could pretend that you weren't aware of my feelings for Noah, but Casey figured it out, and she's notorious for oversharing with you. You were willing to let me lose him too. How fucking selfish is that? I've done so much to protect you, so has Alex, but it should be the other way around. Shouldn't it? A parent's job should be to protect their children. I would call you a coward, but I love you too much."

Pops's voice shook when he said, "It *was* cowardly and cruel. I want to make it right."

She bowed her head and took a moment to rein in her rage. Wrath was one of the deadlies, after all. Fletch released her grip on the grass and let out a shaky breath. "I'm going to forgive you for this, Pops."

"I—"

"Few people can claim their actions are one hundred percent pure." She shrugged. "I can't."

"No."

She dashed away the tears on her cheeks. "I have a couple of conditions."

Her father's gaze shot to hers. "Go ahead."

"I want you to see a headshrinker; there's a lot you need to work through. Julia can recommend someone for you. It does help." It had helped her on more than one occasion.

Pops swallowed. "I can do that."

She wanted to tell him to stay the fuck away from Reed, but that was her anger talking. "You have to promise that, no matter what happens between me and Reed, you'll never use Noah like that again."

He recoiled. "I didn't—"

"We've established that you didn't do anything on purpose." If she believed he had, there would be a much scarier outcome. Fletcher stood and helped her father to his feet. "It's going to take some time and effort, but we'll be okay again, Pops."

"I love you."

"I love you too." She kissed his cheek. "You okay?"

"I'll let you know after I come clean to your mother."

She smirked. "You deserve whatever Ma throws at you." And her mother had impeccable aim.

His lips quirked upward. "Yeah."

Thunder rolled, and Fletcher looked at Pops. "I've got someplace I need to be."

****

It took Fletch a while to get to Noah's house on foot. His truck wasn't in the driveway, so she let herself in. Alexandra was right, the place was a disaster. Quickening her steps, she went upstairs to the attic, booted up her laptop, and waited. She hadn't shut down her surveillance, so she opened the program and entered the date of the last time she was here.

She used the discarded blanket to dry herself. The rain had turned to mist when she'd arrived, but the thunder and lightning had different ideas. She wiped her face and hit play.

She fast-forwarded through her leaving, then bit her lip when Noah came back in the house and started destroying his things. Fletcher switched cameras when he went into the kitchen. She put a hand to her chest when he slid to the floor on the screen. "Oh, Noah."

"Getting an eyeful, McKay?" Noah asked, holstering his weapon.

Fletcher jumped. Her mouth opened, but nothing came out. That was twice in one day someone had snuck up on her.

"Enjoying the program?" The glint in his silver eyes was harsh. "You let yourself in…now you can let yourself out." He glanced around the attic, shook his head, then turned on his heel.

Fletcher shut her laptop and hurried down the steps. She found him in his bedroom, changing out of his uniform and into a pair of jeans and a collared shirt. "Noah, I's…"

His hands stilled on the buttons. "What? You're here to fuck with me? I'm not in the mood."

He moved toward her, and she froze. Her throat was closing up, and her heart was beating so hard it would surely break out of her chest. "I'm too late, aren't I?"

"Too late for what? To spy on me? To give me hope only to snatch it away? Yeah, you're too late."

She swallowed. "I'm so sorry," she said, then spun around and ran down the stairs as fast as her legs would take her. She got to the front door and stopped. Hell's bells, what a chickenshit she was becoming.

Fletcher pivoted and raced back upstairs. Noah was standing where she left him. She shoved him. Hard.

"Fuck that. I'm not too late. You's love me." She cleared her throat. "You love me. You've said so a thousand fucking times."

Noah stared at her. Fletcher's eyes were bright, and her cheeks were flushed. When he had found wet footprints in his kitchen, he'd drawn his weapon and gone in search. Never in a million years had he expected to find Fletcher in his house, in his attic, but there she was. She had a whole setup there, which meant she'd stayed up there when she was in hiding. He shook his head. Only Fletcher would have the balls for that. "I—"

"And I love you." She moved closer to him. "I love you so fucking much it hurts." Fletcher put her hand to her heart.

Noah was afraid to move. Afraid to breathe.

"I'll fight for you, Noah. I'll fight for us. To the death." She stood a hair's breadth away from him. "Will you?"

He ran a hand through her wet hair. "Yes."

"No matter what fuckery Pops tries to get you to go along with."

Noah dropped his hand. "You know."

Fletcher snorted. "Pops came clean." She cupped his cheek. "But I'd already decided to forgive you for your dumbass plan."

He leaned in to her hand. "You did?"

She nodded. "I love you too much to let you go because you're a noble fucking idiot."

He laughed, then lifted her up and spun around. "I promise to take no part in any fuckery."

Fletcher's smile lit her eyes. "Good, that's settled. Now kiss me already!"

She didn't need to tell him twice. Noah kissed her with everything he was, everything she'd helped him become, and all he hoped they would be. Together.

Epilogue

Fletcher J. McKay Reed sat on the back porch in the swing her father had made for her and Noah's fifth wedding anniversary last spring. She sipped her coffee and sighed. She had chili on the stove and cornbread in the oven. Now all she needed was her husband to come home from the station.

The fine people of Blue Creek had elected Noah sheriff in the last election, and they'd had a huge celebration. Fletch missed police work, but she helped Reed out whenever he needed her. People nicknamed them Law and Order if they showed up on a case together. She loved it when he introduced her as his secret weapon.

Married life was different, but Jasper had been right, it suited her. She was still her own person, still independent, but she shared her life—the good and the bad—with Reed. He was her rock, and she was his. They were a damn force to be reckoned with, and she loved him more with every passing day.

Law and order reigned over Blue Creek, and the kids reigned over the family. Casey and Ryan's oldest son, Emmit, was five, and his little brother Marty was two. Unlike his older brother, Marty was a hellion who was always getting into everything. Emmit was quiet, but those were the ones you watched. There was plotting behind the boy's violet eyes, just like his ma's.

Casey ran her garage, while Ryan ran the hardware store. The kids were learning both trades, which was nice. Little Emmit listened intently while Marty tried to taste everything. Theirs was a happy family, and Fletcher couldn't be more thankful for it.

Mack was eleven and turning into a little priss like her auntie Alexandra, while five-year-old Anita could be sweet as pie one moment, then prickly the next. Mack was the peacemaker like Charlie had always been, and Anita was crafty like her dad. They had Craig wrapped so tightly around their little fingers that they got away with most everything. But that was to be expected.

Charlie and Tiny were still feeding the people of Blue Creek the best home-cooking around. And with the addition of the bakery, they were pretty much unstoppable. Jake, Tiny, and Charlie worked well together, though Charlie would get furious when Ryan would come over from the hardware store and start bickering with Jake. Always wanted peace, Charlie did.

Alexandra and Jake were expecting their first baby this winter. Fletcher was happy for them. They'd had a hard time getting pregnant and had to get help from a specialist. It had been difficult, there had been issues, but it was happening for them. The B and B was doing fantastic business during the fall, spring, and summer, but Alexandra had decided to keep the place closed during winter months. Which worked well for everyone.

Ma and Pops hosted couples group therapy twice a month at the diner and had just returned from touring Europe. Pops said if anyone deserved a vacation, it was Savannah Frances Walker McKay. They'd come back seeming more in love than ever, which did everyone's heart good. Now they had the entire gang over for Sunday get-togethers. Everyone would show up, and the house would be chaos. Fletcher loved it.

She smiled when Noah came out on the porch carrying a mug of coffee. He'd changed out of his uniform into jeans and a polo shirt. She loved his shirts; in fact, she'd slipped a couple in his closet that were a size smaller so she could drool over his body.

Fletcher glanced at her hands and fiddled with her rings. She had three: the engagement ring, the wedding band, and the ring tattooed on her finger. She smirked, thinking of their wedding day. She'd worn a dress because she'd lost to Noah at Clue again. But she was secretly glad. Alexandra had gone above and beyond, finding a dress with a breakaway skirt and pants underneath for the reception. Fletcher had never seen or worn anything so lovely in her life; she'd actually cried about it.

Even Noah had gotten tears in his eyes when Pops and Jasper walked her down the aisle. The day was a memory she would cherish. She hadn't even cared that she'd cried in front of the whole damn town when the preacher pronounced them husband and wife. Noah was hers forever, and she was his.

"Hi, cupcake," Noah said. He sat next to her and put his arm around her shoulders.

Fletcher rolled her eyes but leaned in to kiss him. She was still conflicted about his choice of endearment. Especially after he'd broken the rules and said it in front of Jake. Who then told his twin, who told his wife, and big sis had had a field day. "Catch any bad guys today?"

"Someone's been pulling up Mildred's flowers again."

"Have you asked your nieces if they know anything about that?" Fletcher smirked when he stopped laughing. Noah adored his nieces and nephews.

"Should I?"

"Charlie and Craig ate over at Mildred's the other night, and the girls were with them. You know they like flowers." She clinked her mug against his. "Your guess is as good as mine."

"Wonderful."

"It's not so bad, Reed. When I was Mack's age, I'd already broken into the police station half a dozen times and been shot twice. They ain't got nothing on me!"

"Thank Christ. Now, what are you doing out here?"

Her cheeks heated. How could she still blush after the things she'd done with this man? "Waiting for you."

Noah's smile was quick. "Oh?"

She rolled her eyes. "Don't get a big head about it."

"Wouldn't dare." He kissed her temple and rested against the swing. "Did Jebb finish moving into the cabin?"

Fletcher smiled. She, Noah, and Jebb had rebuilt the cabin together a couple of years ago. She'd known when they were building it that she was going to give it to Jebb at some point. She'd handed him the keys two days ago when he came home from the academy. He'd graduated at the top of his class and was going to start working with Noah next week. "Yep, he's all moved in. I already warned him I'm not taking sides if you two asshats get into an argument."

Noah chuckled. "That's big of you."

She snorted. "I thought so."

"How are things at Laura's?"

"We had a new arrival this morning. They're shaken, but safe."

Laura's Heart had opened four years ago. Fletcher had bought the Thomas's bankrupted estate, bulldozed it, then built a shelter. Tiny's wife, Julia, and Judge Mason had both helped Fletcher set up and staff the non-profit. It was off the radar to keep the residents protected; of course, everyone in town knew, but the location of Laura's Heart was one secret the people of Blue Creek would take to their graves.

Laura's Heart was a place for victims of domestic abuse to stay without fear. Not only was it a safe haven, but they also offered long-term and temporary housing, counseling, self-defense training, job training, and, in the direst of circumstances, extraction.

Noah gave her a squeeze. "That's good news."

She nodded. "It is." No matter how victims arrived, they left Laura's better equipped to handle whatever came next. Being able to give someone the tools to feel safe, to be safe was something Fletcher didn't take for granted. Nor did she take for granted that her entire family volunteered at Laura's whenever they could. Jasper especially.

Jasper had officially retired after his ordeal but was always ready to lend a hand at any of the McKay businesses when needed, and he was a fixture at Laura's. Fletcher wouldn't have been able to do it without him. He came to Sunday supper every week at her parents' house. The kids would circle around Pa to hear stories about the "McKay heathens" and all the grief they'd given him.

"Jasper's coming for dinner."

"I figured when I saw what was on the stove."

Fletcher grinned. "He loves my chili and cornbread. I think he's finally gonna tell us."

Noah turned to her. "Really?"

She bit her lip. "Yeah." Tiny's sister-in-law, Rita, had been working at Laura's for over a year, and Jasper was sweet on her. Not only that, but Mildred and Trixy both said they'd seen the old man out on a date with Rita on two separate occasions!

"Maybe he'll bring her tonight."

Fletcher sat up. "Hell's bells, you don't really think so, do you?"

"It wouldn't be so bad, would it?"

"Hell no, but I'll have to get another plate and—"

Noah set down his mug, pulled her on his lap, and kissed her.

Fletcher pushed away. "Stop that. Jasper's coming, and you can't get me all riled up."

He laughed, then headed inside. Before he shut the sliding glass door, he toasted her with his mug. "I wouldn't get you riled up without giving you a happy ending, cupcake," he said in that sexy-ass tone that shot straight to her lady parts.

Fletcher checked her phone. They did have almost half an hour… She forgot about her coffee and went after her husband. There weren't any hidden doors or bunkers here. There wasn't anything to hide or anyone to hide from. No web of lies to shroud the truth. Fletcher's secrets were safe with Noah, and so was she.

A word about the author...

W. L. Brooks likes to write like she reads with a bit of mystery, steamy romance, suspense, and, to keep it interesting, the occasional dash of the paranormal. Living in Western North Carolina, she is currently working on her next novel.

Thank you for purchasing
this publication of The Wild Rose Press, Inc.

For questions or more information
contact us at
info@thewildrosepress.com.

The Wild Rose Press, Inc.
www.thewildrosepress.com